You'll a...
Reuben Frost mystery

MURDERS &
ACQUISITIONS

"All Frost books are pleasing combinations of the old-fashioned and the up to date.... *Murders & Acquisitions* is the most absorbing of his books so far."

The New York Times

"A classic murder mystery ... Mr. Murphy writes with the conviction and eye for detail of someone who has seen these corporate imbroglios from the inside."

The Wall Street Journal

"Reuben, who rides in limousines and dines on occasion at his private men's club, is a courtly and pleasant companion for an evening's read."

Publishers Weekly

Also by Haughton Murphy
Published by Fawcett Books:

MURDER FOR LUNCH

MURDER TAKES A PARTNER

MURDER & ACQUISITIONS

MURDER TIMES TWO

MURDER SAVES FACE

MURDER KEEPS A SECRET

A Reuben Frost Mystery

Haughton Murphy

FAWCETT CREST • NEW YORK

A Fawcett Crest Book
Published by Ballantine Books
Copyright © 1989 by Haughton Murphy

Library of Congress Catalog Card Number: 88-7982

ISBN 0-449-21788-4

This edition published by arrangement with
Simon & Schuster, Inc.

This book is a work of fiction. Names, characters, places and incidents are either the product of the author's imagination or are used fictitiously. Any resemblance to actual events or locales or persons, living or dead, is entirely coincidental.

Printed in Canada

First Ballantine Books Edition: March 1990
Second Printing: May 1992

For Louis and Anka Begley. Friends.

And for Alpheus Thomas Mason and Jerome Blum, who many years ago tried to teach me something about biography and history.

—H.M.

PRIZEWINNER

REUBEN FROST STOOD IN THE BAR CASHIERS' LINE AT THE
side of the grand ballroom of the Sheraton Centre, waiting
his turn to buy two red tickets that would enable him to
obtain a weak martini for himself and a Scotch and soda
for his wife, Cynthia.

He was patient, but also wary. Those around him were
prosperous New Yorkers, gathered for the annual charity
dinner of the Reuff Foundation, at which the Reuff Prize for
American History would be awarded. They were basically
polite, but in their quest for prebanquet drinks might be
tempted to sneak into the queues at the understaffed cashiers' table. Frost, at seventy-six (albeit a vigorous seventy-
six), might be thought to be a likely target for the survival
tactics most residents of the city had instinctively learned
and which even the most proper could be tempted to employ
if the circumstances were desperate enough. And having the
comfort of a small, cold glass in hand, even if the contents
were meager and the whiskey cheap, might be enough to
set off a sneak attack.

Frost recognized a few familiar faces in the black-tie
crowd, but in the line he was in he knew only his wife
of forty-odd years, who was standing beside him. Then
he felt a hand on his shoulder and turned to face, in the
parallel queue, the aristocratically craggy visage of Stanley

1

Knowles, a well-known New York publisher. Knowles was the head of Hammersmith Press, a small, respectable house and one of the few American publishing firms independent of German or British, or even Australian, conglomerate ownership.

"Reuben, you're amazing!" Knowles roared.

Before Frost could say hello, the man shook hands vigorously, kissed Frost's wife, Cynthia, on the cheek, and once again pronounced Reuben "amazing."

"You know, most men your age have had a pacemaker put in, but you got a computer chip instead. One of those Silicon Valley gizmos that connects you to everyone and everything. What the hell is an over-the-hill Wall Street lawyer like you doing at a party like this?"

"I don't know what to say, Stanley," Frost replied. "I presume you're here to pay homage to David Rowan, one of the many authors you so shamelessly exploit."

"That's nice talk! And it's unfair. If you knew what I've just paid Rowan as an advance for his new book you wouldn't say things like that."

"The Ainslee biography?" Frost asked.

"Yes. David's living high in Manhattan and it's costing him a lot of money."

"I'm sure you can afford it, Stanley," Cynthia said. "After all, David isn't exactly one of those Brigham Foundation monograph writers that you underpay so badly." Cynthia, who had become the head of grants for the arts at the Brigham Foundation after her retirement as a ballerina, had worked closely with Knowles in bringing out a series of highly regarded studies on arts funding and management.

"I think we've had that argument before, Cynthia. So now, if you'll excuse me, I'm going to the bar." Knowles had succeeded in buying his tickets and was anxious to join a second line where he could cash them in. (The Reuff Dinner was a fancy affair, but not that fancy. The price of admission was $250 a person; it was considered low enough that the guests could be asked to pay for their own drinks.)

The publisher had not received an answer to his question about why the Frosts were present. The reason was simple:

Reuben was David's godfather and was a guest that evening of Harrison Rowan, David's father. The elder Rowan was a contemporary of Frost's. They had become close as undergraduates at Princeton and had remained in touch ever since.

The friendship between Reuben and Harrison had flourished despite a divergence in their career paths. Graduating from Princeton in 1932, Rowan, after tramping around Europe for a year, had gone to Washington to work in Franklin Roosevelt's Treasury Department. Although a gifted economist who could have achieved great prosperity in the private sector, he never left the Government. His superiors had begged him to stay at Treasury during World War II, and again in the days of international monetary reform after the War. By the early 1950s, he had lost his inclination to change and stayed in Washington until his retirement to Fairfax, Virginia, in 1976.

Frost, by contrast, had joined the eminent Wall Street law firm of Chase & Ward right out of law school and remained there until his own retirement as a senior partner in 1982. Despite the obvious differences in their lives—and their financial statuses—Frost and Rowan had remained good friends. And Harrison's late wife, Valerie, whom Harrison had married in 1937, and Cynthia had also gotten on well, despite the contrast between Valerie's life as a Washington housewife and Cynthia's international fame as a ballerina in the thirties and forties.

Harrison Rowan's career had not been without interest, particularly in the early New Deal days and then again when the world economy was restructured in the late forties. But his greatest satisfactions had been vicarious, through his son, David, who had been born to the financially strapped Rowans in 1938. With much celebration, Reuben had gone to Washington, a prosperous young associate at Chase & Ward (then making the grand sum of $5,000 a year), bearing champagne to toast David's arrival and to be the godfather at his christening.

Fortunately for the Rowans, their only son became a brilliant student. Through scholarships and fellowships, he had blazed a remarkable path through Yale, where he received his A.B. degree in history *summa cum laude*, and then Harvard. (The Frosts, childless themselves, had made occasional subventions to David, but these had not in any way been essential to his success.)

At Harvard, the young scholar wrote his dissertation (subsequently published) on the Social Security Act of 1935, getting his Ph.D. in 1965. The History Department at Princeton, then notorious for hiring from its own ranks, nonetheless eagerly pursued David and hired him. Nine years later, he had become a full professor, to the delight of his Princetonian father and godfather.

Once he had reached the pinnacle of academic success, David, married since graduate school and the father of a son and two daughters, became restless. Princeton started to feel confining. He succeeded in finding a new outlet for his energies, however, becoming the moderator of a well-regarded intellectual talk show, called simply *Point*, on NBC television.

This part-time diversion temporarily relieved his disquietude, and then fundamentally changed his life. *Point* was telecast in New York, and in the course of things he met Grace Mann, then an up-and-coming NBC television reporter and subsequently the early-morning anchor on a rival network. Close proximity soon grew into a clandestine romance—"familiarity breeds," as Frost often said—and then into an open relationship. In 1980, wife Nancy, the three children, the Tudor house in Princeton and the Princeton History Department were all forsaken for Grace Mann and the glitter of minor celebrity in New York.

David Rowan's new social and sex life did not impede, but indeed seemed to stimulate, his work. Using his television expertise, he dabbled as a ghostwriter for several liberal candidates including a Governor of New Jersey and the upset victor of a close Senate race in the Sunbelt. At a more scholarly level, he undertook a massive history of the powerful Ways and Means Committee of the House of Representatives. Published by Hammersmith Press as *Ways and Means*, the work was a critical success with reviewers, both popular and academic, and sold surprisingly well. In recent months it had won both the Pulitzer and Bancroft

Prizes for the year's best work in American history and had been the basis for David's being awarded the Reuff Prize.

Ways and Means helped David's career in another way. It came to the attention of Marietta Ainslee, the oft-married, ambitious and rich widow of Garrett Ainslee, a pillar of the United States Senate for sixteen years and a Justice of the Supreme Court for twelve more, until his sudden death in 1980. Mrs. Ainslee was determined to have a biography of her husband written that would preserve, and perhaps even enhance, his reputation. She liked the comfortable sophistication of *Ways and Means* and, even though knowing that David Rowan did not have experience in writing biography or any special knowledge of the Supreme Court, she decided that he was the person to write it.

Negotiations between the historian and the Justice's widow were easy; he was given complete control of whatever he might write and also full access to the personal papers Ainslee had left behind. These papers had been deposited with the University of Tennessee, in the Justice's native state, but the widow had retained control over them. At her direction, they were moved in their entirety, after considerable grousing by the university's library personnel, to the capacious one-room office David had rented on West Forty-fourth Street in Manhattan.

As the honored guest of the evening, David was not present in the reception hall where the Frosts and the other ordinary participants had gathered. Instead, as was the custom at these testimonial dinners, he was probably at a much more intimate gathering (where drink tickets were not necessary) in an adjoining room with such special guests as his father; Grace Mann; Senator Wheeler Edmunds of Michigan, a candidate for the Democratic Presidential nomination and the evening's guest speaker; and Elliott Reuff, donor of the Reuff Prize.

Knowing the usual protocol, Frost was surprised to see Reuff circulating in the crowd of the unwashed with his beaming wife, Micella, in tow. He was working the room like a seasoned politician, and soon approached the Frosts.

"I'm very glad to see you, Mr. Frost," he said. "And you, too, Mrs. Frost. It's a great occasion, isn't it?"

Before they could reply, Reuff had shaken their hands and moved on. His wife, wearing a very short skirt with a wide ruffle at the bottom, said nothing but nodded cheerfully as she followed her husband, wide smile in place.

"That was a heartfelt greeting," Cynthia muttered to her husband.

"Funny little fellow, isn't he?" Reuben commented.

The Frosts were hardly intimates of Reuff's, but he was a ubiquitous fixture on the New York party scene, so they had met him many times.

Elliott Reuff was one of the great real estate developers in New York, erecting office towers or apartment buildings on every inch of Manhattan real estate he could purchase. His buildings were utterly without distinction and invariably raised anguished protests from community groups and those concerned with decent architecture.

Like the evening's prizewinner, Reuff had become restless in the last year or two; edifice-building had come to bore him. Everyone knew he longed for a political career, but since there was no visible evidence that he had talent for anything except stacking up boxes, nothing had happened. (As part of his presumed campaign for political recognition, Reuff had become an energetic fundraiser for many candidates, including Wheeler Edmunds; hence, the Senator's presence at the Reuff Dinner.)

In an effort to brighten his public image, Reuff had hired a clever public relations operative named Eamon O'Farrell, who could boast of his successful promotions of, among others, a Mafia *capo* craving respectability, a movie starlet without discernible talent, and the Palestinians—or at least promotions as successful as could be expected amid an urbane citizenry that had little enthusiasm for organzied crime, artistic mediocrity, or the PLO.

Reuff had wanted to endow a prize for architectural distinction, but O'Farrell had dissuaded him, since such an award could only call attention to the developer's shortcomings in this regard. Studying his subject carefully, O'Farrell discovered that Reuff had majored in American history at New York University and therefore suggested funding a history prize. Though Reuff had been a C student at NYU, he had liked the idea and the prize had been established two years earlier. And it carried an enormous stipend of $100,000, dwarfing the Bancroft ($4,000) and the Pulitzer ($3,000, recently raised from $1,000) in richness, if not prestige.

Once Reuff left them, the Frosts began looking around for friends, a quest interrupted by the dimming of lights, announcing the start of dinner. Taking his wife's arm, Reuben moved toward the ballroom, picking up a seating list from an attendant at the door.

Frost quickly thumbed through the list. He knew he was sitting with Harrison Rowan, but he did not know who else might be joining them. The list resembled a Bulgarian train schedule and he had to look first in the alphabetical section, to find out that he was at table ten, and then had to flip to a table-by-table list where he found out who his fellow diners would be: Harrison Rowan "and guest"; Alan Rowan, David's eldest child; Stanley Knowles and his wife, Donna; Grace Mann (what prudery kept her from the dais? Frost wondered; after all, she had lived with David for eight years); and Richard Taylor and Patricia McNiece, whom Frost did not know.

A diagram of the tables indicated that table ten was in the front, but clear across the cavernous ballroom. He and Cynthia headed toward it, but were waylaid over and over by friends, making it appear as if they, like Reuff, were working the room. (And giving the lie to any modest assertions by Reuben that the Frosts were not well-connected.)

By the time they reached table ten, the other guests were assembled and seated. Harrison Rowan jumped up and greeted them warmly, introducing them to those they didn't already know, and showing Cynthia to a seat at his left and beside Richard Taylor and Reuben to one between Grace Mann and Donna Knowles.

"Here comes the walking computer chip!" Stanley Knowles proclaimed. "Or are you a mobile modem, Reuben? Damn well-connected, whatever you are!"

"Do I have to take this, Donna?" Reuben asked, as he sat down amid laughter around the table.

"Don't pay any attention to him," the publisher's wife

said, lowering her voice. "He's just published his first book on computers and he's crazy about all the terminology."

Frost was glad to see that Harrison Rowan was joining in the laughter. He, of course, had every reason to be happy, given the occasion. But Frost knew he had been lonely and depressed since the death of Valerie, from cancer, two years earlier. Perhaps the surprise "and guest"—or "date," as Harrison had quaintly called her—was partially responsible for the new cheerfulness. The "date" was the former Emily Bryant, a woman the two men had known in their college days. A cheerful, slightly plump extravert and an exceptionally good sport, she had been a party to many of their bachelor antics in Princeton and New York but then, to their shock, and that of most of the other young men who knew her, she had married Barton Sherwood, a stuffed-shirt lawyer and a heavy, ponderous bore. Harrison and Reuben had reluctantly excommunicated Emily from their bachelor rites, having been unable, like most, to abide the new husband. But now Sherwood was dead, and Frost silently congratulated his old companion for having rediscovered her.

Reuben was sitting too far away to talk to Emily and so, after taking a sip of the California plonk and glacial fruit cocktail at his place, he turned to Grace Mann.

Ms. Mann was a woman Frost had at first disliked. In his role as godfather, he had not approved of David's flight from the hearthside, though since the miscreant was then forty-two, there had seemed to be very little that he could say. But he had been reluctant to blame his godson and therefore concluded that the television newswoman was a home-wrecker.

As time passed, Frost realized that David appeared happy in his new life, whatever misery he had caused for Nancy and his children. So forgiveness had come for Grace Mann, made all the easier by her stunning, blond good looks, her wit and her obvious intelligence. Though neither he nor Cynthia (who was usually a good judge of such things) had ever detected under her cool demeanor much evidence of a very deep love for David.

"How's the prizewinner bearing up?" he asked.

"Just fine. David's not averse to praise, you know. Though I must confess, these award ceremonies are a strain on me."

"Really? Why is that?"

"They last long past my bedtime. I'm usually at home at this hour getting ready for bed."

"At eight o'clock?"

"You forget I go on the air at seven in the morning. With every hair in place, both eyes open and the overnight news digested."

"Where is Alan, by the way?" Frost asked, nodding toward the empty chair next to Ms. McNiece.

"His mother wouldn't let him come."

"Nancy?"

"Yes. She has a real hold on that boy."

"How old is he? He must be twenty-one."

"Just. But that doesn't matter. She's got him very firmly in her clutches. He's living at home with her, so his freedom's restricted."

"I thought he was at Vanderbilt."

"He was, but he left in the middle of his junior year, last January. Said he needed a rest."

"Grace, I don't know about young people today. You'd think they'd want to finish college and get on with it."

"That's a very old-fashioned attitude, I'm afraid."

"I suppose it is, but as far as I'm concerned there's too much lounge-lizardry around."

Grace Mann laughed. "And that's a nice old-fashioned term, Reuben. Today it's called couch potatoism—sitting in front of the television and doing nothing by the hour. Though I suppose in my line of work I should be grateful for couch potatoes."

"I'm sorry about Alan. It would have pleased his grandfather to have him here."

"I know. It's doubly too bad because he's the only one of the children who even speaks to David."

A burly waiter came between Ms. Mann and Reuben, hurriedly scooping out a green salad.

"That's your plate on the left," the waiter said to Frost.

"I'm aware of that," he replied, astonished at the silly

remark, wondering why the man hadn't told him to eat his salad with a fork.

As the tired salad greens were ladled out, Stanley Knowles turned to speak to Grace Mann on his right. Frost, obeying the switching-partners convention, himself turned to Donna Knowles. She was gray-haired and craggy-faced like her husband; they could have been brother and sister. She had never been a close friend, but Frost knew that she was considered a good editor at Hammersmith, where she was responsible for new fiction and poetry. She was also rumored to have sunk her modest inheritance into the publishing house.

Donna Knowles began her end of the conversation by complaining about the food. "This food is terrible," she said. "I know I eat like a bird, but these portions are much too big."

Frost looked at her sympathetically and then turned away to scan the dais, where he saw David laughing and talking with animation with Micella Reuff on one side and Professor John Wilson Torrance of NYU on the other. Frost remarked to Donna that the guest of honor seemed in very good spirits.

"Oh, he is—as he ought to be. The reception for *Ways and Means* has been exceptional and his research for the Ainslee book seems to be going well."

"I'm delighted for him. And for you. It seems to me Hammersmith has had all the prizewinners this year," Frost said, referring not only to David's achievements but the National Book Award for fiction, won this year by a Montana novelist published by the firm, and, the previous fall, the Nobel Prize for literature, awarded to a Siamese poet Hammersmith published in English translation.

"Yes, it's very nice. But I can assure you those prizes and one dollar will get you a ride on the subway." Her cheerfulness disappeared as she began talking about the book industry.

"Oh, come, Donna. You're still publishing Sylvia Simmons, aren't you?" Frost asked, referring to a hack novelist whose romances about the antebellum South consistently headed the bestseller list.

"Indeed. But you must realize the only thing Sylvia Simmons likes better than fame—she would admit this herself, so I'm not being indiscreet—is money. She helps pay the rent, there's no question about that, but she escalates her demands with every book. Whatever all those foreign investors raiding American publishers think, publishing isn't the pot of gold at the end of the rainbow. And everything's more expensive these days.

"Take that girl over there, Patricia McNiece," she went on, lowering her voice once again and, by now, completely ignoring her food. "She's a brilliant editor and we're very pleased to have her. Twenty years ago, she would have made a pittance and would have—or at least should have—been grateful for the chance to learn her profession. Not today. She can command a handsome salary, and if we don't pay it, she'll get it somewhere else. Of course, Reuben, I hold you responsible—you and the other rich lawyers who pay your new recruits such obscene amounts of money."

Frost ignored the jibe; he knew the complaint about the extravagant pay scales of Wall Street law firms and often heard it in social conversation, but he didn't feel like debating the subject tonight.

"Is Ms. McNiece David's editor?" he asked, scrutinizing the pert, freckle-faced woman of perhaps thirty almost directly facing him.

"Yes, she is. She did a magnificent job on *Ways and Means* and I know is going to have a bigger job working with David on the Ainslee book."

"Why so?"

"Force of circumstances. You know about Horace Jenkins, of course?"

"Jenkins? No, I can't say that I do."

"He's been David's research assistant. A brilliant, brilliant young man who wrote his Ph.D. thesis with David at Princeton. David was elated because he'd persuaded Horace to take off two years or more to help him with the biography. But then he was diagnosed."

"Diagnosed?"

"I'm sorry. That's a sad term going around the publishing

industry these days—and I guess just about every other
profession as well. He has AIDS."

"Oh, God."

"It's a tragedy. And a real setback for David. Horace
was an indefatigable worker and his work was the best.
Unfortunately, what little time for recreation he had seems
to have been spent at the baths."

"How sick is he?"

"He's in Tyler Hospital. He was working up until two
months ago, but he got too sick to go on. He's dying.
Cancer and heaven knows how many other infections."

"I hate hearing about these things."

"So do I, but you can't avoid it these days, can you?"

Frost thought it was time to change the subject and, in any
event, he was curious about Cynthia's dinner companion,
with whom she seemed to be carrying on a very animated
conversation.

"Who's the fellow next to Cynthia?" he asked. "Burton
was it?"

"No, Taylor. Richard Taylor. He's Senator Edmunds's
administrative assistant. Somebody said before dinner that
he'll be the head of the White House staff if Edmunds gets
elected."

"Isn't he a little young for that?"

"After the Reagan administration?"

"Good point."

Frost was fascinated with the conversation he was observing, though his wife and the AA were speaking too low to be
heard. Taylor, with tiny horn-rimmed spectacles (the kind
the British National Health passes out, Reuben thought)
perched on his pink-cheeked face, was gesturing forcefully
with his large hands as he made a point to Cynthia. She, in
turn, was making almost balletic gestures as she dramatically gave her side of the argument.

Reuben's surveillance was interrupted as Grace Mann
began talking across him to Donna Knowles.

"Did I overhear you discussing the Senator?" she asked.

"Yes. What do you think of him, Grace?"

"I'm mildly impressed. Though given the candidates this
year, that may be faint praise. He's got a good record and

he can talk in sentences. He was on the show a few weeks ago and I liked him."

"What does David think? Is he going to go to work for him?" Donna asked, alluding to the historian's speechwriting avocation.

"I don't know. David loves ghostwriting, but I think the book's going to keep him busy. There's been a feeler or two, though I haven't been told any of the details. Knowing David, I'm sure he'll be tempted."

"What do you think, Reuben?" Donna asked.

"Oh, I'm afraid I'm tired of politics. Too many pip-squeaks—in both parties. All the same, I've only heard good things about Edmunds. And I guess if he wins the New York primary next month he'll pretty much have the nomination sewed up."

The political conversation was interrupted by another benefit-dinner rite: the few moments, usually between the main course and dessert, when the prominent guests descend from the dais, like gods coming down from Olympus, to mingle briefly with the hoi polloi.

David Rowan went at once to table ten and quickly made the rounds. He was without question in an "up" mood, his receding black hair, without a trace of gray, framing the top of his shiny and happy face. His toothy, but not unattractive, smile was bestowed in turn on each one at the table though, as he greeted each guest, the smile dissolved into mock gravity as he called each of them by a facetious nickname—"Pops" in the case of his father (whom he embraced), "my queen" for Grace Mann (whom he also embraced perfunctorily), "Emms, dear" for Emily Sherwood, "my patron and protector" for Stanley Knowles and "la bella Donna" for his wife, "amanuensis cara" for Ms. McNiece, "old friend" for Richard Taylor, and "dear godfather" and "the queen mother" for Reuben and Cynthia.

Hands shaken as he went around the table, he stopped briefly between his father and Cynthia, embracing them both.

"You're all coming to Stockholm, I assume?" he asked, his eyes darting about the table as his listeners caught his reference to the Nobel Prize, his staccato laugh making clear that he was not serious—or at least not quite serious.

"See you there!" he said, patting both Harrison and Cynthia on their backs, then retreating back toward the dais, waving at table ten as he moved away.

Once the dais guests were reassembled, Elliott Reuff, never the shrinking violet, took the podium to act as master of ceremonies at his own Foundation's dinner. After a tepid joke, he introduced Professor Torrance, the head of the Reuff Prize selection committee. (Torrance, years before, had given Reuff a D in American History 201 at NYU, but bygones were apparently bygones.)

Torrance, round as he was tall and with the hair of a wild violinist, gave a graceful, if not especially warm, encomium to the evening's prizewinner. He made only one crack about David's television career—a subject anathema to most academics, either as a matter of principle or as a matter of green-eyed envy. Then, taking a plaque and what appeared to be a check from the shelf beneath the podium, he presented them to David Rowan.

David's acceptance speech was witty, gracious and brief.

"Everyone knows that historians covet professional acclaim," he said. "What is less well known is the dirty little secret that they like money. And when you put the two together, the combination is downright irresistible."

Senator Edmunds, who spoke last, gave an impressive speech. It was not an all-purpose oration, equally suitable for award dinners, fundraisers, photo opportunities in Iowa farmyards and television debates, but one carefully crafted for the occasion. He spoke of the value of learning the lessons of history and of the importance of higher education in general (the latter reference giving him a chance to remind his audience of his record of support for education funding in the Senate).

As the Senator talked, Frost observed the Secret Service agents who had positioned themselves in front of the dais, facing the audience. Was this a waste of taxpayers' money or not? he asked himself. What if someone in the audience got up suddenly and appeared to threaten the speaker?

Would a sharpshooter in the agents' ranks pick him off? Or would they simply yell at the candidate to duck? Either eventuality would be a trifle embarrassing if the unfortunate spectator had merely leaped up because he had a charley horse.

Reuben also thought of the dowager who lived around the corner from his townhouse who had entertained the First Lady recently—even though the electricity in the woman's apartment had been knocked out earlier in the day by a freak accident in the basement of her building. From what he knew of the guest list, there had been at least one or two present whom he would not have been willing to encounter unless all the lights were on. Had it really been wise to let the First Lady visit an apartment illuminated only by candles? Well, he was not running the Secret Service. Given the recent course of American history, he concluded that it was probably a necessary, if possibly ineffectual, evil.

Frost then observed Richard Taylor anew. The young man was listening to his boss with a look of intense concentration, and perhaps of rapture, on his face. His body English, slightly anticipating the rhythms of Edmunds's speech, indicated to Frost that Taylor was its author. David Rowan might not find it easy to penetrate the candidate's inner circle, even if he wanted to do so.

The Senator ended his speech with a flag-waving flourish, albeit of the First Amendment–free speech variety, as befitted the gathering he was addressing. The applause at the end was hearty, and Elliott Reuff called the evening to a close.

The audience immediately rushed out of the ballroom, not out or boredom or relief, but because the city's movers and shakers, although of all ethnic and religious persuasions, were supposed to behave like rigorous Protestants and get to bed early.

Harrison Rowan urged Reuben to join a small after-dinner celebration with David, but he declined, pleading that he was tired. After kisses for the women—and a promise to Emily Sherwood to call her—and handshakes for the men, Reuben piloted Cynthia toward the exit.

Saying good night to Harrison, Reuben instructed him to tell David that he would see him soon, not realizing that he would see the Reuff Prizewinner only once more: on the television news; dead; and covered with a blanket.

POST-MORTEM

2

As was their custom after an evening out, the Frosts relaxed with a nightcap in the living room of their East Side townhouse. Their light Scotches and soda tasted good on the unseasonably warm night.

"Why do people go to those things unless they have to?" Cynthia asked her husband as she stretched out on the sofa. "Of course, I know why we were there. But wouldn't people who had the choice rather be at the theater, or even at home in front of the TV, than eating a microwave dinner in a hotel ballroom?"

"You know the real reason as well as I do, Cynthia," her husband answered, sitting across the coffee table from her in an armchair. "You scratch my back and I'll scratch yours. It's reciprocity, not generosity, that makes these dinners successful."

"What if you just sent out a letter and said, 'We'll spare you the agony of a hotel dinner—just send money instead'?"

"I think somebody tried that once and no money came in."

"I guess people like to be seen. All dressed up and some place to go."

"Like Mrs. Reuff, for example?"

"Micella! Wasn't that incredible? Skirt up to her behind and ruffles sticking out about two feet. It's that new French

17

designer, Christian Lacroix. He must have a wicked sense
of humor to dress women that way. Micella's no chicken,
either."

"I was hoping to see her sit down, but I didn't."

"She wasn't dressed, she was upholstered," Cynthia commented.

The Frosts laughed quietly and sipped their drinks as
they thought about the incongruously dressed Micella Reuff.
Then Reuben asked if Cynthia had learned anything of
interest on her side of the table.

"No, not really—oh, yes, there was one thing. A hot
little tidbit at that. Did you know that Garrett Ainslee was
quite the ladies' man?"

"No, I've never heard that."

"It seems that he went to bed with anything that
moved—female, of course. According to Harrison, it was
a well-kept secret. He'd never heard about it in all the years
he lived in Washington."

"How did this come out, if it was such a secret?"

"Apparently the old goat kept a record of his conquests.
I don't know the details, but he had a code letter for
sex—O, Harrison said—that he meticulously entered, with
the number of times, in his daily engagement book."

"That's weird. He wasn't a Catholic, was he?"

"I don't think so. Southern Baptist I would've guessed.
Why?"

"Well, as I understand it, Catholics tell their sins in confession. Maybe he was just keeping track for the priest."

"Oh, Reuben," Cynthia said, with some exasperation.
"But I agree with you, it's pretty strange behavior."

"Where did Harrison get this bit of dirt?"

"David cracked the code while going through Ainslee's
papers. Don't ask me how. Harrison didn't explain."

"Well, well, the Ainslee biography may have some spice
after all."

"Ainslee's widow knows about David's discovery. He
bragged a little too much about it and word got back to
her. She's fit to kill, Harrison says."

"Does that mean she'll withdraw her support for the
book?"

"Harrison doesn't think so, since that could lead to a public scandal. But David's worried. It seems the widow has a new live-in—younger than she is—who's a real brute. I gather he's been egging the woman on."

"That's pretty good gossip," Reuben said. "What did you learn from your other dinner partner, that young fellow Taylor? You were certainly chatting him up!"

"Me? Chatting him up! I had to *fight* to say a full sentence to him!"

"Hmn. What was the big topic of conversation?"

"Wheeler Edmunds, of course. Richard's . . ."

"Richard, is it?"

"Why, yes. Are you jealous?"

"Of course not. I'm always glad to see my poor, aged wife making new friends."

"*Richard* is absolutely devoted to Edmunds. He began working for him as a volunteer when he was an undergraduate at the University of Michigan, then full-time when he got back from Oxford and Edmunds had gone on to the Senate. He's been with him ever since."

"What's the Oxford part?"

"Richard was a Rhodes Scholar. Magdalen, I believe."

"My God, you found out everything about the kid."

"Not exactly a kid. He's thirty-three, he told me."

"He looks younger."

"He runs."

"Oh."

"To answer your question, though, we were talking about Presidential politics. I expressed the view rather gently . . ."

". . . of course . . ."

". . . that I didn't think *anyone* was qualified to be President, that the job is just too tough. Well, I got a hand-waving argument that I was wrong. Or at least wrong as far as Wheeler Edmunds is concerned. By the time he finished, I was surprised he wasn't telling me that the Senator could walk on water."

"Did you like—Richard?"

"I guess so. But his dedication to Edmunds was really overpowering. I felt like I was being preached to by—what do they call holy rollers now?—a television evangelist."

"I think a lot of smart young men do what your Richard has done. Tie their fate to an up-and-coming politician and hope for glory."

"It's interesting. Having your career, even your life, so dependent on someone else."

"Yes, yes it is," Reuben agreed, before lapsing back into silence. Then Cynthia suddenly leaned forward as if she had just remembered something.

"What about seeing Emily Sherwood again? Isn't Harrison the sly old devil, ferreting her out after all these years?"

"Indeed. I didn't talk with her much, but Barton Sherwood apparently didn't ruin her. She seemed her old, ample, jolly self."

"Thank heaven for that."

"I told her we'd get in touch."

"Where does she live?"

"Port Washington, I think."

"And what about the Knowleses? Stanley seemed absolutely manic. I've never seen him like that before. All that joking, and in such a loud voice, about you being connected up like a computer."

"You know him better than I do. Still, I agree with you. I didn't mind his kidding, but he was pretty heavy. She, on the other hand, seemed a trifle down."

"Oh, Reuben, she always is. You can't ever talk to her about publishing without her poor-mouthing and whining."

"Maybe she sees her money going down the drain."

"Very possibly."

"She eats like a bird, too, as she herself admits. She scarcely touched her food."

"I'm afraid I don't like her much," Cynthia said.

"How do I know the name Peter Jewett, by the way?"

"He's a member of the Foundation's advisory history panel. Professor of History at Amherst. I've probably mentioned him. As a matter of fact, I'll probably be seeing him tomorrow. I'm sure he'll be in town for the panel's semiannual meeting. Why do you ask?"

"Apparently he and David don't get along. Donna

Knowles said that when they awarded David the Bancroft Prize for history, Jewett was the winner of the companion Bancroft Prize for American diplomatic history. When David found out, he refused to go to the ceremony."

"Peter can be ornery, arrogant and rude, I'll say that. But what exactly does David have against him? It must be more than a clash of personalities."

"Donna didn't elaborate. It was just another item in her litany of problems with her authors."

Before they could discuss the matter further, the telephone rang. Reuben went into the library to answer it.

"That was Nancy Rowan, for God's sake," he said on returning.

"What on earth did she want?"

"Wanted to know if we'd seen Alan."

"How strange. Why didn't she call David, or Harrison?"

"I suppose she guessed they'd still be out. Or she probably knows Grace Mann goes to bed early and she might have to talk to her if she called the apartment."

"But why you?"

"I'm sure she knew we'd be at the dinner tonight. Alan left the house yesterday and she's probably checking up to see if he went, too."

"That's really vindictive."

"What other explanation is there?"

"I don't know, but it's certainly not a good situation."

"Did she have anything else to say?"

"No. She asked if I'd seen Alan and I said I hadn't. End of conversation."

"No questions about the dinner, I suppose."

"No, nothing like that. She's very clearly written David completely out of her life."

"For which I can't blame her."

"True enough."

"Well, at least her call roused us. I'm falling asleep and must go to bed. What are you doing tomorrow?"

"Not much. Going to the office to get some postage stamps, I guess."

"Sounds more interesting than Peter Jewett and his history panelists. Or lunch with a young man who wants to do a Pirandello festival in North Dakota."

"Give him a grant. Just so long as we don't have to go out there," Reuben said as he and his wife headed upstairs to bed.

MORNING AFTER

3

TUESDAY MORNING, FROST WAS UP AND READING THE
Times when the telephone rang. It was Harrison Rowan,
who asked to talk to Cynthia. Frost tried to thank Rowan
for inviting him the previous evening, but the caller was
interested only in talking to his wife.

Reuben got Cynthia out of the bathroom to take the call
and hung up when she picked up on the bedroom exten-
sion.

"What did Harrison want?" he called out when he heard
his wife coming down the stairs.

"Silly old Harrison. He was all upset that he'd told me
about Garrett Ainslee's sex code. Nervous as a tick about
whether anyone else had overheard him at the table, which
I doubt. He said I absolutely couldn't tell anyone and that
it was very wrong of him to talk about it."

"Did you tell him you'd spilled the beans to me?"

"Yes, and of course he trusts you'll keep it quiet, too.
He said David really is worried that Marietta Ainslee will
take the book away from him."

"Well, his secret's safe with me—and I trust with you."

"Reuben! Are you saying I can't keep a secret?"

"No, no, no. You learned the cardinal rule for a lawyer's
wife—discretion at all times—many years ago. I was only
kidding," Reuben said hastily.

"I hope so."

* * *

An hour later, Reuben took the subway downtown to the offices of his firm, Chase & Ward, at One Metropolitan Plaza. Even though retired, he still kept a small office at the firm. He did not go there often, though it was still a useful place to buy postage stamps and cash checks. And to have a stenographer's help in answering correspondence.

As he went down the hall, encountering a fair number of young associates (or were they paralegals, a substratum in the office new since his time as an active lawyer?), messengers and the occasional secretary, he was depressed at how few of them he recognized, not realizing that the growth of the firm had made it impossible for even the active partners to know more than a fraction of the staff.

Once at his office, there was a message to call Keith Merritt, a tax partner with whom he had worked closely. Frost walked over to see Merritt immediately. He found the tax lawyer eager to test his recollection of a nearly forgotten corporate merger that had come under attack in an Internal Revenue Service audit. Frost tried to reconstruct the decade-old events, but was not sure how helpful he had been to his former colleague.

Returning to his own office, he ran into one of Chase & Ward's youngest partners, Frank Norton, now in his mid-thirties. During Frost's last years before retirement, Norton had been of invaluable assistance to him. He was a feisty and ambitious lawyer, but had nonetheless worked for Frost without a trace of condescension or resentment, which could not be said for all those with whom Frost had come in contact toward the end. Frost was fond of him.

The younger lawyer greeted his old mentor warmly and seemed genuinely glad to see him.

"You're not free for lunch, are you?" Frost asked.

"I am, to tell the truth. Things are pretty slow at the moment." Norton was being unusually candid; the work ethic at Chase & Ward demanded that one always purport to be busy, even if the financial markets were in the doldrums, as they now were, and project after project had been postponed or canceled outright. "Shall we go upstairs?"

Frost grimaced slightly. "Frank, one of the glories of

being retired is that one no longer has to face the menu at the Hexagon Club or the eat-and-run pace of the Training Table," Frost said, referring to the lunch club atop One Metro Plaza, and the nickname for the common table at which the firm's partners customarily ate.

"I agree. And we all know what terrible things can happen to you there," Norton said, recalling obliquely the scandalous death by poisoning of senior partner Graham Donovan at the Training Table two years earlier. "But what do you have in mind?"

"How about Bouley?"

"What's that?"

"Honestly, you young fellows have tunnel vision. You come to the office in the morning, dash up to the Hexagon Club, and then work until dark, when one of the finest French restaurants in New York is a stone's throw away."

"Where is it?"

"Up just north of City Hall. It's magnificent, but it does take a little time."

"You're on. Let me get my coat and I'll meet you at reception."

"Let me make sure we can get a table first. That fellow in the *Times* wrote the place up a while back and it's gotten very crowded."

A reservation made, the two lawyers walked uptown in the near-perfect spring weather. Norton discussed his latest activities, expressing worry about the slackening in legal business.

"I suppose the firm's in the red," Frost said.

"I'll say! We've been running a deficit for three weeks!" The firm, as a partnership, paid out its cash, once expenses had been taken care of and a small rainy-day reserve provided for, as soon as it came in. Norton, who had become a partner in extremely prosperous times, had never seen a downturn before, even for such a short period as three weeks.

"Don't worry, Frank. The firm's business does reflect what's going on in the markets. But it always comes back. Plenty of businesses have to raise money, even in bad times.

And when the stock market's down, companies that aren't affected find it's a good time to buy others.

"And if worst comes to worst and everything goes haywire, there'll be a whole new demand for lawyers to help pick up the pieces. Financial lawyers are like undertakers, you know. Businessmen need us in good times and bad, as much as they may deny it, or resent it."

"Maybe," Norton said, more than a trace of doubt in his voice.

"I went to work in nineteen thirty-five, Frank, so I've seen the firm ride out the cycle plenty of times."

As he reassured his unnecessarily nervous junior, he led him down Duane Street to the tiny square where Bouley was located. Bayard, the maitre d', gave them a friendly reception and seated them at a table by a window, the afternoon sun streaming through the curtained glass.

"Hey, this is a nice place!" Norton said.

"Yes. I'm not that much of a boulevardier, but that light, and the square outside, remind me of Paris. Right here in the shadow of the Hexagon Club."

The two men ordered from the tempting, slightly *nouvelle* menu.

"How about some wine?" Frost asked, fully realizing that temperance was the usual daytime rule among working lawyers. (A rule Frost strongly approved of. One would not want a surgeon taking a drink before an operation; a lawyer's client was, Frost maintained, entitled to the same clearheadedness.)

"As I said, I'm not all that busy, so why not?"

After a quick consultation, Frost ordered a bottle of Chablis, one of the less expensive bottles on a not especially cheap list.

"What's the gossip?" Frost asked, drinking approvingly from his glass.

"You mean at the firm?"

"Yes." Frost missed being in touch with the latest rumors and scuttlebutt, false as often as true, that inevitably whirled about the office. And there was always an item or two of petty office politics that interested Frost, as the former head of Chase & Ward.

"The only news is that we may actually be moving. There's a new skyscraper going up in midtown where we can get all the space we'll need for the rest of the century."

"That's what everybody said when we moved to Met Plaza twenty-five years ago. And now I think they want to put a new associate in my little office."

"By 'they' you mean Bannard?"

"Right," Frost said, referring to the current Executive Partner.

"Has he said so?"

"No, but all he talks about whenever I see him is how hard up you all are for space. He even brought it up when we ran into him at the theater the other night."

"I'd ignore him."

"I do. But where is this building?"

"That's the catch. It's on Eighth Avenue, practically in the porn district."

"That may present whole new opportunities for legal practice, if the financial business doesn't come back. From Wall Street lawyer to Eighth Avenue lawyer. Pornography, dope, mugging. The possibilities are·endless."

Norton laughed. "You know, Marvin Yates was at a dinner celebrating the closing of one of his mergers the other night and the investment bankers presented him with a box of condoms. Said it might come in handy at Pierpont Plaza, as the new building's called."

"Condoms! That's all one hears about these days. Coming down on the subway this morning, there were two posters in the car about using them, right between the ads for an abortion clinic and a warning about AIDS. I don't think there's any fun to sex these days. AIDS, herpes, all of that. Why, I remember years ago when one of our young lawyers—*not* a partner, I might add—took up with a girl in the files. One night her regular boyfriend came to the office and chased the lawyer down the hall with a baseball bat! It was the talk of the office for weeks. There was real *feeling* there! Today it would probably all turn into a very boring *ménage à trois*."

The sautéed oysters both lawyers had ordered arrived,

served on a glistening bed of arugula. As they ate enthusiastically, Frost changed the subject. "Do I recall correctly that you clerked after law school?" he asked.

"That's right. A year for Judge Marder on the D.C. Circuit, then a year for Justice Carroll on the Supreme Court. It was a time I'll never forget."

"Why do you say that? I didn't do it and I've never been quite sure that clerking was that valuable, unless you're a litigator."

"You're right, unless you've got a really good judge. Dine Carroll was, and he treated his clerks like his own sons. It was almost like having a second father."

"That I can understand," Frost said. "By the way, was Garrett Ainslee on the Court when you were down there?"

"Oh, yes. I was there in seventy-eight. Ainslee died two years later, as I recall. Quite a man."

"Tell me about him. I'm curious, because my godson's writing his biography."

"He and Justice Carroll were very close, though miles apart politically. Remember Ainslee was an old-line liberal and Carroll was a conservative, though not as much so as the ones Reagan appointed—or wanted to. Ainslee had a fine intellect, which surprised some people, since you don't necessarily expect that in a former Senator . . ."

"I'm convinced that any more than two terms in the Senate rots your mind."

"I agree with you. But Ainslee was different. He wasn't just a knee-jerk liberal, but a very thoughtful man. Carroll respected that, and they argued and debated cases all the time behind the scenes. Some of the arguments were pretty strenuous, but there was real affection between them."

"Interesting."

"I think my judge had only one reservation about him," Norton said thoughtfully. "That was his lechery."

"Really? Even at the end?"

"He was only in his late sixties when he died."

"That does slow some people up," Frost observed. "Besides, I thought he had a wife."

"Two. His first wife died about nineteen sixty-five or -six and he married the vivacious Marietta Greer after he went on the Court. But neither marriage kept him from cutting around."

"Was his nightlife public? I've heard that it wasn't."

"Justice Carroll certainly knew a considerable amount about it. He brought it up to me many times, though he always swore me to secrecy. He was afraid it would reflect badly on the Court if Ainslee ever got caught."

"Well, well. Dirty linen in the Supreme Court." Frost laughed, and was about to tell Norton about the late Justice's date books, but remembered in time Harrison Rowan's strictures earlier that morning. Instead, he called for the check, both men having declined the tempting Bouley desserts after their oysters and entrées of seared slices of fresh salmon.

"I should pay this," Norton said, "I'm still on percentage."

"Percentage of what?" Frost asked, teasing his young companion once again about his anxiety over the fortunes of Chase & Ward. "Besides, this is *my* restaurant, so I'll treat."

As they reached the door, Frost again assured Norton that the economic fortunes of Chase & Ward were bound to improve.

"I'm not worried, Reuben. And besides, having a little breathing time is good once in a while. Especially when you can have a great lunch like that one. What are you up to these days, by the way?"

"Oh, not much," Frost answered. "I hang out at the Gotham Club and read a lot. I'm perfectly content. Besides, something always turns up to keep me busy."

FALL

4

THE NEXT MORNING, CYNTHIA FROST AWOKE BEFORE
Reuben, shortly before eight. In accordance with her morning ritual, she went down to the kitchen to squeeze fresh
orange juice for them both. She flipped on the portable
television on the counter and was instantly shocked and
horrified by the first item on the local news: David Rowan,
prizewinning historian, had jumped or fallen to his death at
a building on West Forty-fourth Street. More details were
promised after a break for commercials.

With her dancer's agility, Cynthia bounded upstairs, put
on the television in the master bedroom and woke up her
husband, all before the opening commercials were over.

The couple sat on the edge of the bed, Reuben fully
awake once he understood what his wife was screaming
at him. They watched in frozen horror as the videotape
on the news showed the open window from which the fall
occurred, and then the body, covered with a blanket, lying
on the street amid an array of fire engines, police cars and
an ambulance.

They could scarcely comprehend the details: the incident
had occurred at seven-fifteen the previous evening; death
was instantaneous; the police were saying nothing; neither
suicide nor murder had been ruled out.

Cynthia threw her arms around her husband and began

30

sobbing. He looked fixedly at the screen, and then fairly shouted to his wife. "My God, Cynthia, that's Grace Mann!"

Indeed it was, though the Frosts had been too stunned to notice at first. David Rowan's mistress was coolly describing the death of her lover.

"I don't believe any of this!" Cynthia yelled at the screen.

"It's insane! What is this show-must-go-on nonsense?" Reuben said. "Christ!"

Cynthia continued to weep and Reuben tried to comfort her, though by now there were tears in his eyes, too. Then Grace Mann went on to the next story, looking vaguely upset, but not enough so that a stranger would have suspected that she was the dead man's lover.

Reuben took a shower and got dressed, turning over in his mind as he did so what he would do next. He had to make at least two calls—to Harrison Rowan, and to his friend in the New York City Police Department, Homicide Detective Luis Bautista.

Frost called Bautista first. By now he felt he knew the police officer well, having worked with him first in connection with the poisoning of his partner Graham Donovan at Chase & Ward. Frost, in luck, reached him the first time he rang. He explained that a friend, David Rowan, had jumped or been pushed out a midtown window the night before.

"Yeah, I know about it," Bautista said. "There's pressure from downtown to take the case away from the guy who caught it at the precinct. If I'm real lucky I may get it."

"If a detective is being assigned, does that mean it's definitely murder and not suicide?" Frost asked.

"Not necessarily. But ninety percent sure, yes. Off the record, the guy's office was all roughed up and there were signs he had a real struggle with somebody. But we've got to wait for the Medical Examiner's report to be certain."

"You don't sound too happy about getting involved."

"I'm not. I hate political cases."

"Political cases?"

"Yeah, when the Mayor or somebody else downtown gets personally interested. I understand the Mayor was friends with this guy, or his wife, or something, so everybody got the no-stones-unturned speech this morning."

"I guess I should tell you I'm interested, too," Reuben told him. "David Rowan was the son of an old, old friend of mine. He was also my godson."

"I'm sorry, Reuben. So what the hell. It looked like I was going to get the case anyway. If you get involved and help me, I'll go and sign up."

"Luis, I'm relieved. I'm going to talk with his father now. Shall we get together later?"

"Sure. What time?"

"I don't know. I can't figure how long I'll be."

"Look, I'm going to be here on other stuff all morning. Why don't you call me when you're finished."

"Fine. I'll do that."

Minutes later, Frost was out on Park Avenue, heading for David Rowan's apartment on Seventy-fourth Street. He had called there after talking with Bautista and had reached a very distraught Harrison Rowan.

As he went up in the elevator to the apartment, Reuben steeled himself for what awaited him. He realized all too painfully that every encounter he had ever had with the man, except at the time of Valerie's death, had been pleasant, sometimes exuberantly and joyously so. The apartment door was unlocked, so he entered without ringing. Harrison Rowan was standing in the living room and he walked quickly to greet his visitor. But the sight of his old friend set him to weeping, in deep, uncontrollable sobs. Frost enveloped Rowan with a bear hug, repeating "Harrison, I'm sorry" over and over in a low voice as he tried to calm him.

Harrison Rowan seemed frail and helpless, his voice weak. He passively sat down after Frost maneuvered him to a chair.

"My life is over, Reuben," he moaned. "First Valerie and now . . . this." He began sobbing again, his eyes pink and his normally jovial face distorted in unkind caricature.

"I know, Harrison. I'm very sorry."

"It's not fair. Just when David's piling up honors one after the other, he has an accident like this."

"You think it was an accident?" Frost asked, as gently as possible.

"What else could it be?" the father answered. "Not suicide. No Rowan has ever done that. That leaves murder, and that's preposterous."

Frost decided not to pass along the sketchy information Bautista had conveyed to him earlier, none of which was consistent with a conclusion that David's death was accidental.

"What does Grace think? Is she here?"

"One question at a time, Reuben, I'm totally drained. Where is she? In her bedroom back there. She was up all night—we both were—and insisted on doing her broadcast this morning. Then she came back here and collapsed."

"Didn't she talk to the police? Doesn't she have any ideas?"

"Two questions again, dear Reuben. Yes, she did talk to the police, but she told me they were noncommittal."

"And does she have any theory?"

"She's uncertain. And with her guilty conscience, I'm not sure her judgment wouldn't be clouded anyway."

"What do you mean, guilty conscience?"

"Why, her relationship with Tom Giardi."

"Who? What are you talking about?"

"Tom Giardi. Owns a restaurant a few blocks from here. She's been having a fling with him for months now."

"How do you know that?"

"I visit here a fair amount, you know. He seems to be on the telephone ten times a day, talking to Grace while David's at his office. He came here to see her a couple of times and the two of us went to his restaurant for lunch once. You can't fool an old man. I could see something was going on."

"Did David ever say anything about it?"

"Oh, no. And I never raised it with him."

"So there was no estrangement, no quarrel that you know of?"

"No. I'm confident it was Grace's little secret."

"She and David weren't married, were they?"

"Not to the best of my knowledge. He only got around to divorcing Nancy about two years ago. Or, I should say, she divorced him. She's a lawyer now, you know."

"So there was no reason for this Giardi to wish David any harm?"

"Reuben, Reuben, what an imagination you have! I'm sure it was an accident. A sad, stupid accident."

Frost drummed on the coffee table in front of him as he thought over what he had been hearing.

"Harrison, I've talked to the police," Frost said, reversing his earlier decision to remain quiet. "The one thing that's clear is that it wasn't an accident. David's office was ransacked. The chances are very, very high that it was murder and very, very low that it was suicide. And I would say zero that it was an accident."

Rowan seemed to take in what Frost was saying very slowly. It was several moments before he asked, "When will they know?"

"I've talked to a homicide detective—actually a friend—who says he hopes to have a preliminary report this afternoon."

"I forgot. You keep getting mixed up with murders—that partner of yours, then the choreographer, and that food heir."

"I certainly wish I'd avoided this one," Frost said. "But since I haven't, who could have done it?"

"My son could be a difficult fellow, but I'm sure there was no one out to kill him."

"You can't think of anyone?"

"He's had a lot of problems with the women in his life," Harrison said. "Not that they would try to kill him."

"Like Nancy?"

"Yes."

"And what about Grace Mann?"

"Oddly enough, I think they were getting along," Harrison said. "She seemed perfectly happy with David as long as she had her little affair on the side."

"And what's her name, Marietta, Marietta Ainslee?"

"Oh, yes. She was mad as hell at David."

"While we're on that subject, can you tell me a little bit about this sex code old Ainslee had? Cynthia told me about it after the dinner on Monday."

"Yes, and I told her yesterday not to tell anybody else."

"I know."

"David didn't say too much about it. Just that Ainslee put down an O each time he had sex. Some days there were as many as *three*."

"Hmm," Frost said. "How on earth did David figure it out?"

"He was obsessed by the Os, which were all through Ainslee's entries in his engagement calendars. Then, when he started interviewing people for the book, he talked with a woman who had gone out with Ainslee after his wife died and before he hooked up with Marietta. She was rhapsodic about a ten-day cruise they took together. David, when he tried to fix the exact dates of the trip from Ainslee's records, saw that there were a really large number of Os during the cruise time.

"At that point he had a suspicion of what the Os were about," Harrison went on. "There were other ups and downs that confirmed it: none at all for the first few days after his first wife's death—decent fellow, there. And Os coming off the page when he first met Marietta Greer."

"That doesn't necessarily sound so scandalous," Frost said. "He could have been a monogamous old fellow, taking one woman at a time."

"David didn't think so. He was convinced that Ainslee kept track of sex *only* if it was out of wedlock. The Os disappeared for several months after he and Marietta got married."

"But then they came back?"

"Yes, yes. Right up to the day he had his heart attack."

"How old is this Marietta, do you know?"

"She must be fifty-five by now."

"Could she have killed David?"

"Good Lord, what an idea, Reuben."

"I hear she lives with some kind of weightlifter. Do you know anything about that?"

Harrison fitfully described what he had read, mostly in

the *Washingtonian* and the *Style* section of *The Washington
Post*, about Marietta Ainslee's "pet," a thirtyish former
championship bodybuilder named Ralston Fortes. The woman had apparently met him at a party, taken him home and
immediately tried to uplift him, thus accounting for his
enrollment in a creative writing course at Georgetown and
the completion of a first (but as yet unpublished) novel
Marietta had publicly declared to be "stunning."

"I take it you haven't met this Mr. Fortes," Frost asked.

"Oh, no. But his picture's in the paper a lot—crew-cut
and block-headed, in a literal, and probably a figurative,
way. Clearly the beneficiary of the new trend that sees
bodybuilders as fashionable." Harrison attempted to speak
lightly, but without success; his voice remained dead and
unanimated.

"Do you think I can see Grace if I wait around?" Frost
asked, changing the subject.

"I think she'll be asleep for a long time," Harrison
answered. "She's exhausted. As I told you, she was up
all night."

"What about a funeral?"

"I haven't even given it a thought. I suppose I've got to.
Me . . . me and Grace, I guess," Harrison said, sounding old and tired.

"Would you like to come and stay with us, by the way?"

"No, no. I'm all right here, as long as Grace will have
me."

"Well, I hope you'll let us know if there's anything we
can do," Frost said, standing up.

"Reuben, if what you say is true about my son's death,
there certainly is something you can do."

"Of course. Anything."

"Find the murderer! Find the one who took away the last
joy I had in my life!" Harrison Rowan shook with anger as
he exhorted Frost, his voice rising.

"Harrison, I will do everything I can," Frost replied.
He embraced his old friend one last time and hurried out
the door.

* * *

Frost briskly walked the four blocks back home. With Harrison Rowan's plea fresh in his mind, he was determined to talk to Bautista immediately and get started. The murder of his godson must be solved, for his own peace of mind and that of his old friend.

GETTING STARTED

FROST CALLED LUIS BAUTISTA ALMOST PRECISELY AT NOON and suggested that they have lunch.

"I want to go to a place I've heard about but have never been to," Frost said. "It's called Giardi's. Do you know it?"

"I've heard of it. But I can't go there."

"Why not?"

"It's a Mafia joint—off-limits to the police."

"You mean Tom Giardi is a gangster?"

"The answer to that is yes. Why are you interested in him anyway?"

"I'll tell you over lunch," Frost said. "If Giardi's is unsuitable, why don't we go to my club?"

"Good. I like that old place. Even if it is sexist. Fifty-sixth Street, right?"

"Yes. At Fifth. Is one o'clock okay?"

"Make it one-fifteen."

"Fine."

Jasper Darmes, the jocular doorman at the Gotham Club, advised Reuben when he arrived that he had a guest waiting in the reception room (a pleasant enough Siberia, but Siberia nonetheless, where nonmember guests were relegated by the portly young Darmes until their hosts arrived; it would not do to have strangers roaming about unaccompanied in the staid premises of the Club).

Luis Bautista rose to greet Reuben when he came to offer deliverance.

"Luis! Good to see you," Frost said. "You've shaved off your beard."

"Yes. You and Cynthia and Francisca win," Bautista said wryly. "None of you liked it so I gave up."

"You did the right thing," Frost confirmed, looking up at the handsome face of the detective. "You've been South."

"Francisca and I went to Florida for a weekend. Only three days."

"It looks like you were in the sun longer than that."

"Not me, Reuben. My ancestors. They were in the sun a lot." Bautista laughed easily as he spoke.

"How is Francisca?" Frost asked, referring to Bautista's long-standing girlfriend.

"She's just fine. Scared there for a while when they announced a big cutback at her firm. But she survived okay. The guy she's secretary to got promoted to chairman of the place."

"I'm glad to hear that. They would have been fools to get rid of someone as capable and pretty as Francisca."

Once seated in the dining room of the Gotham, Bautista apologized for not being able to go to Giardi's, and added, "We're also safer here. Don't forget there was a gang killing at Giardi's about six months ago."

"So there was. But that doesn't mean you'll avoid the Mafia by coming to the Gotham."

"Here?" Bautista said, looking incredulous.

"Not the kind you mean—the crime Mafia. But every other kind. Look over there: the editorial director of a major publishing house, one of the city's most successful literary agents, the editor-in-chief of one of the news magazines and a couple of *capos* I don't know. The literary Mafia.

"Or over there. The President of the City Council, the head of the Metropolitan Transportation Authority, the Chairman of First Fiduciary Bank, a Deputy Mayor. The political Mafia. Or the political Mafia meeting the chief of the banking Mafia."

"I see what you mean, Reuben," Bautista said, laughing. "What are we? The homicide Mafia?"

Bautista's attempt at humor had a sobering effect on the two men, and focused their attention back on the serious business that had brought them together again.

"Any word from the Medical Examiner?" Frost asked.

"Not yet. But, as I told you, I think you can assume the decedent was murdered."

"No chance of its being a suicide?"

"I don't think so."

In response to Bautista's request, Frost described the late David Rowan, his work and his private life, including the three women—his former wife, his mistress and his patroness—who might have been angry with him. He told the detective, as best he could, about the women.

"It's curious," Bautista said after Frost had completed both his narrative and his chopped steak.

"What?"

"Those women. All three of them seem to have a man under their thumb, or at least around. Mrs. Rowan has her son, Grace Mann has Tommy Giardi and Mrs. Ainslee has her bodybuilder."

"What do you make out of that?"

"Nothing right now. Except that any one of those able-bodied men could have heaved Rowan out the window."

"I have no idea whether they're all able-bodied. I certainly don't know about Tommy Giardi, since you won't let me get a look at him."

"Reuben, if Giardi isn't able-bodied, I can assure you he has a lot of friends who are."

Over coffee in the Club library, Frost and Bautista continued their discussion in lowered tones.

"Who else might have killed him?" Bautista asked.

"I've told you everyone that I know about. Couldn't it have been an ordinary robber off the street?"

"Not likely, as you can tell by looking at the mess in his office. You want to see it? I think you should."

"Sure."

"Now?"

"Why not?"

* * *

The two men walked down Fifth Avenue to Forty-fourth Street. Turning right, Bautista pointed out the building from which David Rowan had fallen.

"Here Reuben. Let's cross the street, so we can get a head-on view."

They jaywalked to the south side, in midblock.

"He fell from the fourth window over on the tenth floor," Bautista explained, pointing upward. "He landed right in front of the curb, there across the street."

What had been a dramatic scene on television had now returned to complete normality; there was no evidence, no mark, that an important American historian had died there less than twenty-four hours before.

"Now take a look at the lobby," Bautista said. Frost did so, and saw a narrow expanse, with an arched ceiling, extending from Forty-fourth Street through the block to Forty-fifth. They stood in the ornate passageway, with its vermiculated arches, as Bautista explained the building's security arrangements.

"At night, the Forty-fifth Street entrance is closed after seven o'clock. After that a guard sits in the lobby, south of the two elevator banks. Everyone who enters or leaves after seven has to go in or come out through Forty-fourth Street and is supposed to sign in or out."

"David fell about seven-fifteen, is that right?"

"Correct."

"So the person who pushed him—if there was one—could have entered the building before seven without signing the register."

"Correct again."

"But that person would have had to sign out."

"Theoretically, yes. But this is a very busy building—two big law firms, an advertising agency and a magazine, all with lots of traffic. Federal Express messengers, photo-finishers, pizza-delivery guys—plus lots of people working late and leaving after regular hours. The guard really only makes people sign the register when he's suspicious—or feeling mean."

"I understand," Frost said. "At night they have guards

and a sign-up register at One Metro Plaza, but I've never had to do it coming in or going out."

"Of course not," Bautista said. "You're old, distinguished looking—and white. But try to get in there without signing if you're eighteen, black and wearing sneakers and a Walkman."

"So you don't think the pusher—if we can call him that—signed the book?"

"I doubt it. Or if he did, he probably used a fake name. We're checking it out, though, just in case. The guard ran out to the street once the decedent's body was discovered. So anybody could have walked out of there unnoticed.

"What's more likely, though, is that the killer went out the fire exit on the Forty-fifth Street side. The burglar alarm on that exit went off a few minutes after Rowan was found. He probably sneaked out the back way."

"Hmm. Not too encouraging."

"No. But come on, I'll show you upstairs."

The stout but creaky automatic elevator stopped at the tenth floor. The directory opposite indicated that the floor was subdivided into many small offices, including Room 1003, occupied by "Rowan, D." Bautista led the way down a dimly lit hallway almost to the end, where a patrolman was standing guard outside Room 1003 and a sign warned off intruders:

CRIME
SCENE
SEARCH AREA
STOP
NO ADMITTANCE BEYOND THIS POINT

By order of Police Commissioner
POLICE DEPARTMENT

"Afternoon, officer," Bautista said to the policeman, who was young enough to have a heavy case of acne and whose uniform, badge, service revolver and nightstick were not sufficient to keep him from being nervous. Bautista showed his own badge, which he was wearing inside his suit lapel.

"I'm from homicide and we'd like to take a look inside. Mr. Frost here is a possible witness."

Frost was surprised to hear himself so characterized, but assumed the representation was necessary to gain him entrance to Rowan's office.

"The CSU gone?" Bautista asked, referring to the crime scene unit specialists from the Homicide Bureau.

"Yessir. About half an hour ago."

"Good," Bautista said. He then turned to Reuben, and in a voice too low for the patrolman to hear, explained that he was going to open the door and would only let Reuben see what he could from the doorway. "The CSU boys may say they're finished, but they never are. They'll be back, and I don't want to be blamed for messing up the scene."

With that introduction, he asked the guard to unlock the door. He motioned Reuben forward to look inside. What he saw was a large, one-room office with bare walls and three casement windows. Along most of the wall space were metal bookcases extending from floor to ceiling, some still containing the letter-box files that had not been strewn about on the floor. And, at one side, a closed and seemingly untouched four-drawer file cabinet.

"This is the way they found the place?" Frost asked.

"Yes. I hope just exactly as you see it. Why, did you think the police made this mess?"

"No, no, nothing like that," Frost said hastily, though that thought had crossed his mind. "What's in the file cabinet over there?" he asked, pointing.

"That appears to have been his personal files—correspondence, newspaper clippings, that sort of thing."

"And it was not touched?"

"Not as far as we can tell."

Turning to the letter boxes, Frost read the labels on the backs of those nearest the door. He saw that most of them related to specific Supreme Court cases, though more distant ones, the labels on which he could barely make out, related to legislation dating back to Garrett Ainslee's Senate days.

The boxes on the floor had burst open with their contents spilling out. None appeared to be empty—except two almost directly in front of Frost.

"I wonder what those are," he asked, pointing to the empty boxes.

"You mean what was supposed to be in them?

"Yes."

"Let's have a look." Bautista produced a rubber glove, which he put on before reaching out and turning over the two boxes. One bore the label "Desk Calendars, 1952–66," the other "Desk Calendars, 1966–80."

"I don't see signs of any desk calendars, do you?" Frost said.

"No."

At lunch Frost had told the detective about Ainslee's sex code, so he now understood Frost's remark that "It looks like we're never going to see the famous Os—or anything else those books might have contained."

"Let me see if the CSU found anything," Bautista said.

"If not, I think we'd better start finding out where the long arm of Marietta Ainslee's been reaching lately," Frost told his colleague.

Contrary to his usual custom, Frost took a taxi home after leaving Bautista; he had done enough walking for one day. And he had become sufficiently absorbed that he now felt very sad and very tired.

6

REUBEN FROST TOOK HIS USUAL NAP THAT AFTERNOON. HE was sleeping soundly when Bautista called, shortly after five o'clock.

"We've got the ME's report," the detective said. "Murder."

"For certain?" Frost asked.

"No question about it. The Medical Examiner's pretty sure he was knocked unconscious—hit on the side of the head—before he was shoved out the window."

"Anything else?"

"Yes. Rowan obviously struggled with his assailant, and it looks like he fought like hell."

"How can you tell that?"

"His fingernails. When they scraped them, they found traces of skin and blood that weren't his. His blood type was A and the blood under his nails was type B. The skin fragments were probably from the neck of his attacker—a white person, incidentally. Rowan must have struggled like a cornered rat."

"Hmn."

"Sorry, Reuben. Forget about the rat. Let's just say he fought back."

"So we—you—have got to find someone who matches the blood type and the skin samples."

45

"Yeah. Unfortunately, there are about forty million living white Americans with type B blood. Got any ideas which ones we start with?"

"No. None at all," Frost said, though what he really meant was that the confirmation that David Rowan was murdered had temporarily crowded out all other thoughts from his mind.

"We're still waiting for the CSU's report on the office. If we're lucky, there'll be a nice, clear, visible print or some other good hard evidence there. Not much we can do until then. But you, meanwhile, might focus on which of those forty million white Americans we look at first."

"I've got to get my thoughts in order," Frost said. "Can I call you later?"

"Sure. But the sooner the better. Meanwhile, just be glad my boys remembered to bag Rowan's hands at the scene and that Rowan didn't bite his fingernails."

Frost went to the bathroom after hanging up the phone and splashed cold water on his face. The effort brought him fully awake, but did not make his thinking any clearer. Following a pattern set in the earliest days of his marriage, he wanted to talk out this latest crisis with Cynthia. He awaited her return from the Brigham Foundation with increasing impatience.

"Where have you been?" he demanded when she arrived home shortly before seven.

"I'm sorry, dear, I didn't mean to be late. I had to have a drink with the culture man from Exxon about the Pirandello festival I told you about. Exxon may put up some of the money."

"Ridiculous idea. North Dakota, wasn't it? *Six Characters in Search of a Pig Farmer*."

"You're in a foul mood, I can tell. What can I do to cheer you up?" Cynthia asked, tousling her husband's gray hair.

"Nothing. I just want to sit down with you and talk about David's murder. In case you had any doubt that it was murder, Luis called two hours ago to confirm it."

"I was afraid of that," Cynthia said, with a sigh. "Shall

we eat here? I had a cooked chicken delivered this afternoon. Is that okay? "

"Fine. That means we can really talk. I didn't particularly want to discuss this terrible business in a restaurant."

"Have a drink and give me twenty-five minutes."

Reuben obeyed his wife's direction, fixed himself a martini and waited patiently for dinner. Then, as Cynthia brought the food into the dining room, he went to the refrigerator and sampled a half-full bottle of Chardonnay. As he feared, it had gone bad. He cursed quietly and pulled out a new, full bottle to open.

"Someday I've got to get that damn nitrogen contraption working," he told his wife, referring to a device that purportedly kept open wine fresh. He had purchased it several weeks earlier with great enthusiasm but had been unable to get it operating.

"Never mind, dear. We'll probably drink a full bottle tonight, anyway."

Cynthia's prediction was correct. They ate quickly and quietly, then pushed their plates aside and drank up the new bottle as Reuben told his wife the details of his day's meetings with Harrison Rowan and Bautista—and of his visit to the crime scene.

"The way I see it," Reuben said, "somebody came to see David in his office, probably to confront him about something, or to make a demand of some kind. They quarreled, the argument got rough, the murderer got physical and then threw David out the window, conscious or unconscious."

"And then messed up the office to create confusion?"

"Yes."

"How about this? What if the murderer was looking for something in the office, probably in Ainslee's papers? And then was surprised by David and had to kill him?"

"Perhaps. But Luis said there was no evidence the lock on the door was tampered with."

"Maybe the murderer had a key."

"This is getting nowhere," Reuben said. "Let's figure out who we know, or know of, that might have wanted to kill David, or to burglarize his office."

"Well, right off the bat, there's Marietta Ainslee. You

say the Justice's engagement books are gone—and that's where his peccadilloes were recorded."

"I've got to get a line on her, you're right."

"And I would think on her bodybuilding friend whom Harrison told you about. It sounds to me as if he could have tossed David out the window without any trouble."

"I know. Ralston Fortes, for God's sake. What kind of a name is that?"

"God knows."

"I agree with you, he's the most promising suspect at this point."

"But we can't forget the former wife and the present girlfriend."

"Not very likely, Cynthia. You remember Nancy Rowan. She's all of five feet four. She couldn't possibly have defenestrated David, no matter how angry she was."

"Yes, but how about her son, Alan? You told me the other night that Grace Mann said he was under his mother's thumb."

"Alan's a possibility. And we know he's been wandering around lately, judging by his mother's phone call Monday night. But there's no way Grace Mann can be. She's pretty slight herself and I don't believe a TV anchorwoman could sneak about and commit a murder like this without being seen by somebody."

"The guards may have been used to seeing her."

"Sure, she may have come to the office all the time. But they'd still think of her as a celebrity and remember her."

"You're right. But what about her friend, Tommy Giardi—or Giardi's friends?"

"Another possibility, that's true. But what motive would he have for killing David? If Giardi's affair with Grace had really steamed up, there wasn't anything to prevent her from leaving David."

"So it seems," Cynthia said with a sigh.

"Is there anyone else? No one that's plausible. Stanley Knowles? That makes no sense. Why would he want to kill off one of his hottest authors? Harrison Rowan? Absurd on its face. Horace Jenkins, the research assistant? He's dying.

But how about that professor, Peter Jewett, whom David apparently disliked so much?"

"I think it would be more relevant if David had killed *him*. Besides, I don't see Peter as a killer. Disagreeable, yes. But not a killer, unless I'm an awfully bad judge of people," Cynthia said.

"No, Reuben, the only person I've met recently who might be daring enough to commit murder was that cool and clever young man I sat next to at the Reuff Dinner," she went on.

"Oh, yes, your new boyfriend, Mr. Taylor."

"But it's unlikely that he had anything to do with David."

"Right. He was only at the dinner because Edmunds was speaking."

Frost drained the wine bottle, democratically sharing the last few drops equally with Cynthia. "I told Harrison I would do everything I could to find David's killer," he said, putting his empty glass down. "I'm going to do that. The only place I can think to start is with Marietta Ainslee. I think I've got to go down and see her. And hope Ralston Fortes pops out of the bedroom long enough to be seen."

"I have one other idea, which I'm sure you won't like much."

"What's that?" Reuben asked.

"Jenkins. He may know something. And since he's dying, I think you, or you and Luis, ought to see him right away."

"I hate the thought. I'm not afraid of getting AIDS, but I can do without seeing its effects. But you're absolutely right, I've got to see him. I'll call Luis first thing in the morning."

GRACE

7

IF REUBEN FROST WAS A WALKING, WELL-CONNECTED computer, as Stanley Knowles had characterized him at the Reuff Dinner, it was not evident Thursday morning; the wires in his semiconductor were decidedly wet, or perhaps there was a fat sparrow sitting on the lines. Whatever the reason, Frost was unable to reach Luis Bautista at the Police Department. He was "out on a case" and was not expected before early afternoon.

Frost felt that Bautista should be present at any interview with Horace Jenkins at Tyler Hospital, and guessed that he would probably be unable to arrange to see him alone in any event. But now Bautista's absence would delay things.

Frost glanced impatiently at the morning *Times*, which carried a front-page story of the police announcement that David Rowan had been murdered. Casting the paper aside, he returned to the problem that had bothered him through a troubled night—how to get to see Mr. Justice Ainslee's widow in Washington. He had decided that his best chance for gaining an audience was through Dotty Sheets, an old friend and a rich Washington culture maven who was a longtime friend of Cynthia's. He looked up the number on the family Rolodex and called her just before eleven o'clock.

"Dotty, my dearest, how are you?" he said once he heard the woman's near-baritone voice (the product of bourbon and Gauloise cigarettes) on the telephone.

"Reuben, what a thrill! My whole body is weak from hearing your voice again!"

"Mine, too, my sweet," Frost said, adapting to the extravagant 1930s movie dialect that Dotty Sheets favored.

"To what do I owe this *delectable* pleasure?"

Frost told Ms. Sheets that he needed an introduction to Marietta Ainslee; that it was very important that he be able to talk to her.

"Reuben, you old scamp! Chasing after the Widow Ainslee! Why?"

"A fair question, Dotty. I'm a friend—or was a friend—of her husband's biographer. He was murdered two days ago, and I'm just doing a little background work."

"Reuben, you are a devil! When did you get so nosy?"

"I'm not really nosy, Dotty, but David Rowan—the biographer—was my godson, and his father is an old friend, so I'm making some inquiries."

"He was *murdered*? My goodness. What on earth could Marietta have to do with that?"

"I assume nothing. But I'd like to talk to her. Could you be a dear and arrange it?"

"I'm sure I can. Marietta is a darling friend. Marietta—and Ralston too."

"You know him, then?"

"Oh, yes. Ralston Fortes, and I do mean *fortes*! He's the most gorgeous thing to land in Washington since Senator Kerry."

"Hmn."

"When do you want to see her?"

"Just as soon as possible."

"You mean today, this very day?"

"If you could arrange it. But tomorrow probably makes more sense."

"Oh, Reuben, I'm so excited. Are you playing detective again?"

"Just trying to be helpful, Dotty dear. Can you aid and abet me?"

"I thought aiding and abetting was a crime."

"Aid and *assist* me then."

"*Certainement*. Where are you, at home?"

"Yes. Two-one-two, seven-four-four-three-three-three-one."

"What a lovely number! I think the First Lady's numerologist would be thrilled. But forget that, I'll call you. And give my love to Cynthia, if she's up yet."

"She's up, and has gone to work. But I'll tell her."

"Oh, sweet Reuben, how lovely. I'll call you. I assume, by the way, I can tell Marietta why you want to see her."

"I don't see any way around it."

"*Va bene*, Reuben. *Ciao, carissimo!*"

Frost had to rest for a moment after Dotty Sheets had hung up the telephone. Her trilingual energy always exhausted him.

When he had recovered, he realized that nothing was likely to happen until the next day, so he decided he might try to talk to Grace Mann. He found her in, awake and willing to see him. They arranged to meet at two o'clock.

Promptly at the appointed hour Frost waited for Grace Mann in the same living room where he had met Harrison Rowan the day before. Her Irish maid explained that Mr. Rowan had returned to Virginia earlier in the day.

"What about the funeral?" Frost asked.

"I don't think there's to be one, sir," the maid replied before disappearing.

For the first time, Frost had a chance to examine the living quarters of Grace Mann and David Rowan—what in former days the tabloids would have called a "love nest" but which, in the advanced eighties, was merely a chic Upper East Side apartment openly shared by its two occupants.

The furniture was an odd, but surprisingly compatible, assortment of severely modern pieces and Art Deco antiques. The stark white walls were covered with large, brightly colored abstract paintings, one of which Reuben was sure was a Helen Frankenthaler.

Grace Mann, wearing a black silk blouse and black pants, came in and embraced Reuben. She was wearing little or no makeup and her face looked drawn, though there was no evidence of tears.

"Oh, Reuben, what a mess! You've seen the papers?"

"Yes. I saw the *Times* at home and the *Post* headline on the way over—PULITZER PRIZER PUSHED. Wonderful taste."

The maid reappeared with a large glass of orange juice for Ms. Mann.

"Will you have something, sir?" she asked. Frost declined.

"I gather there's to be no funeral," Frost said while Grace drank her juice.

"That's right. David always said he hated funerals. He had no particular religion anyway, so we decided against it."

" 'We'? You and Harrison?"

"Yes," she said. "We'll have a memorial service after things quiet down."

"Have you talked to the police?"

"Yes, they were here a couple of hours ago when I was scarcely awake. But there was a nice young officer. He was named Bautista, I believe."

"Yes, I know him," Frost said, realizing that Bautista's morning appointment "on a case" had been with Grace.

"You do?"

Frost explained his past connections with the detective and asked what she had told him.

"What could I tell him? I don't know of anyone that wanted to hurt David."

"You weren't able to give him any leads?"

"I'm afraid not. Nancy Rowan's the only person I could think of, and that little creature isn't in the business of killing people."

"I agree," Frost said. Then he told her why he had come—how he had promised Harrison that he would do everything he could to solve the mystery of David Rowan's death.

"What I'd like to do, Grace, is to ask you some questions—some of which may be a trifle embarrassing. And most of which will probably duplicate what you've already told Detective Bautista. But if I'm going to be of any help to you, or to Harrison or the police, I've got to get David's death—and the life he led before he was killed—in focus. All right?"

Grace Mann looked fixedly at Frost as he spoke. She continued to rein in any emotions she might feel, though she seemed in earnest when she said she valued Frost's assistance and wanted to be as helpful as she could.

"Fine," Frost said, the preliminaries over. "We agree that Nancy could not be the killer. But what about Alan?"

"That's impossible. He's really a good kid."

"Do you know him well?"

"Pretty well. For years he had nothing to do with David, but he'd been reconciled the last year or two."

"They got along all right?"

"As well as any father and son these days. They had a big fight over Alan's leaving Vanderbilt. And, yes, there was a big blow-up last summer, but everything had healed over."

"What was the fight about?"

"Alan wanted to go to Europe with some friends. David was still angry about the boy's dropping out, so he refused to put up the money."

"Which meant he couldn't go?"

"Right. Alan's a nice kid, but he's never worked a day in his life, so he had no money for a trip. And Nancy doesn't either."

"She's a lawyer now, isn't she?"

"Yes. She works for some legal aid outfit in Trenton. Not much money there."

"How long since you've seen Alan?"

"How long? A couple of weeks," she said firmly, though there seemed a touch of nervousness in her voice. "He stayed over here one night when he came in for a rock concert at Madison Square Garden."

"And as far as you know, that was the last time he was in the city?"

"Yes, but he doesn't always check in here when he comes in."

"Could he have killed his father?" Frost asked, looking directly at Grace Mann.

"*Anybody* could have killed David," she answered, then paused for what seemed to Reuben a long time. "But Alan a killer? No way."

Frost then asked casually about Marietta Ainslee, trying to conceal his great interest in the Washington widow. He did not receive much help.

"I never met her. All I know about her is what David told me."

"Did he see her often?"

"Quite a bit, yes. First, when the terms of his deal were being worked out, access to the Justice's papers and all that. He flew to Washington several times for that last year.

"He went back later, several times," she continued, "to talk to her about personal details of the Justice's life. But after a while he gave that up."

"Why?"

"He never could see her alone. She was always with her new boyfriend, Ralston Fortes. Do you know about him?"

"I've heard some things."

"David didn't like him. Didn't like him at all. He said the man always seemed unfriendly, and even menacing. He was a bodybuilder before he met Marietta, you know."

"Yes."

"He was very aggressive in controlling Marietta's interviews with David. David thought he might even be jealous—that maybe he wanted to do the Ainslee biography himself."

"A curious idea."

"Well, he did think he was a novelist."

"Yes. Was the widow being cooperative at the end?"

"No. She was threatening to bring down the curtain on David altogether—to take back the papers and to discourage anyone from talking to him. But she hadn't yet done anything about the threat."

"I gather the trouble was over the sex code in Ainslee's diaries."

"Yes. How did you know?"

"Harrison told Cynthia about it at the dinner the other night."

"It's so silly. David was so pleased with himself he couldn't keep quiet about his discovery—great cocktail party talk. Inevitably she found out and was furious."

"What did David do about her threats?"

"He told her the publicity she'd get by breaking their agreement would be far worse than having the 'code' mentioned in the biography."

"When did he tell her that?"

"About two weeks ago."

"That recently?"

"Yes. She didn't move against him, but she did refuse to come to the Reuff Dinner."

"Very interesting."

Frost hesitated before bringing up the final item on his agenda—Tommy Giardi. He eased into the subject, if not especially gracefully.

"Were you and David getting along?"

"Now you sound like the police, Reuben," Grace said, fixing him with a direct gaze. "But the answer is yes. Do you have any reason to doubt it?"

"No, no, except . . ."

"Except Tommy Giardi, is that it?"

"Well . . . frankly, yes."

"I suppose Harrison told you about him."

"That's right."

"Harrison can be a dirty old man sometimes. But I'm not going to conceal anything—the police asked me about him too. I'll tell you the whole story." She paused and lit a cigarette.

"Tommy Giardi is basically a pal, nothing more. We discovered we had a lot in common—like having our afternoons free, me after finishing the morning telecast, Tommy before dinner began at his restaurant.

"For better or worse, David and I just didn't have that much time together during the week. Every morning when I got home, about nine-thirty, he'd already have gone to that office of his. He always ate lunch at his desk, so I didn't see him until he returned, usually around six, when I was already thinking about going to sleep.

"Anyway, about three months ago I met Tommy Giardi. I liked him—he's amusing, considerate and handsome, in his macho, Italian way. So, yes, we've seen a lot of each other—in the afternoons."

"Did David know about this?"

"He knew we were friends," she said. "Which is basically what we were."

" 'Basically'?"

"You mean did we ever sleep together? It's none of your damn business, Reuben, but we did. Once or twice. But we weren't in love, and our times in bed were, well, sort of frolics."

"Did David know about your, ah, frolics?"

"No. There was nothing serious going on at all. David did know we were pals and didn't seem to mind—he was glad I had company in the daytime."

"I gather Mr. Giardi doesn't have the best reputation in the world."

"Oh, you mean the Mafia business? All ridiculous. Tommy's a nice, hardworking man whose name happens to end in a vowel. That's enough to get the rumors started in this town. Put it this way, Reuben. Tommy and I were—are—friends. David and I were lovers."

"You weren't married, were you?"

Grace Mann smiled and shrugged her shoulders. "Now that he's dead I can tell the truth. We were married. Sixteen months ago, in Maine."

"You say that now that he's dead you can tell the truth. What do you mean?"

"You probably won't believe this, but there's great pressure on me to remain single. The powers that be at the network think it's very important for my image and the ratings. And with my contract up for renewal this year, I haven't been about to quarrel with them."

"But it was in all the papers that you and David were together."

"Oh, that was all right. In fact, that was just fine. Made me seem a *contemporary* woman. But marriage was out."

Frost tried to absorb what Grace Mann was telling him, but her network's values had him confused. He was eager to leave, but there was one more detail.

"Grace, you said that David usually came home at night around six?"

"Almost like clockwork. After all, it was our only real time together."

"But the night he was killed, he was at his office at seven. Do you know why?"

"No. I was out in the afternoon and when I got back there was a message from David on the answering machine saying he might be a little late. It was our last communication—and by recording at that." Mann's statement was matter-of-fact; no sentimental tears were shed over this last, remote electronic contact.

"Did he say why he'd be late?"

"No. I figured he must have an appointment with someone. And I inferred from his voice that he wouldn't be terribly late."

"That tape isn't still around?"

"No. No. I erase messages on the machine as soon as I receive them."

"You guessed that he had an appointment, but no idea with whom?"

"That's the big question, isn't it? No, and as I said, I was only guessing that he was going to meet someone."

"I've kept you too long," Frost said.

"And I haven't been very helpful, I'm afraid."

"You know where to reach me if you think of anything—*anything*—that might be a clue to David's death."

Grace Mann promised that she would call if she thought of something, and showed Reuben to the door.

HORACE

REUBEN FROST WAS CHARY OF THE ANSWERING MACHINE in his town-house. Like all mechanical devices, it terrified him, though he had mastered the Japanese/English instructions that had come with the contraption. As a result he was more or less pleased with its efficiency, though it still reminded him that he no longer kept a full-time office, where one could expect calls to be handled.

Flipping the switch on the machine when he got home from Grace Mann's, he found that Dotty Sheets, Luis Bautista and Cynthia all had called.

He reached his wife at the Brigham Foundation; she wanted to know if they could go out to dinner that night.

"Of course, dear," Frost said. "Orso okay?"

His wife allowed that it was.

"Before you hang up, let me give you one morsel to chew on. Remember last night when you said Grace Mann and Mr. Giardi had no reason to kill David, since she could leave David at any time? Well, she and David *were* married. So think about that." He promised fuller details over dinner.

Then Frost called Dotty Sheets, by now in a high state as the intermediary in a *murder* investigation. She had done her work well; Frost could see Marietta Ainslee—but unfortunately not until Monday. Mrs. Ainslee and Ralston Fortes were leaving Washington on Good Friday for the Easter weekend.

Finally, he found Bautista at his desk.

"I talked to the widow."

"Widow?"

"Grace Mann."

"Oh, yeah. She was married to the guy."

"Yes. That was a big surprise to me, Luis. What about Giardi?"

"Yeah, I talked to him this morning. A greaser. Nothing to say."

"What else did you learn?"

"Not much. Your lady friend down in Washington sounds more interesting."

"I agree. I'm seeing her Monday morning."

"Oh? I was about to get the D.C. police to have a look-in."

"Let me have a go first."

"Sure. That's good."

Frost then told Bautista of Cynthia's concern that Horace Jenkins be interviewed.

"Yeah, I thought of that. I'm going over to the hospital in forty-five minutes."

"I want to go—well, not exactly *want* to go, but I think I should," Frost said.

"That may be hard. He's dying, you know. And in about fifteen different ways, poor bastard. I had a hard enough time getting permission to see him myself."

"I can imagine. But I want to go with you if I can."

"Can you be ready in twenty minutes? I'll pick you up."

"I'll be out front on the sidewalk."

Frost was grateful for the short respite; he was still trying to sort out what he had learned—or not learned—from Grace Mann. Basically she had confirmed things he already knew, though the admission that she was married to David certainly made Tommy Giardi of greater interest. And his hunch was that more than palship and "one or two" rolls around the bed were involved.

And the coldness of the woman! Continuing to go on the air each morning—even on the day after her husband was killed—and the total absence of tears, or even an expression of regret, had succeeded in making Frost suspicious. Maybe she was sublimating her grief through work and maintaining a stoic manner, but Frost wondered.

Riding to Tyler Hospital in the unmarked police sedan Bautista was driving, Frost confirmed that Grace Mann's story to him matched what she had told Bautista earlier in the day.

"What's your impression of the Giardi affair?" Frost asked.

"Intense and steady—like every day," Bautista replied.

"You mean they slept together every day?"

"During the week, yeah."

"Any special reason why you think that?"

Bautista looked over from the wheel, grinning. "Nope. Just male intuition."

"Well, I happen to agree with you."

"I've done a little more work on Giardi," Bautista added. "There's a racketeering investigation going on, and a federal income tax audit as well. His restaurant's packed every night, but it still loses money."

"I suppose that's possible."

"Sure. But the Feds are pretty certain he's laundering money for his mob friends, and skimming it out of the restaurant as well. They say he could be indicted any day."

"I wonder what her network would say about *that*."

"Probably nothing. But I'll bet you she dumps him. Those big six figures she pulls down are going to look better to her than a two-bit mob tax cheat."

As they came closer to the hospital, Bautista warned his companion that the visit they were about to make would not be pleasant.

"I take it you've seen AIDS patients before?" Frost asked.

"Twice. And if I had my way, never again. You just don't understand how awful it is until you see somebody who's got it. It's terrible to say it, but if they'd tack up a few pictures of guys dying with AIDS, you could forget about condoms, and education and all the rest of it. You probably wouldn't even have 'safe sex' if they did that.

"It's terrifying, Reuben," he went on. "Lots of people who don't live like we do—but harmless and decent. Talented quite often, too. And then the new trend..." Bautista seemed unable to finish his sentence.

"New trend?"

"Twenty percent—*one-fifth*—of the new victims are my people. Hispanics so high on drugs they can't take a Boy Scout's precautions and save themselves. *And* their women *and* their babies."

As they entered the Tyler parking lot, Bautista explained that he had called ahead to get permission for Reuben to accompany him. "The nurse said okay, there wasn't much that could harm Jenkins at this point. She said normally we couldn't come at the dinner hour, but it doesn't matter. Nobody eats dinner on the AIDS floor. They're all on IVs."

At the hospital, the two men were detained at the nursing station by the no-nonsense supervisor Bautista had talked to, Ms. Creighton.

"You're lucky, gentlemen," she informed them. "Mr. Jenkins is lucid right now. He slips in and out all day, and he could do so again without any warning. He's also on oxygen for his *pneumocystis carinii* pneumonia—PCP for short. We can't take him off that for very long. I understand the purpose of your visit, and I know how important it is, but I must ask you to keep your questions brief."

Her listeners nodded agreement.

"Have you ever visited an AIDS patient?"

"I have," Bautista said. "Mr. Frost has not."

"I'm not going to give you a medical lecture, Mr. Frost," the nurse said, "but a couple of things may help prepare you for the tragic sight you're about to see. Acquired Immunodeficiency Syndrome destroys T-cells—the basis of the body's immunity system for fighting disease. Someone with the AIDS virus is vulnerable to every sort of opportunistic infection. Horace Jenkins has three of the worst of them—PCP, the type of pneumonia that I mentioned; Kaposi's sarcoma, which is a form of cancer. And oral candidiasis, or 'thrush,' as it's called. His body is covered with purple spots from the Kaposi's sarcoma and his mouth is full of white spots from the thrush."

Frost closed his eyes, unwilling to visualize the person he was about to see.

"Now," the nurse continued, "I have gloves and masks here if you like. Since you won't be touching the patient, there's no need for the gloves. And, for that matter, there's no need for the masks either. But some people feel more comfortable wearing them."

"If there's no need, we won't bother," Frost said. Confronting the stricken man with the news of the death of his friend and mentor was enough of an assault, Frost thought; there was no need to add the affront of protective masks.

"Very well. Come this way."

Bautista and Frost followed the nurse into a ward with four beds, all occupied.

"We've arranged it so you can talk privately," she said in a low voice, pointing to a bed surrounded by white curtains in the corner. She approached the patient and called him by name. He turned, his eyes wide and staring at his visitors.

Frost was shocked by what he saw. He had steeled himself for the ugly purple lesions of Kaposi's sarcoma, which covered every visible part of Jenkins's unclothed body. What he was not prepared for was the cadaverous, skeletal parody of a human form, which could not have weighed more than seventy or eighty pounds. Jenkins must be very near death, he thought.

The nurse removed the oxygen mask from the man's face and told him in a firm, but not domineering, voice that there were "two gentlemen" to see him.

Frost looked at Bautista. Who should begin talking? Bautista did not hesitate.

"Mr. Jenkins, we would like to ask you a couple of questions about David Rowan. I'm Detective Bautista from the New York City Police Department and this is Mr. Frost, who was a friend of Mr. Rowan's."

The hollowed eyes shifted back and forth between the two men; they could not tell whether he had understood what had been said.

"I am very sorry to have to tell you that David Rowan is dead," Bautista announced. Now there was no mistaking that Jenkins understood. The already bulging eyes widened further and his sore-covered lips drew back. "He was murdered."

Jenkins moved his jaw up and down; he was trying to form a word. "W-w-w-where?" he said finally.

"At his office," Bautista replied.

After a painfully long silence, Jenkins asked "How?" and Bautista described the circumstances.

"Awful," Jenkins said slowly, and then again, "awful," in a choked voice. A tear rolled down his left cheek. Ms. Creighton gave Bautista a "get on with it" look.

"Mr. Jenkins, I know this must be a great shock for you," Frost said. "But I would like you to think if there was anybody in the time you worked for David who might have done such a thing. Please think very hard as we *must* find David's killer."

Jenkins stared straight ahead for a long time; his questioners were sure they had lost him. But then once again he was trying to form a word, raising his head slightly from the pillow as he did so. The effort seemed to defeat him and his head fell back. Then he tried again. "It's so hard to remember . . . Elizabeth's the best I can do . . . look into Elizabeth . . ."

Jenkins spoke so softly that Frost and Bautista leaned forward over the railings on the side of the bed to make sure of what they had heard. They would hear no more; Jenkins fell soundly asleep, and the nurse quickly placed the oxygen mask over his sepulchral face.

As they walked out, Frost could not help but notice the other patients. All looked as ravaged as the victims of a Third World famine, vacant eyes bulging as the somber trio passed them. He was relieved when they were at last outside the ward, almost as if they had gone from Hades to the land of the living.

"Miss Creighton, thank you very much," Frost said as they shook hands. "I admire what you're doing here."

"Thank you," she replied. "What we're doing is desperately little. I'm a nurse and I want to cure my patients.

But the rules are different for Horace and the other AIDS victims. It's different...and it's horrible. There's no cure. But thank you, Mr.—"

"M'am, let me ask you, did you ever hear Mr. Jenkins refer to Elizabeth before?" Bautista cut in.

"Never."

"And what about his records? It's not his mother's name, is it?"

The nurse went to check. The answer was no.

"Okay, that's it," Bautista said. "Thank you, m'am."

"Are you off duty?" Frost asked once he and Bautista were back in the police sedan.

"Afraid not. Why?"

"I need a drink."

"The hell with it. So do I."

They went to a deserted bar on Lexington Avenue. They drank in silence, both overwhelmed by the inexpressible sadness of what they had seen.

"You're right about those pictures. Put up a picture of poor Jenkins and sex would be driven out of New York."

"Thank God for Francisca," Bautista said.

"And for Cynthia."

They silently contemplated their heterosexual safety. And tried very hard, without success, to figure out who Elizabeth might be.

FROST WAS UP EARLY MONDAY MORNING, IN TIME TO catch the nine-thirty Pan Am shuttle to Washington. His luncheon with Marietta Ainslee was not until one-thirty, but he had arranged a meeting with a Washington lawyer and old friend, Dawson Evans, for eleven.

Evans had begun work as a lawyer at Chase & Ward at roughly the same time as Frost, but had soon been attracted to Washington, where he had several times been through the revolving door that separated Government service and private practice. He was a legal, political and social eminence in the capital, as well-connected there as Reuben was in New York.

Frost wanted to learn as much about Marietta Ainslee as possible before meeting her. There was no entry on her in *Who's Who*. He had considered briefly trying to get a peek at the morgue file on her at the *Times*, an indiscreet device he had resorted to once or twice in the past, but there simply had not been enough time to activate one of his "moles" at the Good Gray Lady. He had also considered mining Dotty Sheet's mental file of the world's, or at least Washington's, indiscretions. But then he decided that Dawson could probably be of more coherent and precise help.

Once on his plane at LaGuardia, he settled back into the

relative comfort of the seat on the Boeing 727, thinking as he did so that competition did have some benefits after all: Pan Am, in an effort to increase its share of the New York–Washington traffic, offered at least a minimal standard of comfort, as contrasted with Eastern, which Frost regarded as a cattle-car airline.

He faced a long day. First the meeting with Dawson at his office, then his lunch, then a Metroliner trip back to Trenton, New Jersey, where he had arranged to see Nancy Rowan at the end of her workday. With this busy prospect before him, he was determined to rest on the way to Washington and was grateful when the seat next to him remained empty, even though it was the morning after the Easter weekend. One of the young Chase & Ward partners was aboard. He greeted Frost cordially and showed some surprise that he was traveling to Washington. Do these youngsters think one curls up and hibernates after retirement? Reuben thought angrily, uncertain whether to be irritated or amused.

Once in Washington, Frost took a cab to Evans's firm, located in an impersonal glass box on K Street. A delegation of midwesterners crowded the waiting room, each with a carry-on garment bag and an aluminum attaché case, undoubtedly waiting to meet their lawyer-lobbyist before descending in search of a favor on their hapless local Congressman or some middle-range bureaucrat.

Despite the confusion in the reception room, Frost was shown promptly to Evans's office, which was in appearance as cold and impersonal as the exterior of the building. The lawyer did have the obligatory Washington display of autographed photographs—what politicians in New York called their "wall of respect"; no serious Washington practitioner was without one, convinced that the garment-bag crowd from beyond the Washington Beltway expected it. Frost's quick perusal of the wall showed that it contained pictures of Evans with the four most recent Presidents and, except for a group photo with the ubiquitous Issac Stern at the Kennedy Center, all the others pictured were of at least subcabinet rank.

"You're looking well, Reuben," Evans said, greeting his

visitor. Hale and hardy himself, with an impeccably coiffed mane of white hair, he could afford to be generous to his contemporaries.

"You, too, Dawson. Washington has certainly agreed with you."

Evans smiled complacently. "So what's all this about Marietta Ainslee?" he asked.

Frost outlined the circumstances of David Rowan's death, explaining that he was working on a biography of Garrett Ainslee when he died. His account was complete, except for any reference to the late Justice's concupiscent diary entries.

"Did you know Ainslee, by the way?"

"Sure. Everyone knew him. He was a major celebrity around town when he was in the Senate. And he kept a very high profile after he got on the Court. A lot of Justices lead a pretty monastic existence, you know, but not Garrett. There used to be a joke that your party was a failure if he wasn't there—he went to everything."

"So you might say he was a high-liver?"

"Gregarious, certainly."

"A ladies' man?"

"Oh, yes. But entirely discreet. None of that stripper-in-the-fountain stuff for him. Why do you ask?"

"Well, there's some indication that David Rowan was starting to uncover some of the underside of Ainslee's love life."

"And Marietta was objecting?"

"Precisely."

"I'm not surprised. Marietta Swenson Leary Greer Greer Ainslee is a very determined woman."

"Greer, Greer?"

"Yes. She married her second husband twice."

"Can you run through the chronology?"

"I think so. I first knew her when she was Marietta Swenson, a charming, red-headed Southern belle. She had no visible talent, except for attracting attention. That was back in the Eisenhower days, when she must have been on the south side of twenty-five. Things were mighty dull around here then, and a sexy, good-looking girl could go pretty far. I don't think she had any money, or any background at all, but that didn't matter.

"She fixed up the money part right away, by marrying Kevin Leary, a self-made shopping-center millionaire about twenty years older than she was. He was a charming guy—fancied himself a polo player. He had only one fault. Drink. Died of cirrhosis before he was fifty. But well before he'd drunk up his fortune, which went to Marietta.

"We're now in the Kennedy era, and she's back on the block. Had quite a following, too. There's plenty of power in this town, you know, but not all that much money. And certainly not much money in the hands of flaming redheads. There was even the inevitable rumor about Marietta and Jack Kennedy, though I personally never believed it.

"Anyway, she married another millionaire named Greer, a cowboy oilman out of Texas who was an undersecretary under Kennedy. Transportation, as I recall. They were the hit of the party circuit for a while, then he wanted to go back to Texas and run for Governor. She would have none of it and they got divorced.

"He did go back to Texas and got the pants beat off him in the Democratic primary. So he returned, Stetson in hand, and they got married again. But it didn't last. He was getting on in years and Marietta was, shall we say, too frisky for him."

"Does that mean she played around?" Frost asked.

"You have such a nice way of putting things, Reuben. But yes, she was sleeping all over town."

"Is that how she met Ainslee?"

"You guessed it. She really set a trap for Garrett, the new widower. Being set-up financially, I think she wanted respectability, and respectability of a kind that shopping-center owners and cowboys couldn't provide. And what could be more respectable than a Supreme Court Justice, and one with a good chance of being Chief Justice in the bargain?

"Randy old Ainslee was captivated, and they got married about two years after LBJ appointed him to the Court. So Marietta was back on the party circuit again, but this time with a husband who wouldn't be anywhere else."

"But he was a good judge, Dawson."

"Didn't say he wasn't. It's just that he didn't spend his evenings sitting at home reading *certiorari* petitions."

"What happened when he died?"

"Very strange. Marietta became the proper matron, though she was still under fifty. Started becoming a mover and shaker in everything—beautification, the National Gallery, cruelty to animals, you name it. And the keeper of the lamp burning brightly at Garrett Ainslee's shrine."

"How does her boyfriend fit with this respectable image? From what I hear, he's a side of beef, what old crocks like us would call a gigolo."

"Now, now, Reuben, you don't understand. Ralston Purina, as he's sometimes unkindly called, is a *serious writer*. He just *happens* to be a side of beef. He's a protégé that Marietta's encouraging, not a gigolo. She's only interested in his *mind*."

"I hear he's rather mean."

"He's a disgrace. Gets drunk and abusive without any provocation. He had to be carried out of the Gridiron Dinner last year. Makes that drunken lout from the Washington Redskins look like a prohibitionist. But Marietta's going to beautify him, as well as the District's parks."

"I'm not sure I look forward to lunch."

"Oh, don't worry. He usually only acts up after dark."

Evans stopped talking, leaned back and ran his hand through his tawny white hair.

"In her new way of life, she's determined to make sure history regards Ainslee as a liberal icon," he went on. "So she probably was furious when your friend Rowan started nosing around. But I'll bet she was equally anxious that he stay out of her past, too. Her round-heeled days are over and, as far as she's concerned, they never existed."

"Let me ask one final question," Frost said. "Could she have put Ralston—Ralston Purina—up to pushing David Rowan out a window?"

Evans paused and gripped the side of the desk, considering the question.

"Christ, I wouldn't think so. She's damned determined

and Ralston's plenty tough. Yes, it's possible, but I doubt it. Besides, Reuben, you're about to have a chance to make up your own mind.

"Have you ever been in a restaurant in the South?" Evans asked. "You know, where they take your money and say 'Y'all come back and see us, y'hear?' When you're sure as anything they hate Yankees and really never want to see you again?"

"Yes, I've encountered that."

"That's Marietta. She's the original steel magnolia—forget Rosalynn Carter. She's charmin' as can be, but bitch-tough behind it all. She used to flirt like crazy—'My, my, don't you scrub up nice!' I can hear her saying to an unsuspecting subject. Then two minutes later cutting her quarry up behind his back. So just watch out."

"Thanks for the advice."

Evans looked at his watch; the meeting was over.

"Let me walk out with you," he said. As they passed his secretary's desk, he took the pile of pink telephone message slips his secretary handed him and sorted through them as he walked with Reuben down the hall.

"You fully retired now, Reuben?" Evans asked.

"Well . . . pretty much. I still keep my hand in some."

"I wish I could take it easy," Evans said with a sigh, though not one exactly ringing with sincerity. "Look at these," he went on, holding out the stack of message slips. "I spend an hour talking to an old friend and have my calls held. The Assistant Secretary of the Treasury for Tax Policy must talk to me urgently. Senator Dennison wants to have lunch. Secretary Foulkes has to meet with me. It just goes on and on. I wish I had time on my hands so I could go poking around in a murder investigation."

Frost felt, for an instant, that his contemporary was putting him down. But Evans had been very helpful and he knew he must not feel that way. So he thanked him and shook hands at the elevator.

"Oh, one other thing, Reuben. I forgot to tell you—Marietta Ainslee's a vegetarian. All part of the save-the-animals thing."

"Good Lord. That's all I needed to hear. But surely bozo eats red meat?"

"Don't think so. He's on some nut bodybuilding diet, I understand."

"Wonderful."

10

FROST WAS APPREHENSIVE IN BOTH A MAJOR AND A MINOR way as he took a taxi to the Ainslee residence on P Street in Georgetown. The prospect of a health-food lunch (after no breakfast except his morning orange juice) was the lesser anxiety; his principal worry was the imminent confrontation with the characters Dawson Evans had so colorfully described.

He rapped the brass knocker on the green front door of the Georgian house at the Ainslee address and instantly he heard footsteps on the stairs inside. The door was opened by a handsome middle-aged woman with flaming red hair, as promised.

"Mrs. Ainslee?"

"Yes. You must be Reuben Frost. Come right in. I'm sorry, it's the maid's day off."

His hostess led him up the stairs to a large parlor that was draped in boldly patterned chintz. The early afternoon sunshine almost burned through the large windows and, combined with the chintz, created an effect of almost fauvistic brightness.

"Please sit down," Mrs. Ainslee said, pointing to an overstuffed chair that seemed to envelop Frost once he was seated. The chair was low-slung and gave him the feeling that he would only be able to get out of it with difficulty.

A large, fat and unfriendly cat immediately leapt into his lap. Imprecations to "Get down, Elizabeth!" did not succeed, and Marietta Ainslee finally had to pick up the cat and shut her behind the door to the adjoining room. But not before Frost had noted, with some interest, the animal's name.

"I'm mighty sorry about that disturbance," Mrs. Ainslee said. She spoke not in an unfriendly way, but already she reminded Frost of the women functionaries at the New York auction houses, Sotheby's or Christie's, who, while impeccably groomed and coldly polite, conveyed with their turned-down mouths their general contempt for the human race. "Would you like some juice? Or maybe some Diet Coke?"

Frost declined, realizing that he would not get the bracing martini that, even on an empty stomach, he craved. He also wondered to himself how Diet Coke fit into the health regime he had been warned about; his own opinion, albeit a totally unsupported one, was that diet drinks were carcinogenic. He concluded that the woman's Southern heritage accounted for the inclusion of Coca-Cola, albeit of the non-Classic, diet variety.

"We'll be having lunch in about fifteen minutes, but I thought we could talk a tiny bit first."

"Thank you. You're very kind to see me on such short notice, and to offer me lunch besides. But I guess I should never underestimate the persuasive force of Dotty Sheets."

"No indeed, Mr. Frost. She could charm a speckled adder."

As Mrs. Ainslee spoke, Frost noticed for the first time that her bright orange knitted suit matched identically the orange whorls in the room's upholstery, all in insouciant contrast to her red hair. This was not a woman who left things to chance.

"I assume she told you the reason for my visit."

"You wanted to talk about David Rowan."

"Correct."

"You're a relative of his, is that right?"

"No. I was a college classmate of his father's. David was my godson, but we're not related."

"I see. But you're trying to solve his murder?"

"In a manner of speaking. I'm trying to assist the New York police, yes."

"Well, I'm sorry to disappoint you after you came all the way down here. I obviously do not know anything about Mr. Rowan's dramatic murder and I have nothing—nothing at all—to say about him." Mrs. Ainslee's sweet Southern tones had not changed as she spoke, but Evans's reference to a steel magnolia became even clearer.

"That makes things difficult."

"Quite possibly. Let me be very direct. I'm seeing you as a favor to Dotty, though I told her it would be useless for you to come here. She said *you* have great powers of persuasion and would convince me otherwise. You're a lawyer, aren't you?"

"Yes. I'm a corporate lawyer in New York." No need to mention retirement, Frost thought.

As he spoke, he heard the front door open and moments later a hulk that he took to be Ralston Fortes came into the room. He was shorter than Frost had expected, but his neck protruded from under a paisley ascot and his arms and shoulders exploded from the tight confines of a body-hugging short-sleeved shirt. His musculature was as formidable as any Frost had ever seen. The man's square tan face, determined jaw and closely cropped brown hair augmented the impression that he would be best suited for a life as a Marine drill sergeant or a California highway patrolman.

"Mr. Frost, Ralston Fortes."

"Hi," Fortes said, looming over the elderly lawyer. "Don't get up." Frost was grateful for not having to attempt a clumsy exit from his captive seat.

"Did you get the bean curd, dear?" Marietta asked.

"Here."

"Take it down to Bessie."

Forbes obediently took the small package he was carrying back downstairs, presumably to the kitchen. Frost's heart sank as low as his posterior in the chair, reflecting that he would have bean curd for lunch and, worse, would have to make his case to the recalcitrant Marietta Ainslee in Fortes's ominous presence.

"Ralston is our writer-in-residence," the woman said when her companion returned.

"Yeah," he said, his large mouth expanding into a thin, wide, and not especially intelligent smile. He took a seat on a hassock next to the sofa where Marietta was sitting, his muscled legs spread apart and his hands clasped. He sat forward in a crouch, looking directly at Frost and giving the impression that he could spring at him with very little effort.

"What are you writing, Mr. Fortes?" Frost asked.

"He's *written* an absolutely wonderful novel," Marietta explained. "About growing up as a poor Cuban boy in Miami."

"I see," Frost said. "You've finished it?"

"Oh, yes," Marietta interrupted again. "It's going to be published next winter by the Hammersmith Press."

Frost recognized with a jolt the name of Stanley Knowles's publishing firm, and David Rowan's publisher.

"You must know Stanley Knowles, then," Frost said to Fortes.

"Yeah," Fortes answered, permitted to speak at last. "I work mostly with Donna, though."

"You're in good hands. Both Stanley and Donna Knowles are friends of mine."

"Really!" Marietta answered, in a fiddle-dee-dee-Rhett voice.

"Hammersmith was going to publish David Rowan's biography of your husband."

"I'm only too well aware of that," she answered.

"By the way, what do you intend to do now that David is dead?" Frost asked, deciding that directness was the best approach.

"It's very simple," Marietta said decisively. "I'll have to find a new biographer. I hate the thought. You know I conducted what I thought was a very discreet competition to find Mr. Rowan. Then word got out and I got letters and visits and calls from every unemployed biographer in America, and half the historians. I got rid of them all, except a really persistent terrier from Massachusetts—and David.

"David was selected, and I thought my job was done. Now I find it isn't. But that doesn't matter, 'cause I've got some very definite ideas this time. My husband's papers were rifled through, I understand. When your police release them, Tennessee will take them back and hold them until I designate a new writer." She looked meaningfully at Fortes. Was she serious, Frost thought, about having this lout attempt a biography? Love conquers all, he knew, but the idea seemed preposterous, whatever Fortes's accomplishments as a "novelist."

"Isn't there a chance someone could pick up and continue David's work?"

"No, we're going to start again," Marietta said firmly. "And speaking of starting, Ralston, go and see if Bessie has lunch ready."

Fortes did as he was told and reported back that it was. The dining room was on the ground floor. Once there, the hostess seated Frost at the head of the table, with Fortes and herself flanking him. Bessie, the elderly black servant, slowly served soup to the three.

"We're having zucchini and wild rice soup to start," Marietta explained. "I hope you like it."

The combination, as expected, was awful, reminding Frost of what might have been served to his less fortunate Navy colleagues in World War II, in a Japanese prisoner of war camp. But he ate heartily, fearing what might come next. He did note with some relief that the bean curd was in the soup, so he would not have that to look forward to.

Frost decided to make a frontal attack as they ate.

"Mrs. Ainslee, I appreciate what you said earlier about not wanting to talk about David Rowan. I respect that, and it wasn't really why I came here. What I'm trying to do, by talking to you and several others, is to figure out who might have committed his ghastly murder.

"Right now, there are no obvious clues," Frost continued, shading the truth slightly. "David seems to have been well-liked. There do not appear to have been any conspicuous enemies. So we must sift through every shred of information that we can find from those who knew him well, hoping that something, somehow, will lead us to his killer."

"Let me correct one thing, Mr. Frost. I did not know Mr. Rowan well. We entered into a straightforward business relationship, designed to produce a first-class, serious biography of my late husband. I never saw the man more than half a dozen times.

"I am, as I'm sure our busy mutual friend, Dotty, has told you, independently wealthy. I'm happy, I'm content, I love Washington and the life I'm leading. My chief concern—Ralston and maybe others might call it my obsession—is that my late husband be recognized for what he was, the most thoughtful liberal voice in American politics in this century. That means I wanted—and still want—a fair and square biography of Garrett. That's what David Rowan was to produce. Since that's impossible, I've got to find someone else."

While the hostess was talking, Bessie returned with the day's *pièce de résistance*—plates of boiled vegetables, including a mousse of sweet potato and spinach that was topped with poached eggs. Once served, Reuben looked around the table for a salt shaker.

"What do you need?" Marietta asked.

"Salt."

"We don't use it," Ralston said.

"I see."

Bessie next brought in glasses of iced tea. Burned once, Frost did not ask for, or look for, sugar.

"Getting back to David," Frost said. "I realize he was not an intimate friend. But you did talk to him and, I understand, were interviewed by him. Did he ever say anything that indicated trouble of any kind?"

"Never," Marietta replied.

"Did he mention Grace Mann?"

"Not that I remember."

"Or his first wife? Or his son?"

"We had very little social chitchat. Our first meetings were all business, about arranging access to my husband's papers, and the others were strictly interviews. He was always very serious and down-to-business."

"Let me ask one more thing," Frost said. "There are indications that you and David were quarreling over the biography recently. Is that correct?"

"Mr. Frost, I told you I was unwilling to discuss our relationship."

"Who told you they were fighting?" Fortes asked belligerently.

"Mr. Fortes, I've known David's family and friends for many years. They were close to David and knew what he was about. And they've told me what I've just told you. Rightly or wrongly, they believe that you, Mrs. Ainslee, quarreled with David about certain matters concerning your husband that he'd uncovered in his research."

"I don't know what you're talking about," Marietta said.

"May I be more specific? I've been told that David Rowan had figured out a system of notation your husband used for recording his sexual activities."

"Just a minute, mister," Fortes barked, his muscles tensing.

"Mr. Fortes, I'm sorry. I don't mean to offend Mrs. Ainslee, or you. But I'm trying to be frank and to put my cards on the table."

"Where did you hear this?" she asked.

"From his father for one. And Grace Mann for another."

"That bastard! I should have known his family would know about our quarrel."

"So it's true, then, that David had found something?" Frost said, very quietly.

"Yes, it's true," Marietta replied reluctantly.

"What did you say to him? What did he say to you?"

"Mr. Frost, for the last time, I'm telling you that I have no intention of discussing this or any other issue between David and me." Marietta looked pointedly at Fortes.

"And if you keep badgering her, I'm going to have to ask you to leave," Fortes added.

"If that's your wish, so be it," Frost told him. "I have no authority to make you say anything. But it won't be so easy to stonewall the police."

"Do they know about this?" Fortes asked, his uneasiness evident.

"Of course," Frost answered testily, though he immediately regretted his tone of voice, since, as soon as he had spoken, Fortes's muscles visibly expanded and a vein in his thick neck started pounding.

"I really think you should level with me," Frost went on. "If the police, and a major television newsperson with an interest in the outcome, know of Ainslee's sex code, there really is no point in trying to conceal it.

"All of which means," Frost declared, looking at his luncheon companions, "that you really ought to tell me what went on between you and David."

"I feel very put-upon," Marietta said. "But you don't leave me much choice. I'll tell you exactly what happened.

"I first heard what your Mr. Rowan was up to from the professor who lost out to him. He called me to tell me that Rowan had bragged about what he'd learned about Garrett at some historians' meeting. I got hold of David Rowan at once and told him what I'd heard. I said that Garrett's sex life was irrelevant to the story of his accomplishments and advised him that he would do very well to keep his mouth shut. And that if he didn't I knew of at least one historian who would be delighted to take over the project.

"What I got back was a lot of folderol about scholastic integrity, warts-and-all biography and so on. I told him I was displeased, and that if he really was going to tout his biography of my husband by sensationalizing trivial, stupid and irrelevant scandal, we could just put an end to our agreement.

"He was angry, and I was angry. But he said he needed time to think about what his final position was. I told him that was fine, but I wanted an answer right away."

"When was this?" Frost asked.

"Two weeks ago."

"And did he answer?"

"No. That was our last conversation. I'd about had it—it didn't take two weeks for him to make up his mind—and was going to call everything off. Then he died. Or was killed, as you and the tabloid newspapers say."

"This guy really upset Marietta," Fortes said. "He shouldn't have done that."

"Let me be clear—he never responded?" Frost asked.

"Never. Total silence. It was obvious to me he was going to use Garrett's little eccentricity to create interest in his book.

"Will you have some dessert, Mr. Frost?" Marietta asked, after a moment's pause.

Reuben looked at his watch. He had to leave if he was to get the train for Trenton. And he saw no point in probing, or provoking, his hostess any further.

"No, thank you. I've got to get back. Can I get a cab here?"

"Two blocks down the street. No problem," Fortes said.

"Then I think I should be leaving. Oh, but before I do, do you have any reason to link the name 'Elizabeth' with David Rowan?"

"None whatsoever," she answered. "Offhand, the only Elizabeth I can think of is my cat, to whom you were introduced upstairs. Oh, I'm sure one of Garrett's famous Os was probably an Elizabeth—or a Dorothy or a Mary or an Ethel. Which brings me to *my* last question. Do you think this silly little matter about Garrett's date books will become public?"

"I can't tell. The police know about it, as I said. And it's a tempting leak to the press."

"Let's hope it doesn't," Fortes said.

On this friendly note, Frost departed for Union Station.

11

THE MERCHANTS' LIMITED, EVER SO SEEDY FROM TOO
many years' use, nonetheless seemed a welcome haven to
Frost. It also give him two hours of reflection before meeting Nancy Rowan in Trenton. Although it was neither the
meal hour nor cocktail time, he gratefully purchased a whiskey and a ham and cheese sandwich offered by an attendant.
The processed ham in the tired sandwich might be execrable, but at least it was meat.

Marietta and Ralston were quite a pair, he concluded. The
diminutive widow could not possibly have killed David,
but there was no doubt in his mind that her burly friend
might have. And he was now convinced that she could have
encouraged him.

He made a mental note to check out the bodybuilder-
novelist with Stanley Knowles, finished his Scotch and soda
and fell asleep. He woke up as the train slowed down for
the Trenton stop, just in time to see a billboard emblazoned
with the city's motto, "WHAT TRENTON MAKES, THE WORLD
TAKES" (or as Princeton undergraduates in his day had said,
"What the world refuses, Trenton uses").

Frost knew that his rendezvous point with the first Mrs.
Rowan was a bar near the train station. She had given him
explicit directions for reaching it on foot. But he felt more
comfortable taking a cab.

Reaching the bar, called the Twilight Room, he realized he was ten minutes early, but went in anyway and staked out a relatively private table in the back.

Nancy Rowan arrived promptly, apologizing as she did so for bringing Frost to the plastic, nondescript Twilight Room, which she explained was convenient both to the train station and her commuter bus to Princeton.

Frost was struck by how little she had changed in the eight or so years since he had last seen her (once David had left home the Frosts, Reuben now realized with some guilt, had not made any attempt to keep in touch with her). Never an impressive dresser—though in her defense, she had had children clinging to her clothes during the years when the Frosts had seen her most often—she now wore a cheaply made navy blue suit and the inevitable working woman's scarf/bowtie. Her black hair was short and straight, held in place with a little girl's barrettes. Only two small gold earrings and cheerful lipstick gave touches of femininity to her not unpretty face.

"It's been a long time, Reuben," she said, lighting a cigarette.

"Yes, it certainly has. What will you have to drink?" There did not appear to be a waiter or waitress, so Reuben maneuvered amid the after-work crowd at the bar to get two Scotches and soda.

"Did you ever find Alan?" Frost asked, referring to the woman's worried call the night of the Reuff Dinner.

"Oh, yes," she said with a sigh. "He was visiting some friends up in New Brunswick, at Rutgers. He'd just forgotten to tell me he was staying out for the evening."

"I'm told he's at home for the year."

"Yes." She did not elaborate.

"How are the other children?"

"Oh, they're fine. Christina's graduating from high school this year and going to Trinity in the fall. Laura's a sophomore at Princeton Country Day, with not a thought in her head of what she might do."

"Lots of tuition to look forward to."

"Yes, yes. What do the sociologists call it? Tuition over-burden? I'm getting ready for that. David was supposed to pay half, but God knows what will happen now."

"You've joined my profession, I understand."

"In a manner of speaking. I went to Penn and finished two years ago. I took the New Jersey bar exam and now work for the Mercer County legal defender."

"Do you like it?"

"It's all right. The work is sometimes challenging, but there's too much of it. And the county doesn't pay your fancy New York salaries."

Frost felt a twinge of regret for Nancy. She had never had it easy, working to put David through graduate school at Harvard, then raising the three children on an academic's salary, followed by begrudging support payments after David moved out. And now living on what he was sure was still a tiny income.

"Well, I'm glad you find at least some of your work challenging. That's all a lawyer can ask."

"I had to do something with my life after David left. I'd never done real work, you know. Just professor's-wife jobs that any competent eighteen-year-old could do. Doing something where you can use your head is a great change, and every so often you do feel as if you're helping somebody. But enough about me. To what do I owe the pleasure of your visit?"

The woman sat back and lit another cigarette.

"I'm sure you can guess. To put it bluntly, I'm trying to find the person who killed David."

"And I'm a suspect?"

"I hardly think so, Nancy. Maybe in theory—God knows you had a motive—but I don't see you overpowering David and chucking him out the window."

"Defenestration, as they used to say in crim law. I'm glad you don't suspect me. But you're certainly right. I had a motive. I've had black moments about David ever since I realized he was never coming back. And I confess I hated him every time I overdrew my checking account or had to tell the children they couldn't have something they badly wanted. Or thought about his leaving just when he was going to get the academic recognition he'd always coveted—until he started coveting that TV woman, that is.

"Most of it didn't bother me—the pictures of her and David at those glittering New York parties, for instance. I didn't care about that at all. But leaving me hovering on the poverty line, that got to me real hard. After all those little wifey jobs I'd suffered through when he was getting started.

"Plus being both father and mother to the children. That's good fun, too. And not exactly the way to meet a new Mr. Right."

"You should."

"I've given up. I couldn't do the dutiful faculty wife number again, and they're the only men I ever really see. Except for a bunch of bright-eyed young lawyers about half my age."

"I'm sure it's been rough and I'm sorry to be talking about David. But I promised Harrison I would do everything I could to help."

"Poor Harrison. How is he? I get reports from the children once in a while, but I haven't seen him since the Big Disappearing Act."

"He was getting over Valerie's death, but now there's the new blow of David's death."

"Poor man. Could I have another drink?"

"Sorry. Of course." Frost repeated his fetching maneuver at the bar, returning with four drinks.

"This isn't my idea. They tell me it's happy hour. The bartender had poured them before I could stop him."

"Don't worry, they're small."

"Getting back to David..." Frost pressed. He had looked at his watch while at the bar and realized that time was running out if he wanted to get the 7:05 Metroliner to New York.

"You know, while I was waiting for you to come back with the drinks, I was thinking of how I felt when I heard the news. I was startled, of course—and I knew from the beginning that it wasn't suicide. David loved himself too much to deprive the world of his genius. It was terrible, I felt that. But then I realized that my reaction was the same as it would be to any tragedy—to a child down a well, for instance. Or some great catastrophe happening to a total outsider. There was no sense that things might have been different had he not been killed, or anything silly like that. I was hearing about the death of a stranger."

"And a stranger that was not the husband you had loved."

"True."

"Nancy, I'm trying desperately to find some thread, some connection that links David's killer to him. Can you put aside your feelings long enough to help me? Is there anyone out of David's past that might have done this?"

"You're delving into ancient history, Reuben. For all intents and purposes David went out of my life eight years ago—fifteen years ago, really. Before that? I can't think of anyone with an old grievance that would fester into murder so many years later.

"There were plenty of people who would've gladly put David down. Or belittled him professionally. Lots and lots of people were jealous of his rapid advancement at Princeton. And there were always those mean, petty turf fights that make academic life so calm and pleasant. Who gets his own secretary, who has an office with an outside view, who gets a research assistant. You know the old saying, Reuben, academic infighting is so intense because the stakes are so low.

"And then there were always battles in the American Historical Association. David was an agile politician. That and his golden boy reputation usually meant he won out. And when he won, somebody else lost. But a person doesn't kill to have his own secretary, does he?"

"People kill for all kinds of reasons. But I agree, academic cat fights usually stop short of homicide. But Nancy, are you *sure* there was no one David hurt, maybe inadvertently, in some major way? Someone whose career was blocked and who might still be resentful years later?"

"I honestly can't think of anyone, Reuben."

"Did David ever mention a professor named Peter Jewett?" Frost asked. "He's now up at Amherst."

"No, I don't recall David's ever referring to him. Why?"

"I've gotten intimations that he and David didn't get on."

"It must have been after my time."

"One more question, and then I've got to go," Frost said. "How did David and Alan get along?"

For an instant, Nancy Rowan gave Reuben a look of impatience, even of resentment. "Why do you ask that?" she said with some petulance. She lit another cigarette.

"To cover all bases."

"Alan used to be very loyal to me. He wouldn't have anything to do with his father all the time he was in high school. Then, once he got away to Vanderbilt, he started seeing David.

"They seemed to get along quite well until last summer. Alan wanted to go to Europe and David absolutely forbade it. He said it would destroy Alan's treatment."

"Treatment?"

"His drug addiction. Surely you know about that?"

"This is the first I've heard of it."

"How strange. You said you'd talked to Grace Mann?"

"Yes, at some length."

"And she never mentioned it?"

"Never."

"I'm very surprised. As much as I dislike her, she's the one who found the therapy program Alan's in."

"Which is?"

"A combination inpatient, outpatient clinic called Fairhaven Gables. It's in New Brunswick. Alan was there for three months after he was arrested . . ."

"Arrested?"

"He was busted, as they say, at Vanderbilt."

"For what?"

"Dealing in drugs."

"How can that be? Surely you and David supported him?"

"Yes, we did. We paid his tuition, bought his books, paid for his off-campus apartment and gave him a generous allowance. But it wasn't enough to support his cocaine habit. And like good, naive, divorced middle-class parents, David and I thought that if we didn't give him the money to buy dope, he wouldn't buy it. It never occurred to us he'd go off and raise money on his own—by peddling the stuff himself."

"Good Lord. Had you known about his habit?"

"He'd fooled around in high school—'experimented,' as the kids say. If I knew then what I know now—I see the effects of addiction every day in my job—I'd have known better. But then I thought it was just marijuana and some of those crazy pills. I was very firm about it and had no idea he was snorting—and dealing—cocaine until he was arrested.

"They didn't send him to jail, though they don't take dope-selling lightly in Nashville. He's on probation as long as he keeps going to Fairhaven. He now goes for outpatient therapy three times a week. That's why I called you the other night, by the way. Alan had disappeared, hadn't shown up for a therapy session, and I was afraid he was lapsing."

Unpleasant as the things he was hearing were, Frost was nonetheless relieved to learn that Nancy's call, the night of the Reuff Dinner, had not been as spiteful as he and Cynthia had speculated.

"I'm very sorry to hear this, Nancy."

"Cross your fingers. Fairhaven seems to be working, even if I go wild every time he's off somewhere unaccounted for."

"Let's hope for the best. And now, I fear, I've got to get my train."

"You mean you don't want another drink here at the beautiful Twilight Room?"

"If I did, I'm afraid happy hour would turn into a most unhappy one for my stomach. So let me just ask one more question. Was there ever an Elizabeth in David's life that you know of?"

Nancy thought hard, then smiled. "I don't think so. David was guilty of a lot of things, but I don't believe an Elizabeth was one of them. Why?"

"Nothing, really. Forget I said it."

"If you say so, Reuben. You know, I appreciate what you're doing. It means a lot, I'm sure, to Harrison."

Outside the bar, Nancy directed Reuben to the station. The route was all perfectly safe, except for enough panhandlers to populate a city in India.

As they parted, Nancy promised to let him know if she thought of any leads. Frost was not optimistic that any would be forthcoming from her—and gloomy about the one that might develop from what she had said.

COMPARING NOTES

12

FROST ARRIVED HOME TO FIND A NOTE FROM HIS WIFE—ON
an impulse she had gone to the National Ballet to look
over a hot new prospect, a male dancer from Finland the
Company had imported as a guest artist with the idea of
perhaps hiring him.

It had been a wearying day, and Frost went almost
immediately to bed. His eccentric lunch and the ancient
sandwich on the train had suddenly seemed enough food, so
he did not eat. He was sound asleep when Cynthia returned
shortly after eleven o'clock.

"How was the Finn?" he asked his wife Tuesday morning
while she busily packed an overnight bag for a one-day trip
to Cleveland.

"Not bad. Big and strong, which NatBallet can use right
now. But he has to do something about his name."

"What is it?"

"Jan Aadlo."

"I don't see why. He'd be first in those alphabetical cast
lists NatBallet insists on using."

"Yes, probably."

"Are you going to have a busy day in Cleveland?"

"No, not for an old trouper like me. There's a reception
this afternoon and a dinner at the museum tonight. I told
you about it. It's the opening of the Eric Fischl show the

museum's put together—with Brigham Foundation money."

"It's a long way to go to see dirty pictures."

"Now, Reuben, we must be broad-minded."

"I saw his pictures at the Whitney last year. Little boys masturbating."

"That's about one percent true," Cynthia said reproachfully. "Honestly, sometimes you're as narrow-minded as our dear Mayor, Norman."

"Hmn. When will you be back?"

"Tomorrow morning. In time for lunch with Stanley Knowles, by the way."

"You're having lunch with Stanley? Good. You can ask him a question for me." He told Cynthia about Ralston Fortes's novel, allegedly to be published by the Hammersmith Press.

"That's rich. What else did you learn yesterday?"

Frost gave his wife a hurried summary, but then rushed her off. "You've got to get going. I'll tell you more about it tomorrow night."

"I hate this. Going a whole day without knowing what you found out."

"I know, dear, but there just isn't time, if you're going to get to Cleveland and socialize with the guest pornographer."

"I understand. Will you take me to dinner tomorrow night?"

"Of course. Where?"

"I'm scheduled to be down at Cooper Union at the end of the day. How about that nice Italian place on Tenth Street? Il what's-its-name."

"Il Cantinori."

"Fine. Can you make the reservation? Eight o'clock, if that's all right."

"Yes."

"Well, good-bye, darling. Will you be okay without me?"

"I'll try. Maybe I'll get a date."

"Oh? Who with?"

"How about Emily Sherwood?"

"You rascal. Still carrying the torch for her, are you?

Well, go ahead, see if I care. I might just call my new friend, Richard Taylor. He's probably out campaigning somewhere in the Midwest near Cleveland."

"Hurry up. You'll miss your plane."

"Be good." Cynthia kissed her husband warmly and dashed out.

Bautista called a few minutes later. Something had come up—he assured Frost it had nothing to do with the Rowan case—and he would not be free until late afternoon. He proposed dropping by the Frosts' house about six.

"How did it go yesterday?" the detective asked before hanging up.

"Interesting. We'll talk about it."

Frost was not unhappy to have the day off, even though he had slept for nine hours, unusual for him. He read the papers thoroughly, fell asleep again, then got dressed and made himself a tuna-fish sandwich; if he was going to have a day of idleness he would forgo lunch at the Gotham Club.

His sandwich revitalized him and he remembered his jocular threat to Cynthia that he might call Emily Bryant Sherwood. He got her number in Port Washington from information, only to learn from her maid that Mrs. Sherwood was spending two days in the city at the Colony Club. Tracking her there, he found that she was at lunch.

Emily Sherwood returned Reuben's call in midafternoon. A godsend, she termed his invitation. She had come to town to take care of some matters relating to her husband's estate but had not thought to make plans for the evening.

"Dinner would be lovely. But could it be on the early side, Reuben? I'm not the same good-time girl you used to know. Too old to do the Charleston anymore. It's early to bed for me these days."

"Perfect. Let's splurge and go to La Grenouille."

"It sounds divine. Will you pick me up here?"

"Eight o'clock."

By late afternoon Frost was restless. Over and over, during his solitary day, he had tried to fit the bits and pieces of information that were all that constituted the Rowan case into a pattern. But the pattern eluded him. By the time Bautista arrived at six he was ready and eager both for company and to discuss the murder.

"Reuben, I asked Francisca to join us here a little after seven. Okay?" the detective asked.

"Of course. You know I'm always glad to see Francisca. We don't see enough of her." Frost genuinely liked Bautista's apparently permanent, and very stylishly beautiful, girlfriend.

"We're going to some damn detective movie Francisca picked out. Tonight's our movie night. How about if you and Cynthia join us?"

"Cynthia's in Cleveland. An art show for a dirty-picture artist named Eric Fischl. Besides, I can't join you because I have a date."

"You don't let much grass grow under your feet."

"Mind your manners, Luis. Let's get down to business."

Frost reported on his previous day's travels, reviewing Dawson Evans's descriptions of Marietta Ainslee and Ralston Fortes and telling the detective his own impressions, that Marietta was a very determined woman and Fortes a thug.

"You're ahead of the NYPD—or almost," Bautista said. "We got a report on him from the D.C. police this morning. There's quite a sheet on him. He's been arrested three times for assault, but he's never been convicted. And a drunken driving charge for which he got a suspended sentence."

"Sounds like he breaks his bodybuilder training once in a while."

"Yeah. He only gets into trouble when he drinks."

"How did he support himself before he met Mrs. Ainslee?"

"Odd jobs. He's worked at a whole series of gyms and health clubs. Been around the gay circuit, too. Bouncer in a gay bar, and a stripper in one."

"Good heavens, do they have such things in Washington?"

"Practically around the corner from the White House, they tell me."

"Is he gay?"

"Bisexual probably. I mean, you thought he and Mrs. Ainslee had something going, right?"

"I'd bet on it."

"Anyway, he's a bad hombre."

"There was another odd detail," Frost added, "though I can't make anything out of it. The Ainslee cat is named Elizabeth."

"Let me write that down," Bautista said. "It probably doesn't mean a thing, but you never know."

"Can I get you a drink, by the way?" Frost asked. "I know you can hold your liquor better than this fellow Fortes."

"No, I'll wait till Francisca gets here."

"You want to hear about Trenton?"

"Of course."

"No surprises. I learned that Nancy Rowan is pretty bitter—not without cause, I might add. She seems to be totally unaffected by David's murder. I did pick up one thing, though. The son, Alan, is being treated for drug addiction." Frost related what he had been told about the boy's drug bust and his treatment at Fairhaven Gables.

"You're up with us again, Reuben," Bautista said. "We got the same information from the Nashville Police. It seems the kid was quite an operator. He got off on condition that he go to Fairhaven. Where, you should know, he failed to show up for his therapy session the afternoon before his father was taken out."

"Did Grace Mann say anything to you about Alan's problem?" Frost asked.

"No."

"She didn't mention it to me, either. But according to the boy's mother, Grace Mann is the one who got him into Fairhaven."

"Funny. One of the things I wanted to tell you was that we've learned some more about her and Giardi. I talked to the Feds again. They've had Giardi under surveillance for like three months. Grace Mann's been his constant companion. Only in the daytime, of course."

"Anything else?" Frost asked.

"Couple of things. We've had a guy going through Rowan's personal files. Nothing unexpected that we could see. Copies of lots of correspondence between his lawyer and his wife's over the divorce. He managed to get away with paying her a grand a month, plus half the kids' education expenses. The rest seemed routine—correspondence about both his Congress book and the new one, old book reviews, clippings, that sort of stuff. Some bitchy letters about other professors, but nothing threatening.

"We also got a call yesterday from the University of Tennessee. A Miss Wyecliffe from the library. She's all hot and bothered about the Ainslee papers and wants them back right away.

"The thing is, we don't really have anybody that could go through them—you saw what was involved the day we went to Rowan's office. We wouldn't know what we were looking for, or how to find it. Except of course what we already know, that Ainslee's engagement calendars are gone."

"I agree," Frost said. "Besides, if there's anything significant about the papers, it's what's *missing*, not what's still there."

"I'm with you on that."

"The catalogers down there are the only ones who can figure out what's not there, what might have been taken. That is, if *anyone* can figure it out. I'd get them back down there right away—put them in boxes and Federal Express them even. And have Miss Wyecliffe and her staff get to work on them."

"Great. We'll do it tomorrow."

"I'd like to talk to this Miss Wyecliffe, by the way."

"Sure. I've got her number right here."

While Frost was copying the number, the downstairs bell rang. It was Francisca Ribiero, who appeared wearing purple lipstick and a bright purple dress.

"You look like a beautiful spring iris," Frost said, kissing her on the cheek.

"That's okay, isn't it? It *is* April, after all."

"My dear, you know you can wear anything you like as far as I'm concerned. I just meant you looked *especially* ravishing tonight."

"I love you, Reuben. Why can't you flatter me like that, L-L?" she said to Bautista, kissing him.

"L-L?" Frost asked. "That's a new one."

"Oh, just my pet name for Luis Lopez."

"I didn't know Lopez was your middle name," Frost said.

"Most people don't," Bautista replied, pleased, but slightly embarrassed, at Francisca's teasing.

"How about a drink?" Orders taken, Frost disappeared into the kitchen.

"Have you boys solved the case?" Francisca asked when Frost returned.

"I'm afraid not," Frost said. "It gets more complicated by the day."

"I don't understand it. Luis—L-L—" she said, pinching Bautista on the cheek as he smiled weakly. "You told me there was good solid evidence—blood and skin under the dead man's fingernails. All you have to do is match your samples up with the murderer's. Right?"

"It's not that easy, Francisca," Bautista said impatiently.

"Why not? Line your suspects up and give each one a blood test. Simple."

"I wish it were," Bautista said, sighing. "But there's something called 'due process.' You just can't go around taking blood samples from people unless you've got reasonable cause. It's like searching your pocketbook, Francisca. I can't do that unless I've got a good reason."

"You do it all the time!"

"Not true! I may have borrowed a dollar once or twice, but I certainly *do not* make a habit of it."

"Luis is speaking like a lawyer now—which of course he almost is," Frost said, referring to the detective's pursuit of a night law school degree. Then he did not continue the thought, but sat upright in his chair and announced that something had just occurred to him.

"Some detective I am!" he said. "When I was down in Washington, that man Fortes was wearing an ascot, covering up his neck. Do you suppose . . ."

"Let me make a note of it. Fortes sure gets more interesting," Bautista said.

"Fortes? One of us?" Francisca asked.

"Cuban," Bautista said.

"A Cuban with scratches on his neck. Sounds good to me," Francisca said. "And now that I've solved everything for you, let's go to the movies. Where's Cynthia, Reuben?"

Frost again explained his wife's absence.

"Then you'll come to the movies with us, won't you?"

"He's got a date," Bautista said.

"Now, now. Just an old friend from fifty years ago. We're going to have a nice, simple dinner."

"I think I better tell Cynthia about this," Francisca said, playfully.

"She knows."

"Tell her I'm going to call her for lunch. I want to talk to her anyway. Besides, at the rate you two are going, we may have to solve the Rowan case for you."

"Fat chance," Bautista said as the three went down the stairs to Seventieth Street.

EMILY

13

THE EVENING WAS WARM, SO FROST LEFT BAUTISTA and Francisca to walk to the Colony Club, at Sixty-third Street and Park Avenue. Emily Bryant Sherwood, resplendent in a silk dress in a bold floral print, was waiting for him.

"You feel like walking?" he asked her. "It's a beautiful night."

"Absolutely. All it has done is rain in the country, so let's enjoy your wonderful city weather."

Picking up his old friend at the sedate, Georgian women's club, and meeting her in its proper lobby, gave Frost a great sense of *déjà vu* as he remembered calling for her at her Wellesley dormitory, also a Georgian building, almost a half century earlier. He took her arm as he savored the memory and they strode together down Park Avenue.

"As I told you, your call was heaven-inspired," Emily said. " "And what a treat! I haven't been to Grenouille in years. Barton was a meat-and-potatoes man and didn't care much for Frenchified food."

At the restaurant they were welcomed by a smiling Charles Masson, the co-owner, and shown at once to a banquette in the front dining room.

"Why don't you sit inside and I'll face you," Frost said. "The better to have a good look at you after all these years."

"Ideal."

"I'm going to have a daiquiri. They make them very well here, with *real* lime juice and not too much sugar."

"Heaven."

"It is a pretty place, isn't it?" Reuben said, gesturing to the huge and elaborate floral displays that graced the room. "One sits a little too close together," he added, lowering his voice so their neighbors on either side could not hear, "but it's damn attractive."

"It certainly is. Let's drink to our everlasting good health."

"You beat me to it," Frost replied, raising his stemmed glass.

"How are you both, anyway? Cynthia's where?"

Frost explained his wife's absence in Cleveland and what she was doing.

"Does she know about *us*?" Emily asked playfully, touching Frost's arm across the table.

"I've made full disclosure."

"I wish she were here. But I can't say I'm sorry to have you all to myself for an evening."

Memories flooded back to both of them as they sipped their daiquiris.

"You look wonderful, Emily. Are you well?"

"No complaints. I'd never pass for a Ziegfeld girl—I weigh much too much—but, yes, I'm passably healthy. You're never sure how long you're going to go on—I don't buy green bananas at the store anymore—but I'm optimistic that I've got a few good years left. How about you?"

"No complaints at all. Getting old and grouchy and enjoying every minute of it."

"Are you still practicing?"

"Not really. I go down to my little cubbyhole now and then, but for all intents and purposes I've retired."

"Do you miss it?"

"Of course. You don't just erase fifty busy years from your memory."

"I'm interested. Barton died with his boots on, of course, and vowed he'd never retire."

"Most lawyers are like that."

"How about Cynthia?"

"She's busier than ever. The Foundation keeps her hopping all the time. She loves it, though, and wouldn't have it any other way."

The captain interrupted their conversation to announce the day's specials. After much deliberation, and a thorough quizzing of the captain, Emily decided on *saucissons chauds* as an appetizer and frogs' legs, while Reuben selected clams Corsini and roast leg of veal.

"How much wine do you think we can put away?" Frost asked his companion.

"I love it, but if I drink too much it keeps me awake."

"I hate half-bottles, but we really do need both red and white. I've got it. I'll simply have a glass of white with my clams and we'll split a bottle of red. Unless you'd prefer white with your frogs' legs."

"No, red is always fine with me."

Frost chose the Chateau Giscours 1979 and, decisions made, the two diners returned to conversation.

"You know, Reuben, I've been thinking how odd it is, how strange that people who were once so close can disappear from one another's lives. Look at us—you and me and Harrison—we were inseparable way back when. Then we went our own ways and didn't see each other for almost half a century!"

Frost did not mention the barrier tiresome Barton Sherwood had been to the continuation of their collegiate friendship.

"You were never very active in the bar association, were you?" she went on.

"No. I've always been a member, but I never got active." Frost did not spell out his generally low opinion of organized bar activities.

"Barton loved it. He went through that long process by which you become president of the American Bar Association, you know."

"I remember."

"I can't say I was ever too happy with that. Traveling all around the country going to banquets, wearing silly big corsages and being nice to the 'ladies.' And as much as I loved Barton, I did get sick of his basic speech for those dinners. 'The Living Law,' it was called."

The very thought of listening to Barton Sherwood delivering a canned speech sent shivers up Reuben's spine.

"Oh, this looks wonderful!" Emily exclaimed, as her pink *saucissons* and warm potato salad were served. Both started eating with gusto, Reuben savoring the garlic-parsley-white-wine sauce in which his clams were served, sopping up the extra sauce with bread.

"Seeing you eat those clams brings back memories, Reuben. Remember the spring of what? Nineteen thirty-one? You and Harrison came up to Wellesley after you finished exams at Princeton. I got my father's roadster and we went to Marblehead. Do you recall it? We ate nothing but lobsters and shrimps and clams for three days.

"I don't think I've thought about that weekend since, till I saw you eating just now. No, I'm wrong. There was one time when I did think about it. When that wonderful French movie came out years ago, *Jules et Jim*. Jules and Jim—you and Harrison. And I was of course the glamorous Jeanne Moreau, caught in the middle."

"A difficulty you eventually resolved by running off with Barton."

"But not before we'd had some pretty swell times. Remember after I'd moved to New York and you came down from law school at Harvard—I think to have an interview at Chase & Ward? We got standing room for *Anything Goes*—the original *Anything Goes*. I'll never forget it. Nineteen thirty-five."

The two main courses were being served but Emily, in her enthusiasm, continued talking. "We were standing in the very back of the theater, but you could see and hear absolutely everything Ethel Merman did and sang."

"Yes, I recall it very well—that part of the evening anyway."

"You may not remember the rest. Afterward you took me to a piano bar down in the Village, I forget the name of it, and you had the piano player do all the songs from the show."

"And got drunk in the process."

"Yes, and got drunk in the process and sang most of the songs yourself."

"You mean like 'You're the top! You're the Coliseum. You're the top! You're the Louvre Museum...'" Reuben, memories overwhelming him, sang in a low voice, keeping time with his hands. He stopped abruptly when the couple at his right stared at him, their disapproval palpable. Chastened, he began eating, though Emily was laughing too hard to do so.

"We had such *fun*, Reuben! Now it's all sex."

"Let's not forget we knew about sex, too, Emily."

"Oh, yes, but it wasn't a preoccupation. There was so much else, so much to do."

"It was a great time, no question."

"We're so lucky, we have memories. What will today's kids have fifty years from now? Recollections of one long anatomy lesson, with a lot of noise thrown in."

"You're right."

The two turned to quiet eating, delighting in the memories that had been brought to conscious recollection.

Once dessert was ordered—*oeufs à la neige* for both—Emily again remarked her good fortune in renewing contact with Harrison Rowan and Reuben.

Frost and Emily had quite deliberately shied away from mentioning Harrison during dinner, knowing that the conversation would slide into a discussion of David's murder. But Reuben also knew that the topic was inevitable, so he asked how often Emily had been seeing his old friend.

"Quite a bit. For two old people, one on Long Island and one in Virginia, we've done pretty well."

"When did this all begin?"

"Last Christmas. You could have knocked me over with a feather when Harrison called me the first time," Emily said. "I was so delighted, so excited, I could barely wait till we met in New York. It was just like sitting through the winter months at Wellesley waiting for one of you to call."

"You could have used the same feather to knock *me* over at the Reuff Dinner when I saw you there. I thought at the time, and still think, that Harrison deserves high marks for finding you. How is he bearing up?" Frost asked.

"As well as could be expected, I guess. That dinner was such a triumph. Harrison was so happy. And then it all got taken away from him a day later."

"I know. He was devastated."

"He was so proud of David, who really did seem to be on the verge of great things. Not only all those prizes and the new book, but politically. He was going to become a speechwriter for Senator Edmunds, did you know that?"

"Now that you mention it, I guess there was some hinting around about it that night. But are you sure?"

"Oh, yes. Harrison told me, just bursting with excitement. The only thing..." She paused.

"What?"

"Well, at the party afterward—you didn't go, did you?— the Senator and David seemed to be having a dispute. They went off into a corner and talked very seriously for a long time. It didn't look entirely friendly to me, and hardly seemed like the way to welcome a new speechwriter."

"Did you have any idea what they were talking about?" Frost pressed.

"No, no. I was some distance away. But I could hear the Senator's voice rising and saw him shake his finger at David."

"How about Harrison? Would he have heard anything?"

"I doubt it. He was on the other side of the room. And besides, he's gotten pretty deaf, you know."

"Yes, that's true. Do you want coffee, Emily?"

"I can't. And that decaffeinated bilge is just too terrible."

"A brandy perhaps?"

"Reuben, I'd love to. But pumpkin time comes really early for me. Cinderella could stay up until midnight, but I can't."

"Shall we go then?"

"I hate to, but I must. Before we do leave, though, let me ask you about the police. When on earth are they going to find the man who killed David?"

"They're working on it."

"Are you sure? It's been a week now."

"There's a good fellow in charge. Named Bautista. I think they'll solve the murder. It just takes time."

"I pray you're right. Harrison told me you're working with them."

"After a fashion. Needless to say, I'd be grateful for any insights."

"Gracious, Reuben. I didn't know anything about David, or his life. I guess the only thing I can say is that Harrison was very uneasy—*very* uneasy—about Miss Mann's relationship with that Lebanese restaurant owner."

"Italian, you mean. Giardi."

"Whatever. He was very apprehensive that there was going to be an explosion there. That's the only thing I know."

"We—Bautista and I—have had the same concern. All I can say is we're trying to make some sense out of what we know. Which I fear isn't very much."

Emily and Reuben walked back to the Colony.

"It's been a wonderful evening, my dear," Frost said, at the door of the Club.

"Oh, Reuben, and for me."

"You're right about memories, Emily. We're lucky with the ones we have. And don't forget, in that old song, when Martha Tilton sang *'We meet, and the angels sing,'* she knew what those words *really* meant, and we damn well did, too!"

Frost embraced and kissed the Widow Sherwood, then watched her disappear through the door, the good-time girl of old, laughing very hard as she did so.

Continuing on home, Frost realized that he should be elated about his evening. The meal, the company and the memories had all been delicious. But he could not conquer a feeling of deep unease, a feeling generated by Emily's description of the apparent quarrel between David Rowan and Wheeler Edmunds. And a feeling made totally vexing by his inability to imagine what on earth the two men could have been quarreling about.

SYNERGIES

14

"THAT WAS A DISASTER," CYNTHIA SAID THE NEXT NIGHT, when she and Reuben had returned home from Il Cantinori. "I don't mean the dinner—that was very good. But why, *why* did we have to be at the table next to that *Times* reporter?"

"You recognized him, I didn't," Reuben said.

"He's a very nice fellow. Used to be on the cultural desk and then asked to be changed to metropolitan so he could get closer to the city's *real* problems. If he weren't so shrewd and clever on the uptake, I would have gone right on talking about David's murder. But I knew he recognized me, and might have figured out what we were talking about if we'd kept on about David."

"You were right. The press and the TV are having a field day with David's murder. They've suggested everything but a Russian spy. You probably didn't see the *News* this morning, which said that the police weren't earning any Pulitzer Prizes for finding the killer of Pulitzer Prize–winning author David Rowan, et cetera."

"No. All I read was the *Cleveland Plain-Dealer* over breakfast at the hotel."

"I think the press sees David's murder as a new way of annoying the Mayor. It's not every day they get a prominent, white victim like David to write about."

"Poor Norman. If he could hold his temper, and keep his mouth shut, he'd have lots less trouble with the press."

"You know the Mayor so well, you ought to tell him," Reuben said.

"Sure. And have the pittance the Foundation gets from the city for its arts education program cut off?"

"Anyway, dinner was quite nice, and I was just as happy to talk about something else. We haven't talked about the state of the world, or our world, in ages."

"Or Eric Fischl."

"I think we've exhausted that subject. And my 'tryst' with Emily Sherwood, for that matter."

"Your *expensive* tryst with Emily Sherwood."

"After fifty years, my dear, it was the least I could do."

"I would have said the *most* you could do. But let that pass."

"Now look. We're both relatively sober, though I know you're tired from your trip. I need a quiet drink with you to get your advice. Are you game?"

"*Game?* I've been waiting since eight o'clock to hear what's going on. And to report on my *very interesting* lunch with Stanley Knowles."

"You're on. Scotch and soda?" Frost did not even wait for a yes as he went to prepare drinks.

"Who goes first? Tell me about Knowles."

"All right. Our lunch was supposed to be a routine little get-together to discuss the latest Brigham Foundation monograph. A fine little study of regional opera."

"Is there any?"

"Reuben, don't interrupt. I've got a surprisingly long story to tell, and I suspect you have, too. 'Dawn-busting' is great—you once told me that's what Emily Sherwood loved to do—but I for one am too old to sit up all night talking. So please let me get on with my story. Which I think will interest you."

"Peace. I agree."

"We ate at the Grill at the Four Seasons. Stanley was doing the Publishers' Power Lunch number. It's like the medina in Marrakech. Agents, authors, publishers, lawyers, all doing literary deals. And of course old Philip Johnson sitting at his banquette in the corner."

"I've always suspected he took his architect's fee for designing the place out in free lunches for life."

"If that's true, they got a bad deal—at their prices. He's going to live forever."

"If I had a calculator, I'd try to figure it out."

"Anyway," Cynthia continued, "we got our business done over oysters. Then Stanley—I know him so well I can tell—seemed to slip into a mopey depression. Not at all the lively partygoer we saw the other night. Midway into our tuna steaks—delicious, by the way—I asked him straight out what the matter was."

"And?"

"And he told me that Hammersmith Press is in bad financial trouble."

"Hmn. Maybe Donna was hinting at that the other night."

"Apparently costs are just going out of sight. Everything from paper to first-class-mail rates. He's had to get rid of his whole sales force, and now has a contract with Random House—I think—to distribute his books. His credit at the banks is exhausted and he really doesn't know where to turn."

"He told you all this?"

"Yes, like Niagara Falls. I had the feeling that he doesn't have anyone to talk to about his problems, so sympathetic Cynthia provided a comforting shoulder."

"He's determined not to sell out—to the aborigines, as he put it. But keeping afloat is more and more difficult. 'Maybe I'll have to go to the Mafia,' he said. 'They can't do much more damage than the banks.'"

"His company is public, isn't it? I know that he and Donna own a majority interest, but I'm sure Hammersmith's stock's traded over-the-counter."

"Oh, yes. There was much moaning about his duty to his stockholders. But then, Reuben, came the best part. I started sympathizing with him about the loss of David, and the big advance he'd paid him. And you know what?"

"What?"

"He wasn't worried about that *at all*. Said he knew from

the beginning that David's book probably wouldn't 'earn out,' as he put it, but it didn't matter. *He took out a life insurance policy on David's life when they signed their new contract!*"

"For the advance?"

"I think so."

"How much was it, did he say?"

"A 'healthy' six figures, was all he would tell me."

"Lord. Maybe four hundred thousand?"

"Of course he never said it in so many words, but he *almost* did—or maybe I just imagined it—that David's death had not been a financial catastrophe for him."

"Do you realize what this could mean, Cynthia?"

"I'm afraid I do. I think dear Stanley, as much as I love him, might be right up there as a suspect."

Reuben took a deep drink of his Scotch and soda and then ran his hands through his hair. "All we need is another one," he said, despair in his voice. "What did he say about Ralston Fortes?"

"Oh, yes. Your conscientious wife raised your question. He said the novel is a piece of trash, but sexy trash. 'Competent' enough not to be obscene. But racy enough to sell."

"What about Fortes? Anything about him personally?"

"Stanley says he considers himself very lucky because Donna has all the dealings with him. They had a meeting on Tuesday last week. He flew up from Washington and they were supposed to have lunch, and then a real working session to start getting the book in shape."

"So what happened?"

"Ralston Purina got totally plastered at lunch. Totally plastered and abusive. Donna had to call off their meeting."

"What did Fortes do?"

"As Stanley tells it, he started shouting at Donna that she wasn't sensitive to the Cuban experience. She left him in the middle of Seventh Avenue. Outside Bellini."

"So we don't know what he did after that, or where he went?"

"No."

"But he could have been in town at seven o'clock on Tuesday night? When David was killed?"

"As far as she or Stanley knows."

"Good God."

"So that's my story, my dear. What's yours?"

"I'm so shocked I'm going to have to think. I went to Washington and Trenton on Monday, you went to Cleveland yesterday. Let's see . . ."

With some effort Reuben collected his thoughts, then recapitulated in greater detail than he had the previous morning the visits to Marietta and Nancy, Alan Rowan's addiction and Grace Mann's friendship with Tom Giardi. For good measure he added the tale of David Rowan's quarrel with Wheeler Edmunds that Emily Sherwood had recounted.

"Let me try something," Cynthia said once Reuben had finished, getting up to go to the library. She returned with four sheets of yellow foolscap and a felt-tip pen, and ripped the paper into quarters. On six of the torn segments she wrote a name, bending over the coffee table that separated her from her husband.

"Okay, dear, here's the conventional wisdom. The great ladies involved could not have committed the murders. But they might have spellbound men who could have. It looks like this." She arranged six squares of paper on the coffee table, grouped in pairs:

MARIETTA AINSLEE   RALSTON FORTES
NANCY ROWAN   ALAN ROWAN
GRACE MANN   TOM GIARDI

"Nothing new there, Cynthia."

"I know. And I also know the only real lead so far is those missing desk calendars. Which is why I have Marietta and Ralston at the top of the list. But we can't overlook the others. Or maybe even some other synergies—isn't that the word? Like this one." Cynthia wrote on two more pieces of paper and put down a new combination:

GRACE MANN   ALAN ROWAN

"From what you said, Reuben, Grace Mann must be close to young Alan. She found the addiction-treatment program for him, and concealed his addiction from the police and you."

"Yes, you're right."

"Or how about this one," she said, laying down two more scraps that read:

STANLEY KNOWLES   RALSTON FORTES

"Desperate publisher and ambitious author, the author trying to make it on his own and willing to help his new-found publisher collect some much-needed insurance proceeds?"

"Oh, my."

"Or, finally, how about this one?" She produced a new combination:

HORACE JENKINS   RALSTON FORTES

"I don't get it," Reuben said.

"Well, poor Jenkins is gay, right? And Fortes knew his way around what you so dramatically called the 'homosexual underworld.' "

"That's going too far," Reuben said.

"It's stretching, I agree. But if we're going to play synergy, let's play the game out."

"Cynthia, I've got to go to bed. I'd like to say you've been no help at all, that you've only confused things. But of course I can't. But tell me, what are those blank pieces you've got left?"

"I wish I knew, dear. But I feel in my bones the synergy game isn't over."

15

REUBEN DID NOT SLEEP WELL AFTER HIS LATE-NIGHT conversation with Cynthia. Visions of the scraps of paper she had put down on their coffee table floated through his head, the names written on them combining and recombining in his mind. When he finally got up, and thought about the situation after coming fully awake, he despaired of ever identifying the murderer.

Still, he realized that the search must go on, however difficult the circumstances. He reviewed in his mind what Cynthia had said about Stanley Knowles and his apparently grim financial situation. And weighed the interesting fact that Knowles had maintained an insurance policy on David Rowan's life.

Could Stanley Knowles have murdered David, or had him murdered, to collect ready cash? And if so, why would he tell Cynthia about the insurance? It was true they were old friends. And also true that Knowles did not have any reason to know that Frost was involved in the investigation of the murder.

Or maybe Knowles was aware of Frost's activities, and telling Cynthia about the policy was a preemptive move in anticipation of Frost's finding out about it elsewhere.

Frost was not pleased with his speculations. He was sufficiently paranoid about the mysterious circumstances of

David's death that he did not dismiss them outright. And he did call Frank Norton at Chase & Ward and asked him to have the firm's library assemble all the information it could find on the Hammersmith Press. He could at least find out what if anything had become public about Hammersmith's financial troubles.

"This will probably be expensive," he told Norton, "and the library people will want to know what client to charge. Just tell them it's a *pro bono* matter of great interest to me and charge everything to the office. Or if that doesn't work, charge my personal account."

Norton assured him that he was certain the digging Frost had requested could be done for free.

Frost next decided that he would like to see David Rowan's personal files. Bautista, once Frost had reached him on the telephone, agreed that another look might be useful.

He learned that the material he wanted was still in Rowan's office. Bautista said he would call the rookie patrolman guarding the premises and tell him to give Frost access to whatever was there.

Before the morning was over Frost was back at Rowan's tenth-floor office on Forty-fourth Street, now watched over by another young policeman with bad skin, sitting on a folding chair outside the office door.

"Can I help you sir?" he asked, looking up from his memo book, which he had been leafing through.

"Yes. I'm Reuben Frost. Did Detective Bautista call?"

"Yessir. I'm Patrolman O'Bryan." He stood up and stuck out his hand, which Frost shook, noting as he did so that this pimply minion of the law would be about the age of his grandson (if he had been lucky or unlucky enough to have had one).

"Detective Baustista said to treat you as a VIP and to let you see any of the files you want. Come on in."

The tiny office was now almost bare, except for a desk and two chairs, Rowan's word processor and the single four-drawer file cabinet. Frost speculated as to what "VIP treatment" might mean in this bleak setting.

"It's these files you'll be wanting, isn't it?" O'Bryan asked.

"I believe so."

The officer took a ring of keys from his pocket and unlocked the cabinet.

"Can I use the desk?"

"Sure. I'll be outside if you need me."

Frost was glad the desk did not face the window from which David Rowan had been pushed. He still was not entirely comfortable, but set to work inspecting the contents of the file cabinet. The bottom drawer contained only office supplies, but the other three were full of neatly maintained legal-size folders, arranged in alphabetical order. Some of them (which it turned out dated back to Princeton days, when a secretary had been available) had neatly typed labels at the top, the others were lettered in what Frost assumed was Rowan's handwriting.

He decided to begin at the beginning, and was soon examining a file labeled simply "Alan." Its contents confirmed what he had so recently learned, that the boy did have a drug problem. And Grace Mann's name was prominently mentioned in correspondence urging the director of Fairhaven Gables to admit Alan.

He next turned to a rather thick file, marked "American Historical Association." As he flipped through it, he recalled Nancy Rowan's observation that David was a participant in internecine struggles within the Association. David apparently had been on a crusade against what he called "gender" history. Frost was particularly struck by a letter David had written to the permanent secretary, and members of the nominating committee:

> I think I am as aware as anyone of the desirability of seeking historical truth from a wide variety of perspectives; looking through a single facet of the prism that is history is unarguably too limiting. After last year's convention, however, I fear that our Association is being taken over by the "single-perspective" historians, notably those who loudly advocate that historical stud-

ies, to be valid, must be based on considerations of sex and race.

I am not so narrow-minded as to condemn panels such as those we had last year on "Sex, Gender and the Constitution," or even "Sodomy and Pederasty Among Nineteenth-Century Seafarers." But if anyone thinks that Constitutional history or the economic history of nineteenth-century trade is really advanced by such skews in focus, I can only say that I think they are very wrong.

Rumors have reached me that Peter Jewett is now being considered by your committee for nomination as a vice-president of the Association, which means, of course, that he would be in line for president two years from now. As I am sure you all know, Professor Jewett several years back loudly advocated the view that history, of whatever period, can only be seen from a Marxist perspective. Now, presumably after achieving some maturity, he appears to believe that history can only be viewed from the perspective of so-called "new history," in which considerations of race and sex—and sexual orientation—are paramount.

I submit to you that Professor Jewett's views, while trendy and fashionable, are outside the mainstream and that, in a position of power, he would lead the Association down an eccentric path that would bring discredit to the Association and cause our most important constituency—our students—to hold us in deserved contempt.

For your information, I enclose a copy of my recent review of Professor Jewett's history of women in the American Foreign Service, which I hope and trust will demonstrate to you the shortcomings of both his point of view and his methodology.

And there are those who think courtroom lawyers are too argumentative! Frost thought. His brush with the AHA made him feel that he needed a break and, quite possibly, lunch.

"Mr. O'Bryan, I'm going out for a while," he announced

to the policeman outside the door. "Can I bring you any-thing?"

"No, sir, I'm fine, unless a cup of coffee wouldn't be too much trouble."

"Not at all. Cream and sugar?"

"Black."

Frost also was about to suggest that he might bring the poor youngster a paperback book or a magazine; he certainly could not really be reading his memo book all the time. But then he thought he would be violating some Police Department regulation, so he did not. O'Bryan must stalwartly guard his fixed post without distraction.

Frost walked to the Gotham Club eleven blocks away, had a most satisfying Gotham martini and a quick lunch, and then returned, stopping on the way back at a delicatessen to buy Patrolman O'Bryan his coffee. The next few files, with such prosaic titles as "Car," "Garage" and "Apartment," plus a lifetime's accumulation of lecture notes, he passed over quickly.

Then, when he got to "Reviews—W&M," he encountered Peter Jewett again. Amid the almost unanimously favorable reviews for *Ways and Means* was one by Jewett, in an obscure historical quarterly, that figuratively blew Reuben's head off. "Seldom has a political institution, in this case the Ways and Means Committee of the House of Representa-tives, been so misunderstood by an author seeking to tell its history," the piece began. Jewett questioned David's basic premise, that the Committee, through much of its history, had been unacceptably antidemocratic by preventing bills from coming to a vote on the floor of the House.

Rowan "had utterly failed to understand" that this bot-tling up of legislation was exactly what the Members of Congress wanted, that it was a means of getting them "off the hook." The Ways and Means Committee had provided the "grease" that enabled the House to function in an orderly way; David had been "extraordinarily naive" for failing to see this. Worse, he had "selectively and promiscuously used the facts available" to support his thesis.

Frost pondered Jewett's extravagant prose. The review

bore a date earlier than David's American Historical Association letter that Frost had uncovered earlier, so that letter had not been the provocation for Jewett's attack.

Frost made a note as to the particulars of the review. He must find out the cause of Jewett's anger; nearly at an insane pitch in his article, might it not have somehow increased to an irrational, homicidal boiling point? The possibility was remote, but Frost did not feel he could ignore the evidence of rage (and counterrage) he had unearthed in his file search.

Then, with some distaste, he began examining the file entitled *"Rowan v. Rowan,"* which contained papers and correspondence relating to David's divorce from Nancy. All the bitterness he had heard about was confirmed as he looked through the file. Communication seemed to have been exclusively through the lawyers for the two parties; written in restrained lawyer's prose, the file letters nonetheless conveyed the rancor implicit in the positions taken by their respective clients.

The pettiness of most of the disputes seemed appalling. The major issues—custody of the minor children, the level of David's support payment—had been settled early on, but the negotiations dragged on over "priceless" phonograph records, a necklace David's late mother had given to Nancy, and goods and chattels even more trivial.

Frost was about to give up on this dreary correspondence, which only served to prove what he knew already, when he came upon a letter, at the very end of the file, from David to his divorce lawyer. The letter was a belated thank-you note to the lawyer for having sent a certified copy of the divorce decree, which David needed to get his license to marry Grace Mann. It was the postscript that particularly intrigued Frost:

P.S. Do you know anything about copyright law? In connection with this Ainslee book I'm working on, there's a guy who wants to keep me from using certain material that he wrote to Ainslee. It's great stuff and I want to use it, and I have it right here in the files. But can I use it?

David

Frost read the postscript again, seeking to find more meaning from its cryptic words. The "stuff" could not be the notorious Ainslee date books that were now missing, but material sent by a third party, presumably male, to Ainslee. He searched through the files to find the letterhead, with the telephone number, of Barry Stevens, Rowan's lawyer.

After seeking permission from Patrolman O'Bryan, he called Stevens and was gratified to find him in his office further uptown. He explained why he was calling and refreshed the other lawyer's recollection by reading the postscript to him.

"Yes, I remember now. David sent me that note. The answer was so easy I just called him on the phone. Told him the new Copyright Act protects virtually anything a person creates and writes down, except if it's done for an employer. I also explained how he could use somebody else's copyrighted property as long as it's limited to 'fair use.' "

"When you called, what did he tell you exactly?" Frost asked.

"As best I recall, he repeated just what was in his letter. Somebody was objecting to David's using material—I assume it was letters—that had been written to Ainslee."

"No other description, either of the person or the letters?"

"I don't think so."

"Was it a man or a woman?"

"My impression was that it was a man."

"How did you leave it?"

"He thanked me and said he'd get in touch if it were necessary. Oh, yes, and then he offered to pay me for my time. I said, forget it. Then he said there might be some real business for me if the problem got 'hot.' "

"I don't mean to cross-examine you, Mr. Stevens, but what did you take it he meant by 'hot'—that the papers involved were 'hot' or that the litigation, if it came, would be hotly contested?"

"I can't say, Mr. Frost. I guess I thought he meant any litigation would be heated. But he could have meant the other."

"Anything else, anything at all you can remember about your conversation? There was only one conversation, is that correct?"

"That's right. It was the last time I ever talked to David, in fact. And to answer your question, I think I've told you everything I remember about our phone call."

Frost thanked his fellow lawyer for his help, regretting at the same time that David had not been more forthcoming about his "problem." He decided to quit his file search for the moment. What he needed to do was to go home and locate the telephone number Bautista had given him for Lucy Wyecliffe, the University of Tennessee librarian. He instinctively felt that if she were careful in doing her inventory of the returned documents, something besides the engagement books would turn up missing. Something of interest—perhaps of crucial interest.

DIGGING

16

LUCY WYECLIFFE HAD GONE FOR THE DAY BY THE TIME Frost got home. The next morning, he called her from home, before a planned trip to Chase & Ward. There was no reason why he couldn't have waited to call her until he reached the office—except for his nearly total inability to use the firm's new, "improved" telephone system.

He realized that the new instruments installed at the firm, which scarcely resembled any telephones he had ever used before, at home or abroad, performed many wondrous feats: conference calls to multiple locations, automatic retries of busy numbers. And, wonder of wonders, with the punching out of a mere eighteen digits, a long-distance call could be made and charged directly to the proper office or client account. Frost knew better than to wrestle with such an electronic monster.

Having identified himself to the librarian, Frost was met with a tirade that lasted several minutes. Ms. Wyecliffe had known all along that there would be trouble if the Ainslee papers were moved to New York, but had been forced to relent when confronted with Marietta Ainslee's demand that they be placed in David Rowan's temporary custody.

Then there had been the matter of photocopying. Ms. Wyecliffe had tried to insist that the entire Ainslee collection—literally hundreds of thousands of pieces of paper, of varying degrees of importance—be copied before being moved to New York. But neither Mrs. Ainslee nor the university—let alone David—had been willing to pay for this precaution.

"So there we are, Mr. Frost. Probably all kinds of things are missing from the papers, but we'll never know what."

"Surely there must be *some* record, Ms. Wyecliffe."

"*Miss* Wyecliffe, if you don't mind."

"Of course."

"Well, many of the Senatorial papers were in boxes relating to specific legislation and the papers from the time on the Court were arranged by case, one case to a box. The boxes were numbered in sequence, and we do have a list of the titles."

"So you could tell, then, if the entire box relating to a particular bill, or a particular case, were missing?"

"That's correct. We have a master list of the files."

"But you couldn't tell if a specific document were missing?"

"That's also correct. Without cataloging and numbering each document, which would have taken years, or without Xeroxing all the papers, which could have been done very easily but wasn't, there's no way we can track down a single missing document."

"I think it would be very helpful to check the files that came back against your master list."

"I've started that already—I began the instant we got the papers back," Lucy Wyecliffe said possessively. "I'm almost through with the Senate papers."

"And nothing has shown up missing so far?"

"No *boxes* have turned up missing. I can't vouch for anything beyond that."

"*Miss* Wyecliffe, I think it's essential that you continue your exercise. I have a hunch that there are papers missing from the Ainslee files—I wish I could be more specific, but I honestly can't. And I also have a hunch that if we can identify what's missing, it may give us a clue to who murdered David Rowan."

"Oh, goodness, Mr. Frost, I had no idea that's what you

were getting at. You think a *murderer* may have stolen something from the Ainslee papers?"

"That's only a guess. But it wouldn't surprise me."

"Then of course I'll continue checking."

"That would be very helpful. And the sooner the better, I'm afraid. Is there any chance you could get people to work over the weekend on this?"

"I *do* have other things to take care of, you know," the librarian said, in a huff. "And the papers came back in such an unspeakable and inexcusable mess. . . . But I'll see what can be done."

"Will you call me if you discover anything?" Frost asked. He gave the woman his number, spoke a few more phrases of encouragement and got off the line before she could start lecturing him further.

At Chase & Ward, Frank Norton had done his homework. Reuben's modest-sized desk was covered with material concerning the Hammersmith Press: the 10-K and 10-Q annual and quarterly reports filed with the Securities and Exchange Commission, the glossy annual reports sent to shareholders, a NEXIS printout listing references to Hammersmith in *The New York Times*, *The Washington Post*, *The Wall Street Journal* and selected other newspapers around the country. A handwritten note from Norton said he had tried to get everything relevant for the past five years, and also suggested skimming issues of *Publishers Weekly* if the information Frost was seeking concerned recent events.

Frost marveled at the accumulation before him. With the telephone, a copying machine and a computer, all measure of information about the Hammersmith Press had been assembled with very little effort and in one day's time.

Plunging in at once, Frost soon discovered that Stanley Knowles's financial troubles were real. Earnings had been falling for the last three years, though Hammersmith had remained in the black. That was not likely to continue in the current year; the 10-Q report for the first quarter of 1988, just filed with the SEC, revealed that Hammersmith had taken a large write-off against its inventory, consisting mostly of books that Hammersmith no longer considered salable.

Frost took young Norton's advice and went to the library to look over copies of *Publishers Weekly* for the current year. The inventory write-off in February was prominently featured, and a later issue of the magazine reported the rumor that Hammersmith was about to eliminate its sales force and would henceforth distribute its books through another as yet unnamed publisher.

Returning to his office, Frost found another note that Norton had dropped off, enclosing a copy of a recent Dun & Bradstreet credit report on Hammersmith. It suggested that Hammersmith was not paying its bills on a current, or even a ninety-day, basis and that at least one of its paper suppliers had put it on a cash basis—no payment, no paper.

All the signs were clear to Frost. Hammersmith was at best on the verge of insolvency, at worst already bankrupt. Stanley Knowles could certainly use the proceeds from the policy on David Rowan's life. Even if his advance had not been paid in full, the insurance recovery could have been two or perhaps even three hundred thousand dollars—a welcome, if temporary, infusion for a cash-starved business. But had Knowles killed to get the money? Or enticed Fortes to do the killing? Frost did not want to entertain such possibilities, but he could not deny that the motive, a desperate means of staunching the fiscal hemorrhaging of the Hammersmith Press, was there.

"Reuben, was any of this junk helpful?" Norton asked, sticking his head in the door and interrupting Frost's musings on the latest turn of events.

"Oh, Frank, yes. It certainly was. No, let me qualify that. It was very useful in providing me with a lot of information. Very unhelpful by complicating the problem I'm working on."

"Can I ask what that is?"

"I'll tell you if you've got the time. Close the door."

Frost swore his former partner to secrecy and then described to him, at least in outline, the impasse reached in the investigation of Rowan's death. "Now, thanks to all this reading matter you foisted on me, I've got to take a closer look at what had been a very remote suspect."

"I'm sorry, Reuben."

"Forget it. You did what I asked you to do. But now, let me ask you another question. Do you know anything about copyright?"

"Not a thing."

"Who does?"

"Neil Sloane."

"Is he around?"

"I think so. I saw him in the hall earlier today."

"How the hell do I get him on this machine?" Frost asked, pointing helplessly to the new-model telephone.

"You've got to move into the twentieth century, Reuben," Norton said, laughing.

"I have, I have. It's just that these damn things have moved into the twenty-first."

"Let me do it," Norton said, looking up Sloane's number on the office list and calling him.

"He'll be down in ten minutes, if that's okay," Norton announced after completing the call.

"Fine. Since you're being so all-purpose helpful, let me ask you still *another* question. Didn't you go to Amherst as an undergraduate?"

"That's right."

"Did you know a professor there named Peter Jewett?"

"Sure, everyone did. One of the best-known professors on campus. I was a history major, so I knew him quite well. Both him and his wife, Elizabeth."

"What was her name?" Frost demanded, sitting straight up in his chair.

"Elizabeth. Why?"

"Nothing, nothing."

"What do you want to know about Jewett?"

"Anything you can tell me."

"He was a strange bird. Chairman of the History Department when I was there and very obviously—obvious even to a callow undergraduate like me—ambitious to go on to other things. Which he probably could have done, except for the scandal with his wife."

"What was that?"

"He beat her up, gave her two black eyes. She was furious and went to the police. The college persuaded her to drop the charges, or Jewett might have been locked up. But it was a big scandal in the town, I'm telling you."

"Did he beat her up all the time, or was this a special occasion?"

"The rumor was that it was a special occasion. He thought he was in the running for a major history chair at Yale, but he lost out. Apparently he just went berserk and took it out on his wife."

"His wife, Elizabeth?"

"Yes. Why are you looking at me like that?"

"Because you're complicating everything."

"How?"

"Because you've just given me a whole new lead I'll have to follow."

"I don't understand."

"Never mind. If anything comes of it, I'll let you know."

"Anything else I can do for you, Reuben?"

"No, Frank, you've done quite enough."

Frank Norton was leaving just as Neil Sloane arrived.

"Come in, Neil," Frost said, "I'd invite both you and Frank to the party, but there really isn't room for both of you in my retirement cottage."

"I've got to go anyway, I can't stay," Norton said. "Be sure and call me if there's anything else you want."

"What can I do for you, Reuben?" Sloane asked, sitting down in the empty chair and relighting the dead cigar end in his hand.

"Copyright. A subject I've never learned the first thing about. Let me pose a hypothetical question to you. I write someone a letter—Norton, let's say. Then Norton writes a book and decides to include my letter in it. Can he do that?"

"No. Norton owns the physical letter. It's his. He can sell it or do anything he likes with it—burn it if he wants to. But he can't publish the contents. You have the copyright in the contents. That's probably always been the law, but the revision of the Copyright Act in nineteen seventy-six made it explicit.

"Now, Norton might be able to paraphrase your letter, or extract quotations from it," Sloane proceeded. "There's always the right of 'fair use.' But his rights are probably going to be pretty limited. You remember the case of that writer, J. D. Salinger, just a few months ago. The Court of Appeals stopped a biography of Salinger from being published because it contained quotes and paraphrases from some unpublished letters.

"So, Reuben, Frank Norton had better watch out if he wants to put you in his book."

"Is there something about employees not being protected?" Frost asked, trying to recall his conversation with Rowan's lawyer, Barry Stevens.

"Oh, yes. Right in the Copyright Act. 'Work made for hire' is the phrase. If Frank Norton were still an associate—and there are those of us who think that might be a good idea—and was working for you, the copyright in anything he wrote for you would be yours or, more likely, Chase & Ward's, 'unless otherwise agreed in a written instrument,' I believe the Act reads."

"Neil, you've been most helpful."

"Somebody going to publish your secrets, Reuben?"

"No, no, nothing like that. Just a little problem I *think* I've run across."

"Fine. Anything else?"

"No. Many thanks."

Frost was hungry, but he was in a dilemma about what to do for lunch. He didn't want to go out to a restaurant and he didn't want to go upstairs to the private Hexagon Club, where all his former partners would be eating. He finally settled on the firm's cafeteria, where he bought a sandwich, chock-full of mysterious and indescribable ingredients, and brought it back to his office.

Closing the door, he ate in privacy as he pondered his next step. There was nothing at the moment he could do about Stanley Knowles except alert Bautista to Hammersmith's troubles when he talked to him later in the afternoon, as he had arranged to do.

There was likewise nothing to be done about the missing Ainslee papers, if indeed there were such. That trail was dead until Ms. Wyecliffe had completed her work.

That left Peter Jewett. It was time to tap the Frost connections and get a reading on him; he needed to get to the root of the mutual enmity between Rowan and Jewett.

After thirty minutes in the Chase & Ward library, using a foundation directory, the Martindale-Hubbell list of lawyers and other sources, Frost came up with a list of individuals he knew who might in turn be acquainted with Jewett.

Returning to his office, he called (after a false start or two) the word processing supervisor and asked for a stenographer.

"Do you need someone who takes dictation, Mr. Frost?" she asked.

"No, all I need is someone who can operate these damnable new telephones," he replied.

Assistance arrived within minutes, and several calls were placed. Frost learned (from another Amherst professor he had met at the Gotham Club) that Jewett's "violent" period had been real, but brief. There had been no known trouble in the town after the incident with his wife—though perhaps the fact that his wife had later left him had contributed to the domestic tranquility. A foundation executive, a New York publisher (*not* Stanley Knowles), and an officer of the American Historical Association, all friends of Reuben's who knew Jewett, had little to contribute. Yes, it was true that Jewett and David Rowan had bashed each other in public (or in history circles, at least) and the quarrels were so bitter that they seemed to go beyond pure intellectual differences. But if there were deeper causes, no one knew them.

Then Frost called another lawyer and a former chairman of the Yale University trustees, Delbert Rodgers.

"Do you recall picking a new Sterling Professor of History at Yale, oh, twelve years ago now?" Frost asked.

"Indeed I do. Why?"

"Was there a fellow named Peter Jewett considered for the job?"

"There certainly was."

"Can you tell me about it?"

"I assume, Reuben, this is all just between us. Completely off-the-record."

"Absolutely, Delbert. But anything you can tell me would be most helpful."

"Jewett was the leading candidate. His credentials were fine and he made a great hit with the search committee—I know, because I was on the History Department visiting committee then. Everybody was for him—except for this one joker on the committee."

"Who was that?"

"That fellow who died recently, the biographer. David Rowan. He was a professor at Princeton then, and was one of the outsiders on the search committee. This was back when you couldn't have a search committee without everybody under the sun on it—students, campus janitors and outsiders. He made a great nuisance of himself, presenting memoranda about Jewett's faulty scholarship, and on and on. But it worked. Single-handed, Rowan kept Jewett from getting that appointment."

"Why was he so opposed?" Frost asked.

"Hard to say. My own guess was that it was entirely intellectual, or maybe ideological. But it sure as hell was bitter."

"I assume Jewett knew about all this?"

"I assume so, too. Our deliberations were supposed to be secret, but you know how these things work. There aren't secrets for very long."

"Delbert, I appreciate your help."

"Help? I can't say as I know exactly how I've helped," Rodgers said, puzzled.

"I'll tell you sometime."

Frost was about to call Bautista when another thought occurred to him. Marietta Ainslee had referred to a Massachusetts history professor as the runner-up to David in the competition to pick Garrett Ainslee's biographer—and as the source for the information that David was talking freely about the Justice's sex code. Could this person have been Jewett?

A quick, if somewhat strained, call to Marietta Ainslee confirmed that the anonymous professor was indeed Jewett. The woman did open up enough to say that Jewett had been turned down very explicitly because his experience, in diplomatic history, just did not seem right for the job. But he had been doggedly persistent and even became abusive when David had been selected. "He doesn't have the right experience, either," she quoted him as saying, after which he had threatened to "ruin" any biography David might publish.

As Frost absorbed this new intelligence, his wife called, inquiring about plans for dinner.

"How are things going?" Cynthia asked.

"I'll tell you later. But the answer is, not well. We even have a brand-new suspect. Your friend Peter Jewett."

"I don't believe it."

"Cook me dinner and I'll tell you about it."

AN ARREST

17

THE FROSTS HAD TURNED DOWN A TEMPTING INVITATION to spend the weekend with their old friends the Merriams in the country. Charlotte Merriam had been particularly importunate, stressing that an April weekend was one of the absolute best times of the year to visit the Hudson Valley.

"I love the Merriams dearly," Reuben had said. "And Charlotte is absolutely right; Dutchess County in the spring is absurdly beautiful. But I'm just too wrought up about David to enjoy myself."

Cynthia had dutifully expressed their regrets, though she was firmly of the opinion that a weekend in the country would have done them both good.

"You talk about 'lounge lizards' all the time," she had said to her husband. "But you're becoming one."

As planned, the Frosts ate at home that night, but not before Frost had reached Bautista to nominate Peter Jewett for the suspects list. He figuratively kicked himself for not focusing on the Amherst professor earlier. The quarrel over the Bancroft Prize should have tipped him off. And why had he not asked Marietta Ainslee in Washington to identify the disgruntled entrant in her competition?

Now, as he relayed his new information to Bautista, he hoped valuable time had not been lost because of his obtuseness. Bautista was reassuring and promised him he would

129

have the local police in Amherst question Jewett at once. Still, Frost told himself that detection was perhaps not for an old man. He should have been sharper.

He began discussing Professor Jewett with Cynthia the instant she arrived home, and continued to do so through dinner.

"I've never liked him," Cynthia said. "Every time he's at a meeting he has a chip on his shoulder about something. Very argumentative, and not very nice."

"Then why do you have him around?"

"Well, like many people who aren't very nice, he's professionally very competent and a valuable member of the Foundation's history jury. So everyone agrees it's worth the price to put up with his churlishness."

"Is he sinister?"

"You mean a murderer? I would be amazed. No, he's not sinister, nothing like that. Just overbearing and rude, as I said the other night."

"And you never heard what I told you before supper, that he's a wife-beater?"

"No, and as I told you, I always assumed he was just a crotchety bachelor. A true misogynist. There's never been any sign of a wife."

"That's because she left before he bashed her skull in."

"Do you really think he killed David?"

"I have no idea. But he had a motive and he's apparently not afraid of violence."

"At least as far as women are concerned."

"Be still. And just to prove there's no antifeminism lurking here, I'll take you to the movies."

Saturday was a splendid day, the weather a silent reproach to Reuben for not having accepted the Merriams' invitation. That evening, he and Cynthia ate at home again, avoiding, as they usually did, the Saturday night crush of tourists and suburbanites in most Manhattan restaurants. They had just finished dinner when the telephone rang. It was Harrison Rowan, in a state of near panic.

"Reuben, my grandson's been arrested."

"You mean Alan?"

"Yes, Alan."

"Where? What for?"

"Dope peddling. He was arrested in a hotel somewhere near Times Square for buying cocaine."

"Harrison, I thought they only arrested sellers these days, not buyers."

"When you're buying a quarter of a pound of the damned stuff, I guess they do."

"Good God," Reuben exclaimed.

"It's not just some cockamamy offense, Reuben. He's accused of possession with intent to sell."

"How do you know this?"

"He called me. Collect. His one free phone call, I guess. He's being held at something called Midtown South. Can you do something, Reuben? I don't know who else to turn to."

"Of course I'll do something. I'll go down there right now." Frost had not the faintest idea what—or where—Midtown South was, but he was too good a lawyer to betray his ignorance to his old friend.

"Reuben, I can't thank you enough. You've got to help the boy. He sounded terrible when he called."

"How do you mean?"

"Scared and not quite coherent. I had great trouble finding out what happened."

"I'll do my best, Harrison. I'll call you as soon as I've seen him."

Frost hung up the phone and cursed quietly to himself.

"Who was that?" Cynthia asked.

"Harrison Rowan."

"At this hour?"

"Alan's been arrested. Buying dope for resale. I've got to go and see him right now."

"Where is he?"

"Midtown South."

"Shouldn't you call someone to go with you?"

"You mean someone from Chase & Ward? I would, but I don't think there's anybody there who knows about messes like this. The last criminal matter the firm defended was a price-fixing case twenty years ago."

"I suppose you have to go alone then. Do you know where it is?"

"Of course not," Reuben said crossly, irritated at the interruption to his evening and uncomfortable with his own nearly complete ignorance of criminal procedures. He looked in the telephone book, guessing that the "Midtown Precinct South" listed was what he was looking for. Should he call there first? No, he must just get there as quickly as possible.

"Be careful. And good luck," Cynthia called to him as he hurried down the stairs.

Frost's destination was way west on Thirty-fifth Street, almost at the Hudson River. It was a part of the city he had never once visited and, as his nerves told him, he had never been in a New York City precinct house before, either. A law-abiding citizen throughout his life—since he didn't drive, he had never even gotten a speeding ticket—he felt, as he made his way through the squadron of police vehicles outside the building, that he was entering truly foreign territory.

The vast waiting room was severely institutional in tone, with fluorescent lights ablaze and a collection of straight-backed chairs scattered haphazardly about. He approached the long counter at the left and stated his business.

"You a relative?" the officer behind the desk asked.

"No. I'm a friend of the boy's family. And a lawyer."

"An attorney, eh? You representing him?"

"Yes, I am."

"Got your Corrections ID?"

"ID?"

"Yeah. You're a criminal lawyer and you don't have a Department of Corrections ID?" the officer asked, incredulously.

"No. I don't do this sort of thing as a regular matter."

"But you say you're a lawyer. Can you prove it?"

Frost was stymied, then remembered that he still had a supply of Chase & Ward business cards in his wallet, identifying him as a partner. He nervously produced one for his interrogator, wondering as he did so if he was committing some sort of misdemeanor by holding himself out as a partner in his old firm.

The desk officer examined the card carefully, and also scrutinized the well-dressed supplicant before him. (Frost had had the presence of mind to put on a necktie and a quiet jacket before leaving home.)

"Okay, Frost, go upstairs—through that door down there on the left—and ask for Sergeant Rafferty in the detectives' office."

Frost dutifully followed instructions and, after several inquiries, found himself face to face with Sergeant Rafferty. He had scarcely introduced himself when he heard a familiar voice behind him, calling his name.

"Reuben! What the hell are you doing here?" It was Luis Bautista.

"Good God, Luis, I could say the same!" It was unclear who was more startled at this surprise encounter, Frost or Bautista.

"That's all right, Dan, let me handle this," Bautista said to Rafferty. "Come with me, Reuben," he added, propelling Frost into a vacant office and closing the door.

"What happened, the kid's grandfather call you?" Bautista asked.

"Yes. But what's this got to do with you? Harrison said Alan had been arrested on a narcotics charge."

"That's true. But he's also confessed to killing his father."

Frost's shoulders sagged as he took in what Bautista was saying. "Oh, my God," was all he could say, in a subdued voice. "I'd better sit down." He did so, collapsing into a battered swivel chair.

"Is it true?" Frost asked.

"I don't know. Let me tell you what happened."

"Yes."

"Alan Rowan was arrested in a Times Square hotel room about four o'clock. He was buying cocaine from a black dealer called Big Jake, a guy the narcs have been watching for weeks. The kid had bad luck, being there when they finally decided to move in on Big Jake. Bad luck also that he was buying enough coke to get every user in New Jersey high."

"So it wasn't just for him? Dope for his own use?"

"Hell, no. He and a buddy make the stuff into crack back home in New Jersey and sell what they don't use themselves. Mostly to high school kids, by the way."

"Awful."

"The drug case is open and shut. Criminal possession of a controlled substance in the second degree, which means he's probably looking at three to five years, unless something can be worked out.

"But that's not why I'm here, obviously. The kid was high as a kite when they nabbed him. As soon as the guys restrained him and got him into a squad car, he started screaming that he'd killed his father. When they got him here, somebody had the brains to realize he meant David Rowan, the guy whose murder has been Topic A on the TV news every night. They called me at home and I came right in."

"Have you talked to him?"

"Let me continue."

"Sorry."

"By the time I got here, they had a video crew from the DA's office here to tape his statement. I talked to him and he was willing to do it, so we made a tape."

"Good God, didn't he want a lawyer?"

"Negative. We asked him several times. So did the Assistant DA, guy named Joe Munson, who's on the case. He kept yelling, 'The hell with a lawyer.' "

"So he's confessed on videotape?"

"Yes. I want you to see it." Bautista left the room and returned with a technician wheeling a monitor on a cart. Soon the tape was rolling, and Frost recognized Alan Rowan, who was wearing a turtleneck sweater and a windbreaker, looking like a perfectly normal undergraduate. Assistant District Attorney Munson, a pudgy young man with Coke-bottle glasses, and Bautista were also present. As Munson took the boy through the technical preliminaries, it was clear that he was disturbed. Then the tape showed the actual confession:

"Do you have a statement you want to make about your father?" Munson asked.

"Yeah. I killed him. He wouldn't give me the money I needed so I threw him out the window of his office."

"Why have you decided to admit this now?"

"What the hell have I got to lose? They'll put me away for drugs anyway. Besides, the cop who arrested me called me a nasty little punk. I decided to let him know I'm *really* nasty!"

Alan appeared on the screen laughing, and soon his laughter was out of control, his nose running and his eyes watering as he rocked back and forth in his chair. Munson waited for him to calm down before asking why he had killed his father.

"Because I hated the sonofabitch! He was really getting on my case—do this, don't do that, that's all I heard. There he was making a bloody fortune with his book and living off that TV babe and he wouldn't give me any of it. That last night I went to see him, I needed two hundred dollars real bad. He got real leaked off, said I was no good and a disgrace, crap like that. The bastard went on and on until I finally hit him and dumped him out the window. Just like he would've done to me if he could."

Munson conferred with Bautista, then said, "Okay, Rowan, show me just how you went about killing your old man. Let's say the window's over there, and this is the desk. Now what happened?"

Alan explained, with dramatic gestures, how he had grabbed his father across the desk and struck him on the right side of his neck, knocking him unconscious, then opened the window, picked up his father's body in his arms and rolled him across the windowsill and out.

"See, it was just as easy as pie—*bye, bye American pie.*"

"Yeah, I see. What did you do next?"

"I looked in his desk for money and then got the hell out."

"That's all?"

"Ain't that enough?"

"Now, Rowan, I want to run through it again. Same thing, this is the desk, window's over there. Except this time Detective Bautista will be your father." Bautista took a position sitting behind the desk. "Go ahead."

Alan came across the desk and grabbed Bautista by the lapels, pulling him up out of the chair. He did so roughly, but Bautista didn't stop him.

"Then what?" Munson demanded.

"I hit him in the neck."

"Where, exactly? Show me."

"Right there," the boy said, aiming an open-handed chop at Bautista's right side, which Bautista deflected.

"Then you opened the window, picked him up, and pushed him off the sill?"

"Yeah."

"You knocked him out?"

"Yeah."

"With one blow?"

"Yeah."

"He didn't resist?"

"Nah. He was a weak bastard. He went right down."

"Then, after you threw your father out the window, the only thing you did was look for money in the desk? Did you find any?"

"No."

"Then you didn't do anything else. Right?"

"No."

"Just got out of there?"

"Right."

"How did you get out?"

"The elevator."

"Didn't anybody see you when you left the building?"

"Nah. They'd found the body in the street and everybody was freaked out. Running around, screaming. Nobody saw anybody."

"Then what did you do?"

"I went home and went to sleep."

Bautista switched off the monitor. "There it is," he said.

"Do you believe him?" Frost asked.

"Maybe, *maybe*, that kid killed his father," Bautista said. "*Maybe* his mind is so cooked that he remembers killing him, but not how. But my hunch is he was having some sort of hallucination and was making the whole thing up. The facts are all wrong. The decedent was hit on the left side, not the right. He didn't go down, he fought like hell. The desk drawer was all in order, not ransacked by anyone. And what about those papers all over the place? Who made that mess, the tooth fairy?"

"I agree, his story is cockeyed. But is it *all* cockeyed, or just the details?"

"He's now denying what he told us. An hour after he made the tape, he started coming down and acting normal. That's when he decided he wanted a lawyer and we let him call his grandfather. And when we asked him again about killing his father, he denied the whole thing."

"What will happen to him now?"

"They'll take him down to central booking and then bring him back here, probably."

"There's no way to get him out?"

"Negative. Not with a potential homicide charge against him. They'll probably arraign him Monday morning."

"Can I see him?"

"Sure. You're his lawyer. Stay here and I'll arrange it."

Bautista soon returned and took Frost to a different office, one with a clear glass panel in the door. Then Sergeant Rafferty and another policeman appeared, flanking Alan Rowan.

"All right, Rowan," Rafferty said. "This man says he's your attorney. You can talk with him, but if there's any funny business you'll go right back to the pen. Understand?"

Alan made a face, but nodded affirmatively. The two policemen left, though Rafferty's junior remained outside the glass door, looking in.

The young suspect had perhaps been crying. And there were now no signs of the wild behavior evident on the videotape. Catatonia had replaced hysteria. He looked weak and vulnerable as he slumped down on one of the two chairs in the room, his legs spread wide and his arms dangling limply between them.

"Granddad told me you'd come," he said by way of greeting.

"Hello, Alan. I'm very sorry to see you under these circumstances."

"It's the breaks. I got burned."

"Yes, Alan, but what about your father? What about killing your father?"

The boy looked at Frost with alarm. "What are you talking about?" he asked."

"Alan, I just saw a videotape of you confessing that you pushed your father out the window."

"Videotape?"

"Yes, Alan. A videotape of you the police made not three hours ago."

"I don't remember."

"You don't remember—don't remember telling the Assistant District Attorney that you got mad at your father and murdered him?"

"No."

Frost was nonplussed. Was Alan playing some weird game, or did he genuinely not remember?

"You're absolutely sure of that—there was no videotape?"

"Yes."

"But Alan, I just *saw* it!"

"I don't know what you're talking about."

"Alan, listen to me carefully. They're going to take you downtown and book you on the narcotics charge. Then hold you over the weekend, probably back here. Monday morning you'll be arraigned in court. I'll have a lawyer there to represent you. Do you understand?"

"Yeah. I can't get out until Monday?"

"That's right," Frost said, tactfully refraining from adding "if then."

"Meanwhile," Frost went on, "I don't want you to say *anything* to *anyone* about the drug business—or your father. Do I make myself clear?"

"Yeah. Big mess, isn't it?"

"Yes, indeed. But we'll do everything we can for you. Shall I call your mother?"

"Don't bother. I don't talk to her if I can help it."

"Take care, Alan," Frost said, clumsily shaking hands. The policeman outside, observing the scene, came in without knocking and took the boy away.

"I now know what they mean about drug users' 'mood

swings,'" Frost said to Bautista when the detective re-appeared. "Do you know he claims not to remember making the videotape?"

"Crack does strange things, Reuben," Bautista said. "Unfortunately I can believe it."

"What do we do?"

"We get a blood sample and a skin sample from the kid ASAP," Bautista said. "But I need your permission to do that. Or a court order. Take your pick."

Frost suddenly realized that Bautista, his friend and colleague, was at least momentarily an adversary. Though his knowledge of searches and seizures dated back to law school, Frost was sure that the boy's admissions were sufficient grounds for getting a court order to compel the tests Bautista was asking for. Was it worth the effort to resist, or should he give permission as Alan's lawyer?

Uncertain of what to do, Frost decided to request Bautista to get a court order. When in doubt, delay, delay.

"Okay, no problem," Bautista said.

"You said they won't book Alan on a homicide charge," Frost said. "Can I count on that?"

"Until we get the test results, that's right. We don't need headlines about arresting the wrong guy for murder."

"I shouldn't be asking you—you're the opposition. But is there anything more I can do for Alan tonight?"

"No."

"And you won't be trying to question him anymore?"

"If you say so."

"I do say so."

"Then I give you my word."

"Thanks, Luis."

"Why don't you wait downstairs? I'll double-check everything with Munson and meet you in a few minutes."

Back downstairs, Frost asked the desk officer if he could wait in the large room across the way and was told, in effect, that he could wait anywhere he liked. He sat down on one of a group of four folding chairs, obviously pulled together for an earlier conference. Of policemen? Relatives? An accused and his lawyers? He could only guess.

As he waited, he observed two policemen standing beside

a group of six women he took to be prostitutes. The policemen were writing down the answers to questions on vital
statistics, and the women all gave the appearance of having
been through the routine before. They performed their parts
as if the play had run too long, a fact obvious to Frost, even
though he was seeing the drama for the first time.

While he waited, an unsettling, steady procession of
arrested men, flanked by policemen, passed from the front
door to the ominous metal doors in the back. A crime wave,
he thought to himself. Or was business always better on
Saturday night?

Bautista reappeared, as promised.

"Everything's fine, Reuben. The kid will be booked on
the narcotics charge and I will spend the night getting a
court order for the tests."

"I'm sorry, Luis."

"Reuben, look, you got your job, I've got mine. Forget it!"

The two men walked toward the outside door. "Under
the circumstances I guess I won't give my adversary a ride
home, but I'll help you get a cab. Unless you want to pick
up one of the beauties over there," Bautista said, indicating
the prostitutes across the room.

"No ladies of the evening for me," Frost replied, smiling.

"Ladies?" Bautista said. "I hate to tell you, Reuben, but
they're transvestites."

"Good God." Frost was genuinely shocked, though he
guessed he'd heard or read about transvestite whores. But
his own naiveté, his uncertainty in representing his godson's
offspring and his being at cross purposes with Bautista suddenly made him very depressed.

"Are you all right?" Bautista asked.

"Fine. I just need to get home to bed."

"As I say, I'll help you find a taxi."

"No, no, I can manage fine."

"Never mind, I'm coming with you. I don't want you to
get mugged. This is a bad neighborhood."

"Mugged in front of the police station?"

"That's what I said, Reuben, it's a bad neighborhood."

GIARDI'S

18

AS USUAL ON SUNDAY MORNING, FROST IMMERSED HIMSELF in the *Times*. An analysis of the New York Democratic primary, ten days hence, caught his eye. The reporter stated flatly that supporters of Wheeler Edmunds were likely to capture a majority of the state's delegates to the party's Presidential convention.

"Contrary to predictions," the *Times* reporter wrote, "the field of candidates for the Democratic nomination has not narrowed appreciably. That may change next week, when the results from the Empire State are in, since there is every indication that the voters will prefer Wheeler Edmunds, the senior Senator from Michigan, and delegates committed to him will sweep the primary races.

"Of all the candidates, Edmunds has been the only one to stake out a consistently liberal position, picking up on themes that Robert Kennedy, as a New York Senator and Presidential candidate, espoused before his assassination a generation ago: an unambiguous stand on racial justice, including strong measures to promote school desegregation; a pledge to enhance racial and sexual equality by affirmative action techniques more sweeping than any other candidate—past or present—has proposed; an announced determination to view increased national defense expenditures with a highly skeptical eye.

141

"These are not positions popular everywhere in the country," the *Times* reporter continued. "Indeed, they are not necessarily popular with all of New York State's Democrats. But Edmunds has been so articulate in making his case that he has struck a chord with the core of liberals who control the party here. Unless there are surprises to come, Edmunds should sweep the primary and gain important momentum toward his party's nomination."

"It looks like your friend Richard Taylor may get to the White House yet," Frost told his wife over breakfast, quoting her the conclusion of the *Times* correspondent.

"Do you really think this is a year for an out-and-out liberal like Edmunds?" she asked.

"I've given up making predictions, my dear. But you have to concede that Edmunds is articulate and seems to believe very genuinely in what he says. He's a pretty appealing character when you consider that all the others seem to be saying what the public wants to hear. Or what the polls say they want to hear."

Frost's analysis was interrupted by a call from Bautista.

"We haven't closed the book," he said.

"What do you mean?"

"Just as I—we—expected, your client doesn't have the right blood type. He's type AB and it wasn't AB under his father's fingernails. We don't have the skin comparison back yet, but we don't need it. He was making the whole thing up."

"Lunacy."

"That may be. But people on crack do crazy things."

"What happens now?"

"I'm through with your client. I strongly suggest you get a criminal lawyer for him and see if he can work out a deal to get the kid back in Fairhaven Gables."

"Thanks for the advice. I already did that about eight o'clock this morning. The whole mess is out of my hands, thank God. I felt like a dermatologist doing brain surgery last night."

"You did okay, Reuben. Clarence Darrow you ain't, but I see a great future for you as a mouthpiece."

"Thanks."

"I tell you what. Francisca and I are going to enjoy our Sunday—or what's left of it. I was up until five getting that damned court order you insisted on."

"I'm sorry."

"Never mind. I was going to propose that we talk tomorrow."

Frost agreed, though he had now been pulled out of the comfortable verbal cocoon afforded by the Sunday newspaper and began, once again, thinking about David Rowan's murder. What could he usefully do to advance things on a quiet April Sunday in Manhattan? He asked Cynthia if he was correct that the meal they were eating was both breakfast and lunch.

"You know very well it is," she answered. "Why?"

"I think tonight we should have a good, solid, old-fashioned Italian dinner. And I know just the place."

"Giardi's, I suppose," she said.

"Precisely. Do you think we should wear steel vests?"

"A bottle of Pepto-Bismol in my purse would probably be more to the point."

Making a reservation that afternoon, Frost was surprised, when looking up the restaurant's telephone number, to find that the place was only blocks away on Third Avenue. It must be one of those dim, nondescript restaurants I've passed a hundred times, he thought.

Continuing his research after making his reservation, he could find no description or rating of Giardi's in any of his collection of city restaurant guides. The only knowledge he could gather was from a large display advertisement in the Yellow Pages, which proclaimed that Giardi's had served "traditional Italian cuisine to a discriminating clientele since 1958" and that it featured "fine wines and liqueurs." He did not find the self-promotion promising, but deduced that the place must have been started by Tom Giardi's father.

Cynthia and Reuben presented themselves to a beefy maitre d' at the restaurant promptly at eight. His greeting, while not unfriendly, was delivered in a rough, raspy voice. Despite several vacant tables, the Frosts were told to "have a drink at the bar and I'll have a nice table ready for you in a few minutes."

Aside from being imprisoned in a barber's chair while having his hair cut, there was nothing Reuben hated more than waiting for a table in a restaurant, most especially after having made a reservation. He particularly resented the "drink at the bar" con game. He and his wife drank quite enough, thank you, when they went out to eat; there was no need to trick him in order to inflate his check by the cost of two cocktails. In the circumstances, however, he did not want to provoke an argument with the rather menacing headwaiter and risk having to storm out of the place to save his honor.

Grumpily he ordered a negroni—"they ought to be able to make that"—while Cynthia had a gin and tonic.

"Do you suppose that's him?" he said in a low voice to his wife.

"I doubt it. I'm sure he's too grand to act as the head-waiter."

"Well, cheers, and keep your eyes open," he said, touching his wife's raised glass with his own.

The circular bar occupied the front part of the restaurant. As they drank, the couple swiveled on their stools to survey the spacious dining room behind them.

"Don't I recall correctly that Renaissance art flowered in Italy?" Reuben asked his wife, nodding toward the works on the plush-velvet walls, amateurish oils of a grotesque, white-faced *arlecchino* and several village scenes featuring donkeys, children and garishly bright garlands of flowers.

"It's appalling," Cynthia whispered. "But you'd better be quiet."

The maitre d' came over and, once their drinks were paid for and a tip left for the bartender, showed them to one of the tables that had been empty when they came in.

"Would you like another cocktail?" he asked hopefully.

"No thank you," Reuben answered, firmly but politely. "Let's just have the menu and the wine list."

Outsize menus, printed in italic lettering, were presented in stony silence, along with an unwieldy wine list bound in imitation leather.

"This isn't *nuova cucina*," Reuben muttered, as he scanned the menu. The fare was old-style Italian, bereft of the currently fashionable yuppie pastas with eccentric sauces. "Everything seems to be made with eggplant," he added, referring to the frequent references to *melanzane*.

"Sicilian, I believe," Cynthia replied.

"Have you decided on a wine?" the maitre d' demanded, returning to their table.

Reuben normally would have told the headwaiter to come back, but he decided to be pacific and hurriedly opened the wine list. Sure that Cynthia was right—the food was Sicilian, or at least Sicilian-American—he ordered a bottle of Corvo.

"What are your specials tonight?" Frost asked when the maitre d' returned with the green-colored bottle of Sicilian white wine.

"No specials. It's all on the menu."

"Thank you."

"Do you know what you want?"

Cynthia ordered the sardines in white wine and the chicken with eggplant; Reuben asked for *caponata* and the pork described as *scaloppe di maiale al Marsala*.

"The entrées come with spaghetti. You want that?"

Both turned him down.

"French fries?"

Again negative.

Their ordering—and their vetoing—completed, Reuben and Cynthia looked around. Here and there were couples who were probably Upper East Side New Yorkers out for Sunday supper. But they were not in the majority. Most of the customers were in groups of four, six or eight and bore the unmistakable signs of the outer boroughs: tacky composition suits on the backs of the stocky men; teased arrangements of dyed hair offsetting the jewelry and heavy makeup of the women.

"I hate to be snotty . . ." Reuben said.

". . . I know what you're going to say, Reuben. And you're right," his wife interrupted.

"The bridge and tunnel crowd, straight in from Queens, Brooklyn and New Jersey. Except, my God, look over there." Frost nodded to a table across the room.

"That's an odd one, isn't it?" Cynthia said, startled, as was her husband, to see Stanley and Donna Knowles.

"You suppose they're regulars here?" Reuben asked.

"Or . . ."

". . . that they're friends of Tom Giardi, too?"

They both pondered the meaning of a link between the two publishers and Giardi.

"I'm sure it's just a Sunday night hangout for them," Reuben said. "Don't they live near here?"

"I think so."

"Well, eat your *sardine* and let's not think about it," Reuben told his wife as they turned to the bounteous appetizers that had been put in front of them.

As they ate, the waiters gathered in a parade and brought a lighted birthday cake to a youngish woman sitting with what the Frosts guessed to be her husband and three other couples. The waiters joined in singing "Happy Birthday" and those in the room applauded. A bottle of spumante and crystal flutes were produced for the group, adding to an already large collection of empty glasses and wine bottles on the table.

Boisterous toasts were proposed by the men—beefy, as so many of the customers were—to the accompaniment of giggles by the overdressed women. Then a tall, dark man with abundant black hair came to the table and shook hands with each of the men. There was more rowdy laughter and shouting back and forth; the man and the celebrants were clearly on familiar terms. He lingered for a few moments, resplendent in his well-cut brown suit, and then returned to a round table in the corner occupied by five other men, all eating heartily.

"I'll bet that's Giardi," Frost said. They both tried to get a better look at the proprietor, but their view was cut off by his table companions.

As they continued to try to get a view of the man, their waiter brought their entrées, the plates groaning with large portions of chicken and pork.

"You know, I'm very relieved about Alan," Reuben said as they dutifully attacked their overflowing plates. "I mean, about the murder part. The drug business is very sad, but Luis seems to think there's a chance he can get off with strict supervision at Fairhaven."

"I don't even like to think about it."

"It's rather pathetic, you know. The boy felt he couldn't call his mother last night, even though by now she's an experienced criminal lawyer. I know you've expressed regrets—and so have I—about not having children. But when you see the messes kids today can get into, we're probably very lucky." As he talked, Frost toyed with his entrée, like a child forced to eat broccoli. His meal was not very good, the Marsala doing nothing to resuscitate the dry, overcooked pieces of pork over which it had been poured.

Still surreptitiously watching the owner's table, they saw Giardi leave his gregarious companions to go over to talk to the Knowleses. He stood over their table and engaged them in animated conversation. Then he grabbed a chair from a nearby table and sat down. The talk was intense, with much gesticulating by Giardi. Stanley Knowles signed a credit-card slip as they talked, after which he and Donna got up and took their leave amid profuse embraces and a kiss for Donna.

"I think they're coming over here," Frost said. Stanley Knowles had spotted the Frosts as he stood up and now, with his wife following behind, crossed the room.

"Paisano!" he said, pumping Reuben's hand. "I had no idea you loved good Italian cooking. Except I should have known, Reuben, that you love *everything!*"

"Do you come here often, Stanley? This is our first time."

"I can't believe it. I know something the Frosts don't— this place is wonderful."

Knowles's boosterism would have done a public relations flack proud.

"We love the food," Donna Knowles chimed in. "We never eat at home, you know. So we're here a lot."

Both of the Knowleses, despite their hearty enthusiasm, struck Reuben as being nervous. Their bonhomie seemed just a trifle off.

"Stanley, was that the *padrone* you were talking to?" Frost asked.

"Tommy? Oh, yes. Good guy. Third generation in the restaurant business. His grandfather was a bootlegger during Prohibition. So was his father. They started serving food to the customers in their speakeasy and've been doing it ever since. Moved up here from Little Italy sometime in the fifties."

"You haven't eaten very much, Mr. Frost," Donna observed, looking at Reuben's picked-over plate.

"Moderation in all things, I'm afraid," Frost replied. "We had a big lunch." He was not about to engage Donna Knowles in a debate over whether the *scaloppe di maiale al Marsala* was execrable or not.

The busy waiters had been bumping into the Knowleses as they stood in front of the Frosts' table. Since there was no place for Donna and Stanley to sit, and no reason for them to, they left, heartily endorsing Giardi's, and expressing the hope they would see the Frosts again very, very soon.

Reuben and Cynthia would have followed their usual custom of passing up dessert, except that they wanted to observe the restaurant—and its owner—further. So Reuben ordered a *tartufo* and Cynthia a *zabaglione* with strawberries.

When their desserts arrived, Reuben inspected his *tartufo* —a frozen block of vanilla and chocolate ice cream, with a raspberry sauce—and told his wife that it "proved his theory."

"You mean your theory that all *tartufi* are made by the Mafia?"

"Yes. Look at this. It's exactly the same as the *tartufi* I've seen people eat in Italian restaurants all over Manhattan. Exactly the same! Hard, frozen ice cream with the same sauce. There has to be a *Mafioso* grandmother who gets this stuff into every restaurant. You'd probably get your kneecaps broken if you tried to make your own."

"Whatever it's like, it has to be better than this," Cynthia declared. "My *zabaglione* was made about three days ago and has been sitting next to the onions in the refrigerator ever since. Reuben, it's truly awful."

Her husband commiserated with her, but didn't help matters by recalling the truly ethereal, fresh *zabaglione* they had

shared in a tiny out-of-the way restaurant in Taormina on a
Sicilian tour two years before.

Seeing that his reminiscing was doing little for his wife's
good humor, he turned her attention to Stanley and Donna
Knowles. "You know, I'm mystified. That meal we had at
the Reuff Dinner wasn't great, but Donna Knowles really
complained about it. I distinctly remember her griping about
the size of the portions. She said she was very uncomfortable eating a lot. And then she and Stanley come to a
pig-palace like this."

"I'm sure you noticed they both had the side orders of
spaghetti and french fries we passed up," Cynthia said.

"No. But you're always more observant than I am."

While they were talking, Reuben saw Tommy Giardi
get up from his table and go to the headwaiter's station.
He looked down the reservation list, consulted with the
maitre d' and turned to look directly at the Frosts. Almost
at once he was in front of them, casting a shadow over
their table.

"Mr. Frost?"

"Yes?"

"Everything okay?"

"Oh, yes, fine," Reuben said, grateful that the proprietor
had not seen the plate of barely touched food that their
waiter had removed.

"Good. We aim to keep our customers happy. By the
way, aren't you a friend of Grace Mann's?" Giardi looked
straight at Reuben as he asked the question.

"Yes, I am."

"You were also a friend of David Rowan, right?"

"That's also true."

"I hear you're playing detective. Going to solve the big
mystery the police—and the media—can't get their hands
around."

"Um . . . I don't know what to say. David was my
godson and his father, Harrison, is an old friend from years
back. I've tried to do what I can, but *detective* is a pretty
strong word."

"I don't know. Pretty good word, I'd've thought. Better
than gumshoe, or snoop or busybody." If Giardi was making

a joke, he did not show it. "But I'm delighted you're here at my restaurant."

"We eat out a lot and are always looking for new spots," Reuben said weakly.

"Well, we've been here since they took the Third Avenue El down, so it's taken you a long time to discover us. But better late than never. Can I offer you an after-dinner drink?"

"Oh, no, we were just leaving."

"I insist. It's wonderful to be discovered by someone after all these years. What'll it be?"

Reuben turned to Cynthia, but got a totally impassive response.

"Very well, I'll have a sambuca," Reuben said. Cynthia nodded her head and said she would have one as well.

"*Con mosche?*" Giardi asked.

"*Senz' altro,*" Frost answered. His amateur Italian brought a slight smile to Giardi's face—his first—and he commanded a waiter to bring the drinks complete with coffee-bean "flies"—mosche. He continued to loom over their table until the waiter had returned with the drinks.

"To your continued good health," he said as the Frosts dutifully began sipping them.

"Thank you very much," Reuben said.

Giardi showed no signs of leaving, until the maitre d' came and whispered in his ear.

"Where?" Giardi asked. The headwaiter gestured toward a table occupied by an older, obviously Manhattan couple, next to Giardi's own. The owner turned, without another word to the Frosts, and went to confront the couple. Reuben and Cynthia watched closely.

"What's your problem?" Giardi demanded.

The Frosts overheard the woman complain, in an indignant voice, about the heavy cigar smoke emanating from Giardi's table.

"They're my friends," Giardi said in a tough, cold voice. "And I own this place. So if they want to smoke cigars they can."

The man at the complaining table said nothing; the Frosts imagined him to be frozen with fear. His wife, on the other hand, was undaunted and registered her complaint again, with even more indignation.

"I don't think you like it here," Giardi said. He beckoned to the headwaiter and asked him to bring the couple's check, though they had scarcely begun their main course. Giardi slapped it down on the table and asked the dissidents to leave, as one of the busboys, at Giardi's beckoning, began to remove their dinner dishes.

The man at the table, by now white and shaking with either fear or anger, bowed to the inevitable, paid the check and fled with his wife as fast as decency would allow. Giardi stayed with them until they were out the front door. He then returned to his table and regaled his vociferous cigar-smoking companions with the tale. Their laughter was loud and ugly.

"Nice fellows," Frost said. "Let's us get out of here before we're invited to leave, too." He got the check from the maitre d' and paid with his American Express card. Signing the American Express voucher, he carefully removed and tore up the carbons between the copies.

"I normally regard people who do this as paranoid old ladies," Reuben explained to his wife. "Scared stiff somebody will use the carbons to make a false chit. But I'm on their side tonight."

As the Frosts walked toward the front door, Giardi loomed up behind them.

"Thank you very much for coming, Mr. Frost," he said, ignoring Cynthia. "Happy gumshoeing."

"Good night, Mr. Giardi," Reuben said, very formally and without shaking hands.

When they got home, Reuben and Cynthia were still upset. They did not talk about Giardi right away; they were more interested in the surprise appearance of the Knowleses at the restaurant.

"Maybe it really is a neighborhood spot for them," Reuben said. "Maybe Donna modifies her birdlike eating habits when confronted with that 'traditional and discriminating' Giardi food. But maybe there's more to it than that."

"Like what?"

"Well, we know Stanley has money troubles. And Luis Bautista says Giardi handles a lot of gangster money. Maybe he's a silent partner in the Hammersmith Press."

"Publishing's not a very likely investment for gangsters, do you think?"

"A lot of funny people have put money into publishing. Besides, as I understand it, organized crime types are willing to invest in almost anything as long as it's legitimate and gives them a chance to launder their money.

"Or there's the insurance policy angle," Reuben went on. "Maybe Giardi supplied a hit man so that Stanley could collect on David's insurance."

"It seems absurd," Cynthia said.

"The whole mess is absurd, starting with pushing a grown man out a window," Reuben replied testily.

"I think it's time we sorted our slips of paper once more," Cynthia said. She went to the library and returned with a new supply of legal foolscap which she tore into quarters, as she had four nights earlier, and wrote names on the torn slips.

"You remember the combinations we put together then," she said, laying out the pieces on the coffee table.

"Now, let's assume we can eliminate Alan—and his mother. We still have some new combinations. We have Peter Jewett to add. Then, after what we saw tonight, we can link up Stanley Knowles and Tom Giardi."

"Fair enough. But just for fun, lay out slips for those who might have done it all by themselves."

"Fine. Let me get more paper."

With new supplies in hand, Cynthia's display eventually looked like this:

MARIETTA AINSLEE	RALSTON FORTES
GRACE MANN	TOM GIARDI*
STANLEY KNOWLES	RALSTON FORTES
HORACE JENKINS	RALSTON FORTES
STANLEY KNOWLES	TOM GIARDI*
RALSTON FORTES	PETER JEWETT

Reuben surveyed the display. "What are the stars for?" he asked, indicating the asterisks after Giardi's name.

"I thought we'd agreed that Giardi, if he's the guilty party, might have had one of his gangster friends do the job. One or two of those cigar smokers we saw tonight perhaps."

"That's right."

"It's an awfully big chart, Reuben," Cynthia said. "It's discouraging."

"Yes, it covers the whole coffee table. But I'll leave you with just one question before we go to bed."

"What's that?"

"Is it big enough?"

MISSING PARTS

19

CYNTHIA FROST, ALWAYS ALERT AND ENTHUSIASTIC IN THE morning, seemed even more so on the Monday morning after the night at Giardi's.

"You're running around here like a dervish," her slow-rising husband complained.

"I've got a lot to do today," she said.

"A new Pirandello festival?"

"No, not a new Pirandello festival. Just a lot of boring things I've been neglecting. Good-bye."

For all intents and purposes the new week began for Reuben two hours later, when Lucy Wyecliffe called.

"I have some information for you, Mr. Frost," she said. "We've been working very hard—overtime all weekend—since I talked to you, trying to put the Ainslee papers back into some sort of order and trying to find if anything's missing. We finished up an hour ago."

Frost was bursting to find out more details, but first had to humor Miss Wyecliffe as she gave her speech once again about the folly of not copying the Ainslee papers before they had been turned over to David Rowan.

"All the boxes relating to Mr. Justice Ainslee's service in the Senate are accounted for," she said, finally. "However, there are three case files missing. Of course, we have no idea what was in those files. Without copies, you know, we just draw a blank."

"I understand, Miss Wyecliffe," Frost said, heading off a second lecture on the merits of photocopying.

"The case files missing are all from the nineteen seventy-two/seventy-three term of the Supreme Court. I have the names if you would like them."

Frost wrote down the case names as Miss Wyecliffe read them to him: *United States v. Rodriguez, Cleveland School District v. Henshaw* and *Carrymore v. United States.*

"Do you have the citations?"

"Not right at my fingertips."

"That's all right, I can get them."

"I hope this is helpful, Mr. Frost."

"I honestly can't say at this point but I hope so, too," Frost said. "By the way, do you know what exactly is in the case files that you do have?"

"Yes. Each file contains a printed copy of the opinion or opinions in the case, the manuscript of Ainslee's opinion, if he wrote one, and proofs of all the drafts of opinions that he wrote or that were circulated to him. Slip opinions, I think they call them. Also any memos or correspondence sent around to the other Justices, and all the memos and correspondence he received from them. Plus any materials his clerks may have prepared."

"I see. That's very helpful, Miss Wyecliffe."

"I'm very happy to oblige, Mr. Frost."

Frost put the sheet of paper on which he had written the three case names in his pocket and set out immediately for his office. Could these missing case files offer up a clue that would lead to the solution of David Rowan's murder? Instinctively, he felt that they could, and he was impatient at a longer than usual delay on the subway.

At Chase & Ward, Frost went directly to the library. He had not used the Supreme Court Reporters in several years and was apprehensive that they might have been replaced by the new electronic research services and been destroyed. If so, he would be in trouble, as he was not about to learn how to use the LEXIS system.

His worries turned out to be ill-founded and, with a minimum of searching, he found the volumes for the Court's

1972–73 term. He took the books to a desk in the crowded library—the firm really did have to move to new quarters, he told himself—and began reading at once. He was oblivious to the stares of the young lawyers around him. Library research was most often done by the very youngest associates, many of whom did not recognize the former Executive Partner of Chase & Ward by sight.

Frost also noticed the profusion of "no smoking" signs in the library, a drastic change from his own early days when nervous cigarette smoking, or a cigar after dinner before an all-night siege with the books, had been almost essential to legal research.

United States v. Rodriguez turned out to be a criminal search-and-seizure case, raising the question whether a search by Federal immigration officers in El Paso, Texas, violated the Constitution's Fourth Amendment prohibition against unlawful searches and seizures.

The hapless Rodriguez's story, even in the dry prose of the opinions, read like an afternoon soap opera. Returning with two friends from an evening's drinking in an El Paso bar, he had been stopped by the border patrol, authorized by an Act of Congress to stop and search automobiles within seventy-five miles of the Mexican border in a quest to find illegal immigrants. Rodriguez and his party were, in fact, legal residents of El Paso, possessed of the coveted green cards that made them legitimate, if not all-American native, inhabitants of the border city.

But in the course of things, the curious border patrolmen found an enormous stash of marijuana in the trunk of Rodriguez's car. So he was arrested on, and later convicted of, a Federal charge of possessing drugs.

Rodriguez's legal aid lawyers had made a persuasive case that the search of the man's battered old Buick had been illegal: he had not consented to the search; the immigration agents had no search warrant; and there had not been any "probable cause" to suspect that the trunk of Rodriguez's car was stuffed with pot. The border patrol's only justification was that they had *carte blanche*, within the seventy-five-mile zone delineated by the Congress, to make warrantless searches.

A five-to-four majority of the Court upheld the lower court's dismissal of the charges against Rodriguez. He was undoubtedly guilty, but Justice Ainslee, writing for the majority, threw out his conviction. The failure of the border patrolmen—who weren't commissioned to pursue drug offenses—to obtain a search warrant fatally infected the proceedings in the trial court. Absent "probable cause" for a search, or a search warrant issued by a judge, a man's home was his castle, and so was his Buick.

No clues there, thought Reuben, who then located *Cleveland School District v. Henshaw*. This turned out to be one of a series of thorny cases—Frost remembered reading about it at the time—implementing *Brown v. Board of Education*, the epic 1954 case in which the Supreme Court had outlawed racial segregation in America's schools. The opinions in the case—a majority opinion, two concurrences and two dissents—took up one hundred pages in the Reporter, and wrestled with the question of whether segregation in Cleveland's schools had been *de jure*, that is, as a result of unconstitutional actions by the city's board of education and zoning authorities, or *de facto*, as a result merely of residential living patterns or other neutral factors not manipulated by the city. Frost grew impatient as he read the Justices' attempts to characterize the patent racial segregation in the Cleveland schools. Did it matter to the black child, he thought, whether the segregation to which he was subject was, in lawyer-talk, *de jure* or *de facto*? If one agreed that segregation was harmful, shouldn't the courts try to weed it out without regard to such legal niceties?

It was clear, reading the lengthy opinions, that a majority of the Supreme Court had not reached Frost's practical conclusion. There had been blatant segregation, fully supported by the local government, in certain Cleveland districts, with both black and white children moved about to create virtually all-black and all-white schools. But in other local areas within Cleveland, it appeared that segregation had arisen unassisted by any improper action of the local authorities.

It was a tricky case, though Frost was impatient with the

painful exposition of the tricks and the intellectual wrestling with the *de jure-de facto* distinction. But in the end, a bare majority of the Court found that a desegregation plan for the entire city, including the "innocent" areas where segregation had spawned without governmental assistance ("it just growed like Topsy," Reuben thought bitterly), was not justified—assuming that the "innocent" areas, on remand of the case back to the District Court, could defend their behavior under guidelines set down in the opinion. Great work for lawyers, Reuben muttered to himself, envisioning the prolonged litigation that surely followed the remand.

Mr. Justice Ainslee did not write in *Cleveland*, but joined in one of the dissents that would have upheld the city-wide desegregation plan.

Again no clues, Frost thought, with a sense of despair. What could David Rowan's death possibly have to do with a Buick full of dope in Texas or black school children in Ohio? Discouraged, he turned to *Carrymore v. United States*. The plaintiff, one Marjorie Carrymore, a woman sergeant in the United States Army, had sued the Federal Government alleging discrimination because of the different criteria applied to award dependency allowances to male and female military personnel. Male personnel, she alleged, automatically received such allowances when they married. But women in the military could only claim them if their husbands were actually dependent on their wives for support.

Again, the disputatious Court divided five-to-four, finding in favor of Sergeant Carrymore under the particular facts of her case and the Army regulations she was challenging. But Reuben found fascinating and compelling a concurring opinion by Ainslee saying that it was time for the Court to stop dealing with sex discrimination on a piecemeal basis, and to recognize that such discrimination was as reprehensible to the American Constitution as racial bias. Frost was struck by the man's eloquence—and his anticipation of the feminist arguments that has come to be accepted years after the late Justice had written.

But what could the case mean in the context of the death of Ainslee's biographer? He was discouraged; the Court opinions told him that Ainslee was indeed a thoughtful and articulate liberal, but they simply did not yield up any useful leads.

Dutifully Frost returned the Reporters to their shelves and went to his office, finding there only an assortment of junk mail, gratis copies of the latest legal gossip papers—a proliferating new phenomenon he despised—and what seemed like an unending series of department store bills.

On an impulse, he called Frank Norton, who came at once to his office.

"Frank, you know all about the Supreme Court. I need your help," Frost said as his young former partner sat down on the sofa in his office. "Close the door," he added as a precaution, though his library searches had not produced any secrets for him to tell.

"I learned this morning that there were three files of Garrett Ainslee's papers that were missing when they got back down to East Jesus, or West Jesus or wherever that college is that keeps them. All dealing with Supreme Court cases, all from the nineteen seventy-two term. I've just spent two hours reading them in that storeroom your firm calls a library, and they don't mean a thing to me."

Frost summarized the three cases and Norton agreed that he, too, could not make any pattern out of them.

"I'm convinced those files are important, Frank. Somebody stole them at the same time that David was killed—I'm sure of it. But what on earth does a Chicano dope peddler, the Cleveland school board, and a disgruntled lady sergeant have to do with David—or Ainslee?"

"I can't help you, Reuben. I draw a blank. Except, didn't you say that the cases were all decided during the same term?"

"Yes. So what?"

"Could that point to one of Ainslee's clerks? They change every year, you know. Maybe those files had something in them damaging to one of his clerks."

"That hadn't occurred to me. Now that you mention it, the mother hen who looks after the papers told me this morning that the case files usually do include memos by the clerks."

"That's all I can think of, Reuben. Who were Ainslee's clerks in nineteen seventy-two?"

"I don't know. How do you find out?"

"That's easy. Call the Office of the Clerk of the Supreme Court. You want me to do that, give him a call?"

"Frank, you're a sweetheart. Would you?"

"No problem. I'll do it right now."

Norton left, and Frost drummed his fingers on his desk as he waited for a response. Norton had had a good idea. But would it produce anything? Given the way things had been going, probably not.

Norton was back in minutes.

"I don't know if this helps, Reuben, but Garrett Ainslee had three clerks in nineteen seventy-two: a woman named Sarah Blake, who's now in the Solicitor General's office; a man named Sheldon Gibbs, who's in private practice in Denver; and Wheeler Edmunds, senior Senator from the great State of Michigan and candidate for the Presidency of the United States."

"Oh, Lord," said Frost, his mind already reeling from the implications of the explosive byte of information his young colleague had given him.

FUNDRAISER

20

Frost left the Chase & Ward offices and walked
with determination to the Brooklyn Bridge stop on the
Lexington Avenue subway. Almost a half century ago, he
had learned that taking an express from Bowling Green,
near his firm's offices, put him on a crowded train, and
one he would have to leave at Forty-second Street in any
event to get the local to his neighborhood. The walk was
a strenuous one, but there was a great deal to be said for
getting on the local at Brooklyn Bridge. The train began
there, and one could always get a seat.

Today, the walk was therapeutic. He ignored the shills,
passing out leaflets for discount video equipment and designer eyeglasses, and the aggressive panhandlers. He was
totally preoccupied with the horrid thought that a leading
candidate for the Presidency of the country was somehow,
in ways not understood, linked to David Rowan's murder.

When he got home, he went immediately to the library,
where Cynthia collected the couple's innumerable invita-
tions to Manhattan social events, great and small. He was
certain that he and Cynthia had been invited to a high-priced
fundraising party for Wheeler Edmunds. And, sure enough,
he found a card created by a well-known, voguish graphics
designer (linking Wheeler Edmund's initials, "W.E.," to the

grand statement that "W.E. ARE GOING TO CHANGE AMERICA").

The invitation was for the next night, Tuesday, at six o'clock. It was from Lowell Oatsman, a preeminent Wall Street investment banker whose fortune rested on extraordinary fees for putting corporate mergers and leveraged buyouts (as they called them downtown) in place, but whose quasi-intellectual reputation rested on *in terrorem* articles in *The New Republic* and other journals about the misallocation of the nation's capital resources (such as the unseemly rush of the major banks to use their loan funds to bankroll Oatsman-sponsored takeovers) and his one-stop-short-of-obsequious support of liberal Democratic candidates for higher office.

Oatsman had egregious ambition. His Wall Street colleagues, most of them far more conservative than he, viewed his political activities benignly, although there was little question that if the Democrats won that year—especially if Edmunds were the winning candidate—Oatsman would be the Secretary of the Treasury or, very possibly, the nation's central banker as Chairman of the Federal Reserve Board. (Or, at the barest minimum, a vocal occupant of the powerless and ineffectual job of Secretary of Commerce.)

By the time Cynthia Frost got home, her husband was stewing about the Oatsman invitation. The ante was $1,000 a person, the maximum contribution an individual could make to a candidate under Federal law.

"I think we'd better go to this, Cynthia," Reuben declared. He then explained why, on the basis of his discovery earlier in the day about Edmunds's uncomfortable link to Ainslee, and hence to David Rowan.

"You were hesitant the other night," she said, "but I didn't throw the invitation away because you didn't absolutely rule it out. You did say you admired Edmunds."

"Yes, yes, I do. He's slightly too left wing for me, but at least he's articulate. And he keeps both his mouth and his pants zipped up, which one comes to admire in politics more and more."

"Then let's go. The Oatsman apartment's such a laugh, anyway."

"It's a lot of money. Two thousand dollars. I suppose that's a cheap price to pay if somehow, somehow, it helps unravel the mystery of David's killing. But can we still get in? It's awfully late to respond."

"Reuben, dear, take it from an old foundation money-grubber—your Morgan Guaranty check for two thousand dollars will be welcome. And if you take a shoe and sock off, Wheeler Edmunds will lick your foot."

"Call them up, Cynthia. We'll be there."

Frost had been to the Oatsman duplex twice before, each time at large dinners served at the two long tables (ever so much resembling, despite all the trappings, the bleak refectory boards in the Princeton dining halls of Reuben's youth) arranged side by side in the banker's mirrored dining room.

On both of those occasions, Frost had been solemnly ushered by Lowell Oatsman into an enormous room adjoining the dining room, which contained a single gray-colored leather chair in the center. The gray of the chair matched flannel-covered gray walls, and a gray pile rug. On each of three walls—the fourth was taken up by a window with a panoramic view of Central Park—was a large Julian Schnabel painting.

"The holy-of-holies," Reuben had muttered to Cynthia the first time he saw it. And, indeed, Oatsman had solemnly explained that the single chair was to allow a solitary visitor to remain quiet to meditate—Oatsman's word—amid the oversize Schnabels.

When the Frosts arrived at the Oatsman party for Edmunds, the double doors to the "meditation room" were closed; politics was politics and art was art. The living room, vast as it was, was packed to overflowing. Thin, agile-hipped waiters from one of the trendy catering services made their way through the crowd, offering drinks. Frost surveyed the claustrophobic scene with amusement, despite his dark thoughts about Edmunds and Rowan.

The crowd was "mixed," he concluded: real estate developers—none quite as grand as Elliott Reuff—and Wall Street investment bankers, many of whom Frost had at

least met; Arthur Mattison, the all-purpose critic of the
New York Press (my God, has he gone from theater and
ballet to politics? Frost thought); a *News* gossip columnist
and assorted editors from the weekly magazines, and a
deceptively innocent looking young subversive from the
naughty new monthly, *Spy*; Anita Stebbins, the toast of
Broadway for three successive seasons (although her current vehicle had just closed); Cindy Walsh, a sexy redhead
who had had a short, but prominent, movie career that
Ms. Stebbins much envied; Harvey Seaver, who had won
a Pulitzer Prize for playwriting in 1964 and done little but
serve on various peace committees since. And then the politicians—a former Kennedy cabinet officer; an ex-Mayor,
forever tainted as a spendthrift and one of the causes of
the city's fiscal crisis in the mid-1970s; a former Lieutenant
Governor of New York, unremembered after service in one
of the country's truly useless positions; a woman who had
had a stormy career as the head of the city's Civil Rights
Commission (even threatening the all-male hegemony of
Frost's beloved Gotham Club); and a brown-suited gent
or two whom Frost knew, from past meetings, to be city
judges, probably hoping that Edmunds could offer them
deliverance through appointments to the more prestigious
Federal bench.

There was an air of excitement about the party; this was
no political duty dance, for which chits had been called in
to produce a crowd. The *Times's* Sunday writer had been
correct—the signs suggested that Edmunds was about to
score an important primary victory. And the guests might
just be brushing shoulders—even conversing with—the next
President of the United States.

The host, whom Cynthia had once unkindly observed
resembled a hyperactive chipmunk, moved with physical
difficulty but psychological ease through the diverse crowd
assembled in his living room. Reuben was making pleas-
antries with Oatsman when Cynthia jabbed him discreetly
but decisively in the ribs. Frost turned to her and Oatsman
continued on his rounds.

"What's the matter?" Reuben asked.

"There's someone here you should meet," his wife replied. "Over there." She gestured toward a tall man in a rumpled brown suit leaning against the wall at the side of the room talking with an attractive young girl sporting a large "EDMUNDS" button. Like many tall men, he had a pronounced stoop, now magnified by his efforts to pay attention to the diminutive campaign aide.

"Who is it?"

"Peter Jewett."

"Let's go."

The Frosts inched their way toward the professor. Cynthia interrupted his conversation, greeted him cheerfully and introduced her husband.

The man was seedy, Reuben could not help observing as he shook hands. Dandruff was visible in his thinning hair and on his suit collar. His horn-rimmed glasses were dirty and his not very becoming false teeth had unsightly food particles between them. The young girl drifted off as her three elders began talking.

"This is a long way to come for a party, Peter," Cynthia said.

"I know. But I love parties, I love New York and I love Wheeler Edmunds."

"You're a supporter?" Frost asked.

"In my modest way, yes," Jewett replied. "I've been giving the Senator some advice on foreign policy. I came to town to talk with him about the speech he's giving at the Council on Foreign Relations next week."

"Speechwriting?" Frost asked.

"Of sorts. He's clearly the best man around and I'm glad to be of whatever help I can." Jewett feigned modesty, but his manner and tone indicated that he felt Edmunds was very lucky to have him aboard.

"How do you get here, Peter?" Cynthia asked. "It's quite a trip from Amherst."

"It is if you rely on public transportation. But I like to drive. The trip isn't half-bad."

The crush around the Frosts increased as more guests continued to arrive. Jewett said he was going to try and get a drink so Reuben, noticing that a breeze seemed to be coming in through the open windows, steered Cynthia toward them. In the noise and the circumstances, they did not have a chance to dissect their brief conversation with one of the murder suspects.

Once at the windows, the Frosts encountered two women sitting on the window seat, one puffing on a cigarette as if it might be the last she would ever be allowed.

"I hope you don't mind my smoking," she said, looking up at the new arrivals. "It's very unthoughtful, I know, and a bad example, but I really need this."

"I'm Ginny Edmunds," she said, thrusting out her hand but not getting up. The Frosts now recognized the candidate's wife, prettier and younger-looking than in her pictures.

Reuben admired her independence, making no effort whatsoever to work the crowd as she smoked away. The woman with her was introduced as Paula Storz, her personal assistant. They acknowledged, with satisfied smiles, Reuben's observation that the primary campaign seemed to be going well.

A flurry of activity signaled the entrance of the Senator and his Secret Service escorts. A single photographer from his staff—the press brigade had been barred from this private gathering—began taking flash pictures as Edmunds, with Lowell Oatsman at his side, plunged into the crowd.

Back by the windows, Mrs. Edmunds was soon joined by Richard Taylor, who had come in with the candidate. He recognized the Frosts and shook hands with them both.

"I see I convinced you to support my man," he said to Cynthia, his pink-cheeked and youthful good looks underscoring the heartiness of his greeting. "I'm glad." She smiled noncommittally.

"How did it go, Richard?" Mrs. Edmunds asked. "The boys are just back from a flying swing upstate," she explained to the Frosts.

"Everything was fine till we got to Syracuse," Taylor said. "We made a quick stop at the airport to generate some local press coverage, and the Senator told the crowd how happy he was to be back in Utica."

"Oh, God," Mrs. Edmunds said. "Now we've lost the Utica vote and the deaf-and-dumb vote in two days."

"What do you mean?" Frost asked.

"Wheeler was at a rally in Queens last night," she explained. "As they so often do these days, they had an interpreter to translate his speech into sign language. This one was truly obnoxious—waving his arms all over the place, standing right on top of the podium—so Wheeler got peeved and told him to go away."

"I'm not worried," Ms. Storz observed. "Little gaffes like that are unimportant—and they make the Senator look more human. That's all to the good."

Further conversation ceased as Oatsman introduced Edmunds from a microphone set up at the side of the room, noting that the Senator was in the middle of a full, three-day swing through New York "and is rapidly becoming one of us" and that Ginny Edmunds, now cigaretteless and at her husband's side, was "the First Lady of New York" who would, in a matter of months, be "the First Lady of the United States."

The applause was warm as Edmunds began speaking, lavishing praise and thanks on his audience and then giving a brief recital of the "vital and crucial issues" of the campaign on which, needless to say, he was on the correct side in every instance.

Frost marveled at the Senator's delivery. He was sure the man must have repeated the same words at a thousand fundraising parties, but he made them sound spontaneous and, with a clever hesitation or two, made up just for this occasion. Taylor, standing nearby, once again listened with rapt attention, as if he had never heard the words before, though Frost speculated that he had probably written them. Frost was sure that he could never master the public performance tricks of either man.

More applause followed the Senator's brief speech. He asked for questions, a look of confidence saying there was nothing, at this late stage in the campaign, for which he would not have an answer. He was right, for the usual New York topics—defense spending, AIDS, relations with Israel, abortion and narcotics enforcement—all were raised and dealt with in deft responses. Finished, he started moving into the crowd in front of him.

Frost, going to Taylor's side, enlisted his help. "I've never met the Senator, you know."

"You haven't? Well, we'll take care of that right now." Taylor motioned to a fellow staff member at the Senator's side, who deftly steered the candidate in Frost's direction.

"Senator, I'd like you to meet Reuben Frost," Taylor said once the two men were face to face. "And this is his wife, Cynthia, whom I personally recruited for you."

"That's wonderful, Richard," the candidate said. "I'm glad to meet you both." He was uncertain whether he should linger or move on. Seeing his eyes scanning the horizon, Frost made his move. He had thought about his approach; it was time to be ingenuous and even a bit folksy—and brief.

"I'm pleased to meet you, Senator, since I understand my godson was going to be one of your speechwriters."

The candidate looked puzzled. "Yes? I'm glad to hear that. What was his name?" he asked finally.

"David Rowan, the biographer."

"Rowan? David Rowan?" Edmunds still looked baffled. "Oh, yes, the fellow who got the Reuff Prize, and then was killed. I spoke at the award dinner. You're his godfather?"

"Yes, and I know he was looking forward to working for you."

"It's a tragedy, Mr. Frost, no question about that. But I'm interested. You say he was going to work for me? I'm flattered."

"Yes, I understood he was going to be a speechwriter for you."

"Well, we certainly can use all the help we can get. Always glad for volunteers. Though I've got a pretty good speechwriter right here," he said, pointing to Taylor. "My indispensable right hand." The younger man, who had listened to Frost's questions without showing any emotion, now smiled back at his employer.

"I'm very sorry about your godson, especially since you tell me he was a supporter. A great loss, not only for you but for the country." Edmunds, having delivered a politician's eulogistic cliché, equally suitable for the death of a senior statesman or a washerwoman, quickly grabbed Reuben's and Cynthia's hands, murmuring as he did so how nice it was to meet them both. Then he pushed beyond them, enveloped at once in a new conversation.

"It was nice to see you both again," Taylor said as he left the Frosts and followed in the candidate's wake. Before the Frosts could decide what to do next, the Secret Service agents converged from the corners of the room and formed a cordon around Edmunds, leading him politely, but inexorably, toward the door; it was time to collect a new stack of thousand-dollar checks at the next party.

Reuben was glad that Edmunds was leaving, since it meant he and Cynthia could do the same. Moments after the candidate and his retinue hurried out, the Frosts headed for the door, stopping only long enough for a perfunctory handshake with Lowell Oatsman.

"We missed the holy-of-holies tonight, Lowell," Reuben said.

"The Schnabels, you mean?"

"Yes."

"This was Wheeler's show. I didn't want to detract from that."

"I trust the broken plates are still in place," Frost said, referring to the pieces of crockery embedded in the Schnabel paintings.

"Yes, they're still there. Maybe I can get Julian to add all the broken glasses from that crowd in the living room. What a mob!"

"It's a good cause, Lowell," Frost said. "Edmunds is a richer man than when he came in here, or at least his campaign is."

Once on the street, the Frosts decided to walk home.

"So your friend Jewett is helping to write speeches for Senator Edmunds, heh?" Reuben said.

"That was news to me, but it's an interesting twist, isn't it?"

"To say the least. Here are two bitter, academic rivals of long standing and they end up competing for the favor of the hottest political prince."

"And they meet, and quarrel, and one of them—David—ends up dead."

"I've got to find out what the constables up in Amherst learned. What a ghastly idea, though."

"What do you mean?" Cynthia asked.

"David's last moments. Let's assume Jewett went to have it out with him and then, reverting to his bullying, wife-beating ways, killed him. It's a ghastly, ghastly thought."

"Of course it is, but what exactly do you mean? Watch out, Reuben, wait for the light."

Frost had been walking down Park Avenue with determination and now barely avoided stepping in front of a speeding taxi.

"I mean, how ghastly to be knocked out by Jewett. So that your last vision as a live human is of a constricted face, surrounded by seedy, dandruff-covered hair, and showing bad teeth plugged up with rotting food particles."

"Your imagination is working, my dear."

"I know. But isn't it possible that I just described exactly what happened?"

"Yes, it's more than possible."

The Frosts walked in silence for a block or two as they took in the reality that Reuben's distasteful reconstruction might be accurate.

"What did you think of the First Lady of New York?" Cynthia asked finally, changing the subject.

"I liked her. Any candidate's wife who has any vices at all appeals to me."

"But, Reuben, what about her outfit?"

"I didn't really notice. It certainly wasn't flashy."

"Flashy! It was a housedress."

"The Pat-Nixon-cloth-coat syndrome, perhaps. Besides, she isn't running for W's 'in' and 'out' list."

"I know, but really."

"Look, never mind Mrs. Edmunds. Let's talk about her husband. Do you have any doubt that he'd never heard of the idea of David's writing speeches for him?"

"That's certainly the way he acted."

"I realize he's probably working on two cylinders about now—still trying to figure out the difference between Syracuse and Utica—but he certainly convinced me. The whole idea was brand-new to him."

"I agree. But what follows from that?"

"Nothing that I can think of. Which is the problem. Just another piece of a hopeless puzzle that I'm supposed to put together. I'd say we wasted two thousand dollars."

"Maybe we'll be invited to the White House."

"To be greeted by Ginny Edmunds in her housedress," Reuben replied, very out of sorts.

DEATH ONCE MORE

21

BAUTISTA WAS ON THE TELEPHONE EARLY THE NEXT MORN-
ing with a report from Amherst. Questioned by the local
police, the professor said that on Tuesday, March 29, he
had driven to New York for the Brigham Foundation meetings and driven back, arriving at his off-campus apartment
around seven o'clock. He had been at the apartment all
evening, he said, reading and correcting papers. Asked if
anyone could substantiate his statements, he had become
extremely angry and refused to answer further questions.

"Do they think he was angry because he had no support
for his alibi?" Frost asked.

"They couldn't tell. They're checking around, but so far
haven't found anyone to confirm or deny his story."

Later in the morning, Reuben, on an impulse, called
Frank Norton at Chase & Ward.

"I remember that you told me the other day that Dine
Carroll, the Supreme Court Justice you worked for, was
close to Garrett Ainslee? Isn't that right?"

Norton agreed with Frost's recollection, and also agreed
with the older man's theory that perhaps Carroll's papers
on the three cases missing from Ainslee's files might offer
some clue.

"They traded memos and notes back and forth more than

most of their colleagues," Norton said. "They usually disagreed, but they trusted each other's judgment. It's worth a try, Reuben."

Norton explained that the Carroll papers were at the Princeton University Library, though they were still sealed and could only be looked at with the retired Justice's permission.

"He's still alive, isn't he?"

"Oh, yes. And very alert. He lives outside of Philadelphia, in Swarthmore."

"What's the best way to approach him?" Frost asked.

"I'll be happy to give him a call. I like to keep in touch with the old boy, and this would give me a good excuse to do that. Can I tell him what you're interested in—and why?"

"Of course. But also tell him it's fairly urgent. I'd like to get in there right away—like tomorrow."

Norton called back before lunch and reported that everything was fine, with one hitch. Carroll wanted to be present when Frost made his visit. "I'll be able to help him," he was reported as saying, except that Carroll could not get to Princeton before Friday morning.

"You sure you can't light a fire under him? Make him get up there sooner?" Frost pleaded.

"You can light a fire under Dine Carroll, but I'm afraid he has asbestos pants, Reuben. You're just going to have to wait till Friday."

A further round of telephone calls sealed the arrangements. Carroll would go to Princeton Friday morning and retrieve the files on the three cases. He suggested that Frost join him at two o'clock.

So be it, Frost said to himself, resigned to the delay.

"We seem to be eating at home a great deal lately," Cynthia said to her husband that evening as they finished dinner.

"Don't you really mean, 'I've done a lot of cooking lately'?" her husband replied.

"Not at all. Usually we're out somewhere most nights, but the last week or so we've been dining *à deux à la maison*. I'm not complaining, just making an observation."

Her husband knew better; Cynthia's "observations" often had an (intended) edge. But before he could make a lavish commitment to take his wife out on the town, the telephone rang.

"Reuben, can I come over?" It was Bautista again, his voice low and constricted.

"Of course. What's up?"

"I'll be there in ten minutes," was the only reply Frost got.

"That's strange," he said to Cynthia. "Something must be happening. Aren't he and Francisca coming to dinner tomorrow?"

"Yes. We're eating here."

Reuben ignored the underlining to the phrase "we're eating here" or, more precisely, the double underline under "here."

Bautista arrived on schedule and barely said hello before announcing that Horace Jenkins was dead.

"I'm sorry," Reuben said. "The poor fellow. When did it happen?"

"Around seven."

"What did he die of, was there any way of telling?"

"*Si, si, si*, Reuben. He died of suffocation from having a pillow stuffed over his head."

Frost had not counted on such a reply. He drank it in, nervously fingering his necktie. "He was murdered, Luis?" he asked, quietly.

"That's right. With five thousand nurses and nurses' aides and interns and residents all over the place."

"And no one saw the murderer, is that what you're saying?"

"No one saw the murderer? Those dumb bastards didn't even see the little red light go out on his monitoring machine when he was asphyxiated. Somebody just came in there, put a pillow over his face and snuffed him out."

"What about the other patients in the ward? As I remember there were three others."

"Christ, they're so full of tubes, or so doped up, they didn't see a thing."

"That's strange."

"Not if you remember how sick those guys were."

"Yes, I suppose you're right."

"Reuben, what the hell are we going to do? First your friend Rowan, now his assistant. And we don't have a single clue that's panned out."

"Could it have been a friend?" Cynthia asked. "A mercy killing?"

"I thought about that, Cynthia. I don't think so. He only had two regular visitors, volunteers from the Gay Men's Health Crisis. His mother and brother had disowned him, and if he had other friends, they've been no-shows at the hospital. Jenkins had a few days, maybe a few hours, to live.

"If anyone wanted to perform a mercy killing, they could have turned one of the dials, or unhooked the IV. Or they could have sneezed, for Christ's sake—that probably would have killed the poor guy right there. But whoever did it chose to smother him. No 'friend' would do that. It's an outsider, I know it!"

"Hmn," Frost said. "What you say makes sense. If the murderer knew his true condition, there was no need to hurry the process along."

"Reuben, I'm desperate," Bautista said. "All the newspapers have got the jitters about Rowan—and now this. Did you see that front-page column in the *Press* tonight by your old columnist friend, Arthur Mattison? How the cops can find the killer of a drug dealer in four hours, but not the murderer of a major author?

"Nobody understands anything, or gives us credit for anything!" Bautista shouted. He jumped up as he spoke and started pacing the room. Frost had never seen him so agitated.

"That drug dealer—you read about it yesterday—his murder was a grounder. Murder weapon with fingerprints in a trash can ten feet from the body. And three separate people all dropped a dime on the killer about ten minutes after the hit. Of course, we collared the guy. What do they think, we're stupid? But now, since we can't finger anybody who pushed your history professor, we're a bunch of jerks!"

"Luis, can I interrupt?" Cynthia asked. "What about the physical evidence you've got—the blood sample and the skin sample? I don't mean to interfere, but can't you take tests? Maybe you can't find the killer that way, but you ought to be able to eliminate some of the people on your list."

"Oh, Cynthia, I agree with you," Bautista replied. "Will you tell that to Joe Munson?"

"Who's he?" Reuben asked.

"The goddam assistant district attorney in charge of the case—you saw him the other night, Reuben, at least on tape. Can't see through his thick glasses beyond the end of his fat face. I tell him about twice a day that all we need is a bunch of court orders and we'd have this thing wrapped up—and Mattison and his press friends back in their cages."

"Well? Why isn't that a good idea?" Cynthia asked.

"Because he's scared out of his pasty, pimple-covered skin, that's why. 'Probable cause' is all he can say. 'Got to have probable cause, Luis. Can't have the police running around taking blood samples for no good reason.'

"He's right, of course, you *do* need probable cause to order a blood test or a skin test. The American way. *I* think we've got probable cause—characters out there with no known alibi and about three motives apiece. Fortes, the muscleboy, known to be in town the day Rowan was killed. That hood Giardi, who probably last gave blood when he took the goddam Mafia oath. The wife-beating professor, Jewett, also in the Big Apple on the big day. Knowles, your bankrupt publisher friend. I keep begging Munson to let me go after them!"

"What does he say?" Reuben asked.

"Like I told you, he's scared, afraid to move. Hell, in a way I don't blame him. Fortes isn't even in the jurisdiction, and he's hiding under the skirts of a broad you tell me's one of the most powerful women in Washington. Not much sex appeal for Munson to go after that one. Then Jewett, also miles out of state and the best-known professor at the col-

lege he teaches at. Or Knowles, big-deal publisher of Nobel
Prize winners. Munson would as soon get a court order
against Mother Teresa as go against him. And Giardi—man,
I agree with Munson, I don't even want to think about that.
He'd have fifty lawyers running to the Supreme Court if
we tried to touch him. And last, but not least, you tell me
you've got doubts about the man who probably will be the
next President of the United States. Munson doesn't even
know about him, but his pimples would be popping if I
even mentioned him!

"I can see it now, *amigos*. Big photo opportunity for
Presidential candidate. Having his blood drawn on television while big, macho Puerto Rican second-class detective
looks on. Good for the junkie vote, maybe? Get him the
sympathy of the Civil Liberties Union? Make him the hero
of the Hispanics, for cooperating with *Lajaras*—me, the
Hispanic cop? Christ, Reuben, do you see my problem?"

"I do," Reuben answered. "It's prickly business. You
think it would help if I talked to Munson's boss?"

"Negative. In a case like this, you can bet the DA knows
everything Munson says or does. If I keep at it, maybe I
can get an order to get tests from Giardi. He hasn't won
any big popularity contests down on Frank Hogan Place.
But that would be all.

"Take me back to street crime where you can finger somebody who isn't famous or well-connected," Bautista went
on. "We're never going to solve this thing, Reuben."

"Luis, we've got to stay calm," Reuben said. "We've
just got to plug away. Unless something more turns up on
Professor Jewett, my hunch right now is that the most promising opening we've got is my meeting with Dine Carroll.
I'm convinced those missing files of Ainslee's are important
and if we're very, very lucky, something in Carroll's files
may shed some light that will guide us."

"Yeah, I'm sorry to be so down. Hell, maybe the Crime
Scene Unit will find some big, fat clue in Jenkins's room at
the hospital. Or, you're right, maybe this guy Carroll can
help. When do you see him, Friday?"

"I'm afraid so. If I had my way, I'd see him tonight. But
he's an old man and Friday was the best I could do."

"What about Jewett? Don't you want to find out where he is tonight?" Cynthia asked.

Both men looked startled.

"Jesus, Cynthia, you're right. I'll call Amherst right now."

"We're seeing you tomorrow aren't we?" Cynthia asked, when the detective returned from the library. "You and Francisca *are* coming to dinner?"

"You bet."

"It's a Bautista festival," Cynthia said. "You tonight, you and Francisca tomorrow night, and Francisca for lunch tomorrow."

"Really? I didn't know that," Bautista said. "What's that about?"

"Just two girls talking. Nothing special—I don't think. Unless we get some ideas."

"Yeah," Bautista muttered.

"And if we do, Luis, you'll be the first to know," Cynthia said as she said good-bye to the detective.

WOMEN'S WORK

22

WHEN BAUTISTA AND FRANCISCA ARRIVED FOR DINNER THE next night, the detective reported that Peter Jewett could not be found. He was not at his apartment and his car was gone.

"Does this mean they put out an alarm on him?" Frost asked.

"Yes, they have. But no results yet. This case is a shitcan," Bautista said as he slouched into the sofa in the Frost living room.

"Luis, you shouldn't use such language," Francisca admonished. "You're with nice people now."

"I know, I know. But that's what we call a hopeless case, one that will never be solved."

"Buck up, my friend," Reuben said. "We're not at the end of our rope yet. And even you seem more cheerful tonight."

"I'm sorry about last night. I was in bad shape, practically an EDP."

"EDP?" Cynthia queried.

"Emotionally Disturbed Person. Not tonight, though. I'm too sleepy to have any emotions."

"Were you at the hospital all night?" Reuben asked.

"Just about."

"Did you find anything?"

179

"Not much. Some fabric hairs on the pillow that was used to kill Jenkins."

"That's something, isn't it?"

"Yeah. It means we only have to look for a person who wears a suit, or at least a jacket. It narrows things down a lot. Poor Jenkins didn't fight back the way Rowan did. So there's no blood sample or skin scraping this time."

Frost was determined to avert still another run-through of the suspects, which he now saw coming. Turning to Francisca, sitting beside him on the sofa, he tried to change the subject. "How was your lunch today?" he asked.

"You mean the pastrami sandwich in Cynthia's office?"

Reuben was confused. Such austerity was not like his wife, who enjoyed going out for lunch.

"Are you on an economy drive, dear?" he asked her.

"No, it's just that Francisca and I had some business to do," she replied.

"Business? Good Lord, you're not interfering in this case, are you?"

"I have to go to the kitchen," Cynthia declared, leaving the room without answering her husband's question.

"Cynthia, what have you been up to?" Reuben called after her. "I demand to know."

Francisca started laughing, and Cynthia returned and addressed the men. "We'll tell you what we've been up to on two conditions—that we wait until after dinner and that we stop talking about these ghastly murders until then. Agreed?" Without waiting for an answer, she returned to the kitchen.

"I guess we've got our orders," Reuben said, turning to Francisca. "You sure you won't give us a preview of coming attractions?"

"Never. You heard the lady." Francisca laughed and patted Reuben's forearm with one hand and swept back her long, lustrous black hair with the other.

"What are we supposed to talk about then?" Frost asked. "Your lipstick?"

"You like it?"

"Well, it's different. But yes, I do." Francisca was wearing fiery red lipstick, a dramatic complement to her black hair and dark features. Bautista stared into his Scotch as this innocent flirtation went on.

"If we've got to change the subject, I've got a question for you, Francisca," Frost said. "What have things been like at Dickey and Company since Black Monday?"

"You mean, since the stock market crashed?"

"Yes."

"Not so great. You know my boss, Mr. Selby, right?"

Frost nodded.

"He's now the chairman, and personally in charge of getting rid of five hundred people. I'm spending lots of my time typing up lists of those who are getting fired. It's very unhappy. Mr. Selby meets with the department heads in his office every morning. The door is shut, but I hear lots of shouting, and then the guys come out looking really mad. I just hope I keep my job."

"If your Mr. Selby has any sense you will," Reuben said.

"It's not good, Reuben," Francisca said. "The company lost a lot of money last year and the bosses are really fighting."

"I realize how lucky I was at Chase & Ward, Francisca. We always managed to make more money each year than we did the one before. Not a lot sometimes, but even if you're growing just a little it keeps down the bitching and the backbiting."

"Yeah, money's great, all right," Bautista said. "Would it surprise you to know that it even helps cut down on crime? Give the guys in a street crew some money and maybe—maybe—they'll stop mugging people."

"I've been thinking," Reuben said. "These murders we've got now, there's only one suspect who might have killed for money. Stanley Knowles. Isn't that odd, Luis?"

"Not really. Robbery and mugging, that stuff's for money. To buy drugs, or radios or fancy clothes. But murder? Anger and jealousy are what you usually find. And we've sure got them in our case."

"We're not supposed to be talking about it," Francisca said.

"That's all right. Cynthia can't hear," Reuben assured her.

"Besides, I don't think Knowles did it," Francisca said.

"What do you know about it, Francisca?" Bautista asked. Both men looked at her intently as she shrugged her shoulders.

"Just a hunch," she said, not convincingly. "Here she comes, so we can't talk about it now."

Cynthia marshaled the group to the dining room table, where they all steered clear of the subject on everyone's mind. Instead, they talked about Bautista's plans after completing night law school at the end of the summer.

"What are your plans?" Cynthia asked the detective straight out. By including Francisca in her sweeping gaze as she asked the question, she could be (as in fact she was) asking about the marital, as well as the vocational, future.

"I wish I knew," Bautista said. "I've got a résumé now—Francisca typed it for me last week. I guess I'll circulate it around to some of the firms that do criminal defense work. Not the single-office guys down on Centre Street, but the bigger firms with good reputations. Of course, now that Reuben's a criminal lawyer, maybe we could start a new department at Chase & Ward."

"Please, Luis, don't remind me of that," Reuben said. "That poor boy Alan would probably have ended up in Attica for life if I'd kept on with his case." (Frost did, however, fantasize for a brief moment a meeting with George Bannard, the stolid Executive Partner of Chase & Ward. In the fantasy he proposed to Bannard that the firm start a criminal department, with Reuben returning from retirement and Luis Bautista assisting him. The meeting would either be a triumph for Bannard, proving once and for all that Frost was senile, or for Frost, with Bannard physically collapsing after hearing Frost's outrageous idea.)

"Or I could stay in the NYPD. The place isn't paradise for a Puerto Rican yet, but it's not just the old Irish gang, either. With a law degree, I might be able to get to Headquarters pretty quick."

"What do you think, Francisca?" Cynthia asked.

"I'm not sure. It's true, Luis is a suit and could get downtown, I know it."

Bautista looked mildly disapproving at Francisca's characterization.

"A suit? What's a suit?" Reuben asked.

"A guy with a college education," Francisca explained. "A guy who wears a suit, not a uniform."

"Cut it out, Francisca," Bautista said. "You've got it wrong. A 'suit' is a guy who can read and write, and they're a dime a dozen in the Department."

"That's not what you told me a 'suit' was three months ago," Francisca said, holding her ground.

"Anyway, I've been thinking about staying on. With Francisca's salary—if Selby doesn't give her the ax—and mine, we could do all right."

Cynthia shot a glance at her husband. It sounded like matrimony to her. He did not comment, but began clearing the dishes.

"What on earth are you doing?" Cynthia whispered to him in the kitchen as she began preparing dessert. "You haven't cleared the table in years!"

"I want to get this damned dinner over so we can find out what in the name of God you and Francisca have been up to!" he hissed.

"Curosity killed the cat. But since you're up, put out those plates."

Frost did as he was told and sat down to eat one of the Bonté raspberry tarts that Cynthia served.

"Shall we have coffee here or in the living room?" she asked when dessert was finished.

"In the living room," Frost snapped, sure that his wife would have to concede that dinner was over once they moved from the table.

"All right, girls, what's up?" Reuben demanded, seated back in the living room.

"Shall we tell them, Cynthia?" Francisca asked playfully. After the healthy quantity of Gruaud-Larose consumed at dinner, she looked to Reuben even more beautiful than usual.

"Yes," Cynthia answered. "We're not trying to play

games. It's just that both of you have been so wrought-up about Rowan's murder—and the appalling sequel yesterday—that I wanted you to have a solid meal where we talked about other things."

Cynthia took a sip from her demitasse cup, and continued. "I'm afraid, Luis, we've been dipping into what you so elegantly called the shitcan. Francisca and I were supposed to have a fancy lunch at Aurora today. Then last night I got to thinking about your frustration with Munson and the barrier of 'probable cause' between your blood tests and the suspects. I changed things around, and Francisca and I had a sandwich in my office. Francisca also took the afternoon off so we could carry out a little plan we worked out over lunch."

"What did you do, Cynthia?" Reuben demanded. "What besides eating pastrami sandwiches in your office? Please get on with it!"

"Reuben, please calm down. And don't interrupt. When I thought about it, it seemed to me that Luis and Mr. Munson of course had to be cautious. The police have to have rules in an 'ordered society'—isn't that what you call it, Reuben?"

Her husband nodded reluctantly, still impatient to get to the heart of Cynthia's maneuvers.

"What I wondered was, do these same rules apply to two nosy women not connected with the police force? Rightly or wrongly, I decided that they didn't. Then I thought about that report about privacy the Brigham Foundation—not my part, but the political affairs staff—put out last year. Do you remember it, Reuben?"

"Yes, I remember it very well," Frost said monumentally, impatient. "Not very original. It came to the not very startling conclusion that personal privacy was more difficult in the age of the computer."

"Oh, my dear, it said more than that. It said that people were getting *used* to having their privacy invaded, that they were *resigned* to it, so that they had given up trying to protect personal information."

"Such as their blood type?" Reuben said, catching on at last to Cynthia's plot.

"Yes, blood types. Blood types of the suspects. Not skin

samples—we didn't go out and attack Tommy Giardi with a knife. We did, however, make some very clever phone calls."

"*Smooth* phone calls," Francisca added, pleased with herself.

"I made the first one," Cynthia said. "To Amherst, where I reached someone in the personnel department. I explained that I was from the Brigham Foundation—I told no lies—and that we needed certain information to complete our records on our trustee, Peter Jewett. I asked for his birthdate and social security number, and a few other dumb things, including his blood type. The woman who took the call was very cooperative, but was stumped at the blood type. She helpfully said she'd call the college health service to see if they knew and would call me back. Twenty minutes later she did, and Peter Jewett is type B."

"Which means he could have killed Rowan," Bautista said.

"Precisely. The next call, to Ralston Fortes, was more tricky. Francisca had the answer for that one."

"Shall I tell?" she asked, unable to conceal the triumphant look on her face. "It was easy if you thought about it. Luis had told me that Fortes was a bodybuilder. Now, I ride the subway every day, and half the Puerto Rican *machos* I see are reading bodybuilding magazines. So why not call Señor Fortes and interview him for one of those magazines?

"I went down and bought one at the newsstand in Cynthia's building—the guy looked at me like I was crazy. *Mega-Muscle*, it was called."

"I don't believe this," Bautista said.

"Shut up. So we got Marietta Ainslee's number from directory assistance and I called. Fortes answered the phone. I said I was a reporter from *Mega-Muscle*, talking real Hispanic, and said we were doing an article on blood—how it relates to bodybuilding, AIDS, the whole business. Could he, Mr. Celebrity Bodybuilder, help little me out by telling me his blood type?"

"And he did? To a *woman* reporter from *Mega-Muscle*?" Bautista asked incredulously.

"As I say, I laid on the Spaneesh accent," Francisca said. "With half the readers of the magazine Puerto Rican, he didn't seem surprised. And he told me his blood type was O."

"So you're telling us Fortes is in the clear?"

"It looks that way," Francisca said.

"Jewett and Fortes were pieces of cake," Cynthia said. "Stanley Knowles was more of a problem."

"I'm not sure I want to hear this," Reuben said.

"It was our best move," Cynthia replied. "I called the public relations person at Hammersmith Press and said I was a freelance reporter doing a piece for *New York* magazine. I told him I was writing about the blood types of famous and prominent New Yorkers and asked him . . ."

"You've got to be kidding," Reuben said. "He believed you?"

"Darling, if you were as desperate for publicity that's not unfavorable as I gather Hammersmith Press is at the moment, you'd believe anything! To be very crude about it, I have an idea I could have told him I was doing a piece on which famous men-about-town were circumcised and which were not and he would have found out about Stanley for me."

"So what is Knowles's blood type?" Bautista demanded.

"This nice young man called me back—half-an-hour this time—and said that Stanley was type A."

"So we can scratch him from the list," Reuben said. "But now, what about Giardi?"

"There we failed. Neither Francisca nor I could think of a way to get to him."

"So you did the three—Jewett, Fortes and Knowles?" Frost asked.

"And one more," Cynthia replied. "The Honorable Wheeler Edmunds. You remember he made a big deal about turning his medical records over to the *Times* when he declared. Through a mole over there—never mind who—we got his blood type as well. Type B, just like under David's fingernails."

"Perfect," Reuben said. "Do you really think a man running for President killed Rowan and Jenkins?"

"I didn't say that. All I'm saying is that his blood is type B."

Both Frost and Bautista bowed their heads and massaged them with their hands.

"You did quite an afternoon's work, Cynthia," Bautista said after a long pause. "All I can say is, thanks."

Frost was suddenly tired, as he remembered his appointment with Dine Carroll the next day. He was amazed at what Cynthia and Francisca had accomplished. His guests, noticing his fatigue, got up to leave.

"Good night, Miss Mega-Muscle of Nineteen Eighty-Eight," Frost said to Francisca as he kissed her good night. "And, Luis, I'll let you know right away what if anything I find down in Princeton. And I'd let the Amherst police know about Jewett's blood type. Just in case they find him and question him again."

"Okay, Reuben. The girls have done great work, but we've still got a shitcan. And maybe a deeper one than we realized."

23

FRIDAY MORNING, FROST ARRIVED AT PENN STATION just in time to take the Trenton local to Princeton Junction. He had drunk the fresh orange juice Cynthia had prepared for him, and carried in a brown paper bag the cup of coffee purchased at the Greek luncheonette around the corner from his home.

As he opened the wax-coated container on the train and sipped its contents with some distaste, he thought of the countless times he had made the train trip to Princeton over his lifetime—as penurious undergraduate returning from magical excursions to Manhattan, as jaunty alumnus going back to his major Princeton reunions, as Princeton trustee going to endless meetings of the Board and its committees. But never had he made the trip—which had changed almost not at all over the many years he had made it—to ferret out clues to a murder.

Once at Princeton Junction he made the transition to the PJ&B—"Princeton Junction & Back"—that took one to Princeton. Undergraduates now called it the "dinky," he had recently learned, but to him it would always remain the PJ&B, the tiny toy train that connected the university to the outside world.

The spring day was perfect, and Reuben, despite the gravity of his mission, recalled with pleasure Scott Fitzgerald's rhapsodies on Princeton in the spring. As the rousing song went, Old Nassau was "the best old place of all," a proposition Reuben devoutly believed.

He walked through the campus, marveling at the green foliage, and glanced only fleetingly at the ground floor room in Henry Hall where he had begun his Princeton journey—and, indeed, his journey into the world—so many years before. It had been a slum then, and he was sure it was a slum now, but the twinge of memory was both strong and affectionate.

A new twinge awaited him at the Annex, the Nassau Street restaurant where he decided to have lunch. This vast basement was much the same as it had been in the early thirties, and still served vast quantities of food priced for the undergraduate pocketbook. "Junk food" was an unknown concept back then, but the Annex had served it, cheerfully ignorant of the pejorative name that would later describe it. With great satisfaction he ate a bowl of spaghetti with sauce rendered from canned tomato paste; the refinement of well-made madeleines was most assuredly not there, but the effect on his taste buds was downright Proustian.

After lunch, he crossed the street to the Firestone Library, which he regarded as the university's most magnificent achievement. He had become familiar with its light, modern and cheerful atmosphere as a trustee, and had often envied the later generations of students who had the privilege of working and sweating there. He did feel regret as he applied for an admission pass inside the front door. For years, the open-stack library had been open to all, the only constraint a routine and friendly examination of bookbags and briefcases on leaving. But theft and vandalism, both of which scandalized Frost, had made inevitable a barrier that optimistically kept out those who were not serious about using the library's riches for the purposes intended.

Pass in hand, he followed instructions and went to the new John Foster Dulles wing, where a cheerful student receptionist directed him to the conference room where Dine Carroll awaited him.

Frost had never met the Justice before. He was now slightly stooped—a quick look at *Who's Who* had indicated he was now eighty-two—but still had a ruddy, patrician demeanor befitting a retired member of the Supreme Court. Frost introduced himself, realizing that this was one of those increasingly rare occasions when the person with whom he was speaking was older than he was. He called Carroll "Mr. Justice," and there was no suggestion that he should change that to "Dine."

"Did you ever argue before the Supreme Court, Mr. Frost?" Carroll asked.

"No. My partners always had the good sense to keep me out of the courts."

"So you were one of those fellows who stayed back at the office and kept people out of trouble—or got them into it?"

"That's right."

"What our British friends call a solicitor?"

"Yes."

"I tried that once. Worked for a big firm in Chicago. Bored silly. I went back to Des Moines and became a trial lawyer. Stayed there until Dwight Eisenhower pulled my name out of the hat and brought me to Washington.

"But enough reminiscing. Let's get down to business," Carroll said, gesturing toward the three boxes of papers on the conference table. "Frank Norton—a fine young man, by the way, one of the best clerks I ever had—tells me you're interested in three cases: *Rodriguez*, *Cleveland School District* and *Carrymore*. He was a little vague about why, but I gather it has something to do with the murder of that young fellow who was writing Garrett Ainslee's biography."

Frost explained the circumstances of David Rowan's death, and the discovery that three of Ainslee's case files had been found missing from Rowan's office.

"And what relevance do my files have?" Carroll asked.

"Mr. Justice, Frank told me that you and Mr. Justice Ainslee were good friends."

"He's right. Garrett was the closest friend I had on the Court. For all his faults, which were many, he was a true Southern gentleman. We disagreed more often than we agreed, but we did *scrap* intellectually all the time. We debated just about every issue that came before the Court.

I think Garrett respected my convictions and I respected his, wrong-headed as they often were."

"I understand, Mr. Justice. What I'm hoping is that there's something in your files on the three cases that sheds some light on what might have been in Mr. Justice Ainslee's. And just possibly points to the killer of his biographer."

Frost further explained that the search was not only for Rowan's murderer, but the person who had killed his research assistant as well. Carroll had not heard or read about Jenkins's death; the lines of sadness in his aristocratic face deepened as he heard what Frost was telling him.

"What do you think my papers might show?"

"I'm not sure. There's just a hope on my part that Mr. Justice Ainslee may have sent you some significant document, some message, that duplicates something that might have been in his own files."

"My files are organized case by case, just as I believe Ainslee's were, and just as those of most Justices are. In fact, there's only one Justice that I know of, and he shall be nameless, who did things differently. This fellow thought that posterity would want to know what he did day by day, so his papers are organized in strict chronology, regardless of subject. I'm told he's now trying to write his autobiography and having a helluva time. Takes him hours to find things. Total confusion, and all brought about by his own megalomania. Not, I think, that there would have been less mental confusion if his papers had been arranged properly. But I'm being indiscreet about one of my brethren."

Frost laughed at the digression, though he was eager to press forward with his quest. "I won't speculate on whom you're talking about, Mr. Justice."

"Good, because I have no intention of telling you."

Frost, despite his impatience, liked his crusty new acquaintance.

"Getting back to your files, Mr. Justice. Do you think there might be something of interest in them?"

Carroll did not answer directly. "You know, you're going back to a period when not everything was Xeroxed. The boys—and that girl—on the Court today drown themselves in paper, I understand. They Xerox everything and pass it around. We didn't have that luxury, or maybe I should say that curse. Unless things were printed, like our opinions and drafts of opinions, it wasn't so easy to bury ourselves in paper.

"But I'm wandering, forgive me. I've looked through the case files you asked about. There may be some things of interest."

"Maybe I could ask you first if you have any recollection of Mr. Justice Ainslee's discussing any of the three cases with you."

"No, I don't. Which doesn't mean he didn't. I remember the cases, all right—all three were pretty important at the time—but I can't honestly say I recall any conversations with Garrett about them. So let's go to the files.

"Here's *Rodriguez*," he said, picking up one of the boxes before him. "You recall that Garrett wrote the majority opinion, saying the appellee's conviction should be thrown out. I disagreed—my God, there was no question the man was caught with a load of marijuana, and the border patrol fellows were just doing their job when they stumbled on it. All I can find in the file is a carbon copy of an early draft of Garrett's majority opinion. There's a handwritten note on it that I'll read to you." He took a bound document from the top of the file and read the note: "My clerks are squabbling over this one. I'd like to have your views. G.A."

"I'm afraid that's all there is that might interest you."

Frost was discouraged. An unidentified quarrel, and one not documented, was not what he had in mind.

"So let's go on to *Cleveland School District*," Carroll said. "That was a hot one. Garrett dissented, but he didn't write an opinion. He clearly wanted to, because I have here a draft opinion he sent me. With a note, which I'll let you read." Carroll turned over a single handwritten page to Frost, who read the text:

Dine,

I'm troubled by the Cleveland desegregation case. I can't overcome being a Southerner, even though I'll admit the Civil War is long over. Fact is, I think the strong desegregation opinions the Court has handed down since 1954 have been absolutely right. Stamping out segregation won't solve the race problem, but it's a necessary start. Lately, however, desegregation has moved into the North and some of our brethren seem determined to make distinctions that will allow Northern school districts to maintain the segregated status quo. I mean the *de facto*, *de jure* dichotomy, which just doesn't cut it with me. If there's segregation, we should order its eradication "root and branch," as our late Chief said. I've tried my hand at a dissenting opinion in *Cleveland* attacking the new Chief on this *de facto*, *de jure* business. I'd like your thoughts, even though I'm sure you disagree with me. God knows my clerks do. There's one who writes me a memo every day saying my position, if adopted, would make the Court even more unpopular than it is now, that it goes too far and would punish the innocent. —G.A.

"If you're interested," Carroll said, "I wrote him a note back agreeing with his clerk. On this one, Garrett was just being too radical."

"Is there any indication which clerk it was who was writing these memos?"

"Nope."

"And you don't remember talking with Mr. Justice Ainslee about the case—or the obstreperous clerk?"

"Nope."

Frost was deflated. The trail was getting warm, but there was no document that identified Wheeler Edmunds.

"You're aware that Wheeler Edmunds was one of Mr. Justice Ainslee's clerks during this term of the Court?"

"Oh, yes."

"But there's nothing to link him to the memorandum I just read?"

"Not in my files."

"How about *United States v. Carrymore*?" Frost asked, almost in desperation.

"Yes," Carroll replied. "Here there may be something that

interests you." He produced an aging copy of a memorandum from Edmunds to Ainslee, dated December 4, 1972, with a cover note: *"Dine—What do you think? G.A."*

The brown paper of the copy was cracking and the text fading. Frost handled it gingerly as he read:

To: Mr. Justice Ainslee
From: Wheeler H. Edmunds

I have read your proposed concurring opinion in *Carrymore* and disagree both with your vote and your reasoning. The majority opinion finds that Sgt. Carrymore, on the facts before it, was discriminated against on the basis of sex, in contravention of the Fourteenth Amendment. I personally don't see why the Army isn't entitled to ask whether a woman noncommissioned officer needs a dependency allowance or not. Why should the Government pay such an allowance if the woman's husband is working and the couple doesn't require it?

But whatever the merits of the case, your concurrence strikes out into completely uncharted waters and finds that *all* sex discrimination is prohibited by the Fourteenth Amendment. At a time when the Court is being attacked—*legitimately*, in my mind—for making new law and changing what had been thought to be solid precedent in so many areas, I don't think it—or you—needs the abuse sure to follow your concurrence.

Men and women *are* different. The legal rules for men are inevitably different from those for women. Under your logic, we could have women firefighters and policemen, and employers could be compelled to overlook the obvious fact that women become pregnant and men do not. The country isn't ready—and probably never will be—for women at West Point.

There's no question that women have the right to vote. If they can persuade the Congress to reconstitute the Army or alter the social mores of the nation, more power to them. But I think you are very wrong to advocate significant changes in the status of men and women by judicial fiat. (You might also consider

taking your logic to its extreme and speculating what
it might do to the status of homosexuals.)

The memorandum went on for two more pages, but Frost
had read enough.

Carroll had been sitting erect in his chair, his bright eyes
shining, as Frost read. When Frost looked up and put down
the memo, he asked, "Is that the hand grenade you were
looking for, Mr. Frost?"

"I think it is—or maybe it is," Frost replied, marveling
at the old Justice's sense of the dramatic in saving the best
for last. "Did you know Edmunds?"

"No. I remember meeting him a number of times, but he
was a rather quiet one to meet."

"He certainly wasn't quiet on paper."

"So it appears. Not exactly what he's been saying in this
campaign, is it?"

"Or since he's been in the Senate," Frost said. "When
did he change his stripes, do you suppose?"

"When he started running for office in Michigan, I
expect."

"Do you mind if I take some notes on this?" Frost asked.
He was not bold enough to ask to make a copy.

"I'm not overjoyed, but I guess in the circumstances I
can't object. I'll expect you to keep what you've learned
confidential."

"That may be difficult, Mr. Justice," Frost said. "I don't
know where the investigation of David Rowan's death may
lead, but this memo may be very important."

"I can't stand in the path of justice," Carroll replied. "But
if there's any way to keep it confidential, I'd appreciate
it. And if it's needed officially, I would expect to have it
subpoenaed in an orderly way."

"I'm sure that will be no problem," Frost said. "Just give
me a few moments to jot down some quick notes."

Carroll got up and stood looking out the window until
Frost had finished. "Unless there's something more, I'm
going back to Philadelphia," he said, once Frost had put
his notebook away.

"By train?"

"Yes."

"I'll walk you to the station." Reuben consulted his time-table and determined that they both could take the same PJ&B shuttle to Princeton Junction.

Walking through the campus, Frost realized that he must make polite conversation, though his mind was hardly engaged in what he was saying.

"How did you decide to leave your papers to Princeton?" he asked the Justice.

"Everyone was after me. The law schools, the University of Iowa, even that Herbert Hoover outfit at Stanford. John Harlan left his papers to Princeton and was very satisfied with the treatment he got. It's near where I live, and I like the building—I don't think being in the same literary mausoleum as John Foster Dulles will rub off. So that's why I decided on Princeton. So far I've kept them closed. They're for future historians. Supreme Court Justices shouldn't kiss and tell."

Frost silently gave thanks that Dine Carroll had let his virtue slip ever so slightly that day. At Princeton Junction, he thanked the Justice abundantly.

"I'm glad to be of assistance, Mr. Frost," Carroll said. "Just keep me out of the tabloids."

"I'll do my best, Mr. Justice," Frost replied.

Then he headed for the tunnel to the New York train while Carroll went straight ahead to the Philadelphia side.

COMPUTING

24

"I HOPE YOU HAD GOOD LUCK TODAY," CYNTHIA SAID TO her husband when he arrived home. "Peter Jewett is off the suspect list."

"What do you mean?"

Cynthia recounted a call received earlier from Bautista, though it was all she could do to keep from laughing as she did so. As the detective had told her the tale, Jewett's car had been found at a motel in the Berkshires early that morning. Jewett had apparently spent the night there with a young woman who was about to graduate from Amherst.

The professor had again flared up in anger when the state police questioned him. But the girl panicked and confessed all. Jewett had been her thesis adviser and she had become infatuated with him. Two weeks earlier—on the night when David Rowan was murdered—she had contrived to deliver her completed thesis to him at his apartment. One thing led to another and she had spent the night. And several other nights after that, ending with the Thursday evening of what was to have been a long, romantic weekend when the police found him.

"Crotchety old bachelor, indeed," Reuben observed. "Some misogynist."

The tale of Jewett's tryst was interesting, and certainly amusing, but Reuben did not take time to savor it. He

was more eager to tell his wife of his own discoveries of
the day.

They didn't even pause for their customary drink, but
discussed the murders until well into the evening. They
had no doubt that the killings were linked to the memorandum Reuben had read that afternoon in the Princeton
Library. But the logical implication, that Wheeler Edmunds
had committed the murders, did not hold up. How could
Edmunds, a highly visible candidate for the Presidency,
recognizable to almost everyone, evade his Secret Service
escorts and the press corps and disappear long enough to kill
two men? It was not possible. Yet the memorandum pointed
to a powerful motive—Edmunds's almost certain desire, as
a Presidential candidate, to keep secret his conservative
writings for Justice Ainslee. And, for what it might be
worth, he had the same blood type as David's murderer.

"Can you imagine what would happen to Edmunds's
campaign if that memo came out?" Cynthia asked her
husband. "The way you describe it, you don't have to be
a militant feminist to find it shocking. Or a homosexual."

"I suppose he could say it was the callowness of youth,"
Reuben said.

"Except that he was an adult when he wrote it. It makes
his liberalism look terribly phony. The hypocrisy of it!"

"We just have to think this through, my dear. But right
now I'm going to bed. Wake me up if you get any good
inspirations, will you?" Frost kissed his wife good night
and went off to the bedroom.

But he spent the night worrying the problem, tossing
and turning so vigorously that Cynthia finally left him to
sleep in the guest room. He was still tired in the morning.

"I've got the jitters and not a single new idea," he told
his wife Saturday morning. "What can I do?"

"You haven't seen the Fragonard show at the Metropolitan. It's delightful, and it's closing soon. Go over there and
calm yourself."

Frost took her advice. Yet all the alluring colors, fantasies
and mild eroticism of the Fragonards did not calm him; his
thoughts remained obsessively on Wheeler Edmunds.

Perhaps lunch would help, he concluded. He found his way to the patrons' dining room, a pleasant and quiet haven away from the Museum's Saturday crowds. As he ate his lunch and drank a glass of wine, Reuben pulled out the tiny notebook he always carried and began making notes. Methodically he wrote down, in no particular order, all the clues, unanswered questions and inferences that might still have relevance after the elimination of Fortes, Knowles and the philandering Jewett from suspicion.

If I put these together right they will tell a story, he told himself. He ordered a second glass of wine, hoping it would stimulate his imagination to organize the miscellany into a coherent whole. He focused on Marietta Ainslee's and Ralston Fortes's concern with Garrett Ainslee's sex-coded engagement calendars; was there any significance to this disappearance now that Fortes was no longer a suspect? Thinking about the missing case files, he tried to imagine who, apart from Wheeler Edmunds, might have been interested in their contents.

Then, sipping his wine, he tried to free-associate on the name Elizabeth, the enigmatic clue furnished by the dying Jenkins. He attempted to recall every Elizabeth he had ever known, or ever heard of. Suddenly, he had an inspiration. He was so shocked by his own insight, bizarre as it was, that he overturned his wine glass. A waiter came running and offered to replace it. But Frost stood up quickly, both to avoid the small stream of wine flowing off the table and to get the check. He had the answer, he knew it, but he had to go off quietly to reflect on whether the pieces now fitted together. And what pieces were still missing.

Frost hurried out of the Museum and walked to the nearest entrance to Central Park. Alone and unbothered, he sat on a bench in the early-spring sunshine and tried to complete the story to which he was sure he had found the conclusion. Nothing that was already known, and on his list, contradicted his theory.

But there *were* pieces missing. He wrote down what he still needed to know and devised a battle plan. His internal computer, with its manifold connections, had to be turned on. Within half an hour he knew exactly what he had to do and hurried home, eager to start what would become a marathon of telephoning.

He was glad that Cynthia was not home. His instincts made him confident that he had solved the puzzle, but there was no harm in buttressing his hypothesis further before trying it out on her. He did, however, call Bautista and tell him his new thoughts. The detective was not dismissive, but he did not display unbounded enthusiasm either.

"Do you think I'm crazy, Luis?" he asked.

"No, not at all. Maybe you've got it. Right now, though, I'd say you had a plausible case—but no probable cause to collar your suspect."

"You sound like your friend ADA Munson. Let's put it this way. Are you willing to help me or not?"

"Of course I am. Any port in a storm. What do you want me to do?"

"Can you get to the Secret Service?"

"I suppose so. They're not the most cooperative bunch of guys, but I'll try."

"Good. I've got some questions for them. Listen carefully." Frost set out his queries and for good measure repeated them a second time.

"I'll get on it right away," Bautista said. "Where will you be?"

"Right here at home. By the telephone—or more likely, on it."

Frost began implementing his battle plan by trying to locate Harrison Rowan and Emily Sherwood. He was going to set up a conference call through the operator with both of them on the line, but was spared the necessity when he learned that Emily was spending the weekend with Harrison in Fairfax. At a less stressful time, he would have speculated pleasurably on the significance of this circumstance, but now he scarcely gave it a thought. They got on separate extensions so that he could question them jointly about what exactly had happened at the party following the Reuff Dinner—a party Frost now deeply regretted not having gone to. He quizzed them thoroughly, rephrasing his questions in slightly different ways to make sure he fully understood their recollection of events.

"Are we getting close to something, Reuben?" Rowan asked.

"I hope to God we are. All I can ask is that you remain patient just a while longer," Frost replied. He hung up the phone with satisfaction. Harrison and Emily had confirmed his educated guesses. So did Grace Mann, an hour later, when Frost quizzed her as to precisely what she knew about the possibility that David Rowan might become a speechwriter for Wheeler Edmunds.

Bautista called back as Frost was pondering his next move. The detective had crisp answers to the questions Frost had posed, including the whereabouts of Wheeler Edmunds when David Rowan and Horace Jenkins had been killed.

"The night Rowan was murdered, Edmunds was finishing up two days of appearances in the city, including that dinner you went to on the twenty-eighth," Bautista said. "On the twenty-ninth, he had a small dinner at Gracie Mansion with the Mayor and went to LaGuardia immediately afterward to fly to Chicago. The night Jenkins was killed he had a fundraising party at the apartment of Monroe Parkhurst, over on Central Park West. He's an architect, I understand. Then he and his party went up to Elaine's for dinner."

Frost's luck was holding. Monroe Parkhurst was an old friend and fellow member of the Gotham Club. But before calling him, Frost roused the duty officer at City Hall to find out where he could reach Kelley Milke, the Mayor's principal assistant. Tracking her down in the Hamptons—after persuading the young child on the other end of the line to please go and get her mother—he learned what he wanted to know about the Mayor's dinner. Then he called Parkhurst and reached his wife, Veronica. Parkhurst was out and not expected back until early evening, so he posed his question to Veronica.

"This is a very strange request, but do you still have the guest list for the party you gave for Wheeler Edmunds last week?"

"I think so," she said. "The doorman downstairs had one to check people in. I'm sure I've still got it, but just let me look." She went off the line and Frost drummed his desk nervously as he waited. "Reuben? Yes I do have it. Why?"

"I'll explain when I see you. Can I come over and get it right now?"

"Why, of course, but . . ."

Frost cut her off without further elaboration. Almost in seconds he was on the street hailing a cab to the West Side.

On the way across town, Frost tried to devise a plausible story for his odd request to Veronica Parkhurst. Could he say that he and Cynthia were thinking of giving a party for Edmunds? No, that wouldn't wash. The Parkhursts' guests had presumably each given the $1,000 statutory limit, so it would make no sense to invite them to a new fundraiser. Nor was the timing right, planning a party when the crucial New York primary was all but over. Truth will out, he finally told himself. He would simply have to tell the woman her list might help in solving David Rowan's murder. She would be mightily puzzled, but that was the best he could think of.

Veronica Parkhurst was indeed perplexed, but handed over her party list without objection after hearing Reuben's sketchy explanation of why he wanted it.

"I also have one other question, Veronica," Frost said, posing a query he would repeat perhaps twenty-five times in the next few hours.

"Thank you," Frost said simply, and noncommittally, when she had given her answer. "If Monroe has a different recollection when he gets back, have him call me at home, would you? And give him my best."

Frost examined the list as he rode back home. It was perfect, from his point of view, the doorman's meticulous checks indicating precisely who had been at the party. And he was gratified to see that he knew, at least vaguely, almost half the names on the list. That would be enough to conduct the telephone poll he had in mind.

Back in his library, Frost looked over Veronica Parkhurst's guest list once again. Then, with the Manhattan telephone book and the Rolodex in front of him, he set to work and began calling the party guests he knew. Since it was a beautiful April Saturday, many of them were in the country. Nonetheless, by the end of the afternoon, through successful calls on the first try, referrals from maids and children to other numbers in the country, and callbacks from messages left with answering machines, he had asked a single question of two dozen of the Parkhursts' guests. To his satisfaction the answers were uniformly negative and to his relief none of those he talked to really pressed him as to why he was calling.

Reuben jubilantly reported the results to Cynthia when she returned from an afternoon of shopping. She was skeptical of her husband's theory as he described it; on the other hand, the pieces did seem to be falling into place and, like Bautista, she did not discourage Reuben from pressing ahead.

"There's one question I have for you, my dear, about the Reuff Dinner," he said finally. He posed it, and his wife, after careful thought, gave him the answer he had hoped to hear.

"Perfect," he said. "Now all I have to do is arrange a meeting with the candidate." After some delay, he got hold of Bautista again.

"Can you find out from your Secret Service friends where Edmunds will be tomorrow or Monday?" he asked. "And who I should talk to about making an appointment to see him?"

Bautista, now sounding more enthusiastic about Reuben's theory, said he would try to find out.

Soon—though not soon enough for the now impatient Frost—Bautista had a report. Edmunds was in San Francisco. He was scheduled to fly East overnight, but was landing in Buffalo in preparation for another round of last-minute upstate appearances before the New York primary on Tuesday. He would be coming into LaGuardia late Monday afternoon for an intensive round of appearances and TV interviews that evening.

"Who should I talk to?" Frost asked.

"Her name is Jean Kirby," Bautista said. "They're all at the Biltmore in downtown L.A."

By now Frost was weary of making calls on the rotary-dial telephone—one of the last in New York City—in his library. Maybe he and Cynthia really should get push-button instruments, he thought, though he knew that the telephone company would try to sell him phones like the infernal new contraptions at Chase & Ward he so much despised. After a preliminary call to Los Angeles information, he got the Biltmore, but could not locate Ms. Kirby. He left a message, with instructions that it was "urgent" (though he suspected that all messages to the scheduler for a major political candidate were "urgent"), and hoped for a call back.

While he waited, he fixed a drink for himself and for Cynthia and, once again, explained to her what he believed he had figured out.

Ms. Kirby called back while he and Cynthia were talking.

"Ms. Kirby, I must introduce myself. My name is Reuben Frost. I'm a lawyer in New York City and it is imperative that I see Senator Edmunds when he gets here on Monday."

"I don't see how that will be possible, Mr. Frost," the woman replied. "As you can appreciate, Monday is the last day before the primary election and the Senator's schedule is completely booked."

"I understand. And you have no reason to think that I am anything other than a crank. But I beg you to give the Senator a message: tell him that it is absolutely imperative that I see him privately about a highly sensitive matter—namely, the murder two weeks ago of the historian David Rowan. Tell him that it is absolutely in his best interest to see me. It won't take long—I won't need more than fifteen minutes. If you care about your candidate's future, you will give him my message."

Ms. Kirby sounded understandably dubious, but said she would convey the message. She took down Frost's number and rang off.

Within the hour, Wheeler Edmunds himself was on the line.

"Mr. Frost, I don't believe I know you," he said.

"We have met, Senator, but there's no reason you should remember me. We met at Lowell Oatsman's last week, where I asked you if David Rowan was about to become one of your speechwriters."

"Oh, yes, I think I do remember," the Senator replied—not without conveying that perhaps Reuben was some demented ancient mariner, dogging his path.

"Mr. Rowan was murdered here two weeks ago. I've been working very closely with the New York police in trying to solve the crime. As circumstances have developed, there are certain matters that I feel I must take up with you."

"I barely knew the man," the Senator protested. "I'd never met him before Elliott Reuff's dinner."

"I'm aware of that, Senator."

After a considerable silence, Edmunds asked if he understood correctly that the police were involved.

Reuben saw his opening. "That is a correct statement, Senator. However, I am not a policeman and have no official connection with the Police Department. My desire is to see you as a private citizen, without any participation of the police." He was about to add, "at this point," but stopped himself in time.

Frost heard muffled talking in the background; he guessed that Edmunds had his hand over the receiver.

"Mr. Frost, your request is highly unusual and my schedule is absolutely packed on Monday," Edmunds said, returning to the conversation. "However, I'm supposed to fly in and go to the Waldorf Towers for an hour before I have any public appearances. Can you come there at five-thirty? It's the one hour I have to rest all day, but I could see you then."

"That would be fine, Senator."

"Come to my suite and I'll make arrangements for you to be let in."

"Excellent."

"You'll be alone?"

"Absolutely."

"I'll see you then."

Reuben and Cynthia went to Elaine's that night, where Reuben asked his final question of the day.

"I understand Senator Edmunds and his party were here Wednesday night," he said to Elaine Kaufman, the owner.

"Oh, sure. He comes here all the time when he's in town. They all do. Secret Service guys all over the place."

Frost posed his question. The answer pleased him, and he and Cynthia ate and drank more than was their custom. It was almost a celebration, though Reuben realized full well that the end of the line had not been reached.

CONFRONTATION: I

25

FROST MET WITH BAUTISTA MONDAY AFTERNOON, AFTER spending a Sunday that his wife later described as "the worst ever." Normally calm and equable, he had been short-tempered and edgy about his prospective encounter with Wheeler Edmunds. His only defense, when Cynthia upbraided him, was that confronting a nationally-known politician with evidence of homicide was not an everyday occurrence.

Bautista, who met Reuben at his townhouse, was insistent that he be present at the meeting with Edmunds. Frost said no, telling the detective, "I gave my word that I would meet him alone."

Reluctantly agreeing, Bautista gave Frost an electronic signaling device to put in his pocket.

"I'll be in an unmarked car down on Fiftieth Street, outside the hotel," Bautista explained. "If anything happens, all you have to do is poke the switch on this."

"Good God, Luis. You must know how hopeless I am with gadgets. If I use this thing I'll probably end up with Waldorf room service—or bring in half the Police Department with drawn guns by mistake."

Bautista painstakingly showed Frost how the device worked and assured him that it could not be triggered by accident.

"I'm surprised you don't want to wire me up," Frost moaned. "Isn't that what they do in the movies?"

"Forget it, Reuben. You said you wanted to be one-on-one with this guy."

Shortly before five-thirty, Frost identified himself to a hotel functionary in the discreet lobby of the Waldorf Towers. He was turned over to a husky man with a plug in his ear and told that it was best that he wait in the lobby. As he did so, press photographers, autograph seekers and curious bystanders gathered outside, all under the watchful surveillance of the Secret Service.

Flashing red lights outside heralded Edmunds's arrival. He hurried through the lobby, oblivious of Reuben and the functionaries who had gathered there, and was shown immediately to an elevator that had been blocked off by the security detail.

When nothing happened for five minutes, Frost approached the Secret Service agent who had told him to wait.

"What should I do now?" he asked.

"What's your name again?"

Frost told him and could not help overhearing the agent describing him on a two-way radio as "an old man named Frost who claims he has an appointment with Stardust."

I wonder what my code name would be if I were running for office, Frost asked himself. It would not be "Stardust," but more likely "Geezer" or "Gramps," he thought bitterly.

"You can go up now," the agent announced. "Take the elevator to thirty-one and someone will meet you there."

When Frost alighted from the wood-paneled elevator, another Secret Service operative showed him to an empty sitting room. After just enough time to allow him to become uneasy all over again, Edmunds emerged from an adjoining bedroom.

"Mr. Frost? Good afternoon," Edmunds said. "We have met haven't we? The Oatsmans, you said?"

"That's correct."

"What can I do for you?" the candidate asked noncommittally as he sat down, looking directly at Frost and giving him his full attention.

Reuben had rehearsed his speech carefully. He told the candidate how he had gotten involved in the dual murder investigation, how he was David Rowan's godfather and how "investigating murders is not my normal line of work—I'm simply a garden-variety corporate lawyer, Wall Street lawyer, I suppose—but for better or worse I can't seem to avoid getting mixed up with the NYPD." To show that he wasn't just a rank amateur, he told Edmunds about the other investigations in which he had become embroiled.

"I have some questions," Frost said, finishing his introduction.

"Join the club. That's all I hear these days—questions. Fire away."

"Senator, on March twenty-ninth, I believe you had dinner at Gracie Mansion with the Mayor."

"If you say so. At this point I barely know what city I'm in or what day it is—let alone what happened last month."

Frost was sympathetic, remembering the candidate's fatigued confusion the previous week between Syracuse and Utica.

"But yes, you're right. I did have dinner with the Mayor. Norman in one of his manic moods. He talked and I listened."

"Was Richard Taylor at the dinner?"

"Richard? Let me think. Normally he would have been, but I don't think he was. It was just Norman, that lady guru of his who's always around, Kelley Milke, and me, and my issues man, Steve Weiner. That's right, it was just the four of us. An early dinner before we left for, let me see, Chicago, I think."

"Fine. Now let me ask you about the fundraising party last Wednesday at Monroe Parkhurst's."

Edmunds sighed. "Fundraising event number three thousand four hundred and twenty-two, I think. What about it?"

"Was Taylor there?"

"I can't honestly remember. But Richard is *always* at them. One of his jobs is to mingle with the crowd, get reactions, meet people who might be useful to us, that sort of thing."

"Would it surprise you if I said that he wasn't there?"

"Oh, no. Richard's his own man. But, as I say, he's usually at our fundraisers. No—wait a minute. I do remember now. Veronica and Monroe took us up to Elaine's afterward. I remember Richard joining us there later."

"I see."

"What's all this interest in Richard? Can I ask you that?" Edmunds said, looking pointedly at his watch.

"Senator, I realize your time is valuable. I know your schedule is full to overflowing. So let me tell you as frankly and succinctly as I can why I'm asking about Taylor. The reason is very simple. I believe that Richard Taylor murdered David Rowan and Horace Jenkins."

"Mr. Frost, I've heard many preposterous things in my life, a good many of them in this campaign. But the statement you just made takes the top bunch of bananas."

Frost realized Edmunds would get up and leave if he didn't talk rapidly.

"Senator, your surprise is understandable. If you'll bear with me for five minutes, I'll tell you why I made the statement I did about Richard." Frost did not give his adversary a chance to reply.

"Richard Taylor was scheduled to go to that dinner at Gracie Mansion. He begged off at the last minute, the Mayor's assistant tells me. Why? Because he was downtown, on Forty-fourth Street, where he pushed David Rowan out the window and walked off with certain files from Justice Garrett Ainslee's papers."

"What files, for God's sake?"

"Ainslee's personal files about three Supreme Court cases —*United States v. Rodriguez, Cleveland School District v. Henshaw* and *Carrymore v. United States.*"

Edmunds visibly drew in his breath, but recovered quickly. "Go on," he said quietly. The nervous glances at his watch ceased.

"Then, on the night of the Parkhurst party, Taylor left your entourage and went to Tyler Hospital, where he smothered Horace Jenkins to death with a pillow. Horace Jenkins, as you may or may not know, worked as Rowan's research assistant until he was hospitalized with AIDS.

"Can I explain my theory, Senator?"

"Please."

"Last fall, shortly after you announced your candidacy for Democratic nomination, David Rowan was selected as Garrett Ainslee's biographer. The story was widely printed, with quotations from Marietta Ainslee, the Justice's widow, saying that David would be given complete access to the Ainslee papers. Do you remember that?"

"Yes, I do. I was delighted. I was one of Garrett Ainslee's clerks, you know. I was especially pleased that Marietta seemed to be doing the right thing by her late husband."

"Pleased but perhaps worried about what Rowan might find? Specifically, what he might find going back to the year when you were Ainslee's clerk?"

"I don't know what you're getting at."

Frost ignored the Senator's disclaimer. "Isn't it true that you wrote to Rowan, telling him that you asserted your copyright in anything that you had written that might show up in Ainslee's papers?"

"I don't remember anything about that."

"You don't?"

"Mr. Frost, I'm a candidate for President. I write—or at least sign—a hundred or two hundred letters a day."

"Hmn. Didn't Rowan get back to you and tell you that you had no copyright in the things you'd written? That, as an employee of the U.S. Government, you had no copyright protection at all?" Frost carefully refrained from saying whether Rowan had responded in a letter or a telephone call—for the good and simple reason that he didn't know.

"Mr. Frost, let's skip the questions. Just get on with your fanciful tale."

"Very well. My guess, Senator, is that you were worried about what Rowan would find. And that you conveyed this worry to Taylor—your 'indispensable right hand,' as you described him to me at the Oatsmans.

"So, your indispensable right hand decided to help. He managed to make contact with Horace Jenkins and started currying favor. Told Jenkins that you were thinking of taking on David as a speechwriter. And, I suspect, through that ruse, managed to get access to Rowan's office, where he saw how the Ainslee files were kept.

"I'm not concluding, by the way, that you ever said anything about hiring David to anyone. But Taylor did. Rowan's widow, Grace Mann, was convinced that David was going to join you, though she admits that the only aproaches her husband had told her about were 'indirect.' Through Taylor, I firmly believe. And David's father and a woman friend of his were also certain you were going to take him on—because Taylor told them so at the Reuff Dinner.

"You denied knowing anything about the speechwriting matter when I asked you directly about it at the Oatsmans'. You were very convincing—and your denial was also consistent with the fact that we know you and David had some sharp words the one time you met, at the Reuff Dinner. Those who saw you at the party afterward said you and Rowan were quarreling. There's no question you weren't talking about speechwriting. What you *were* discussing with him was the memos you wrote for Garrett Ainslee fifteen years ago.

"You didn't resolve anything with Rowan in that argument. Everybody who saw you two together knows that. But Taylor, your faithful assistant, tried to resolve it for you a day later by killing David and destroying the troublesome papers."

"I just came from California last night," Edmunds interrupted. "They talk about La-la Land a lot out there. Meaning, as I understand it, Los Angeles, but also what goes on in some screwed-up heads. Can I suggest, Mr. Frost, that you're in La-la Land right now?"

"Let me continue," Reuben said, ignoring Edmunds's putdown. "At Lowell Oatsman's, a week ago tomorrow night, Richard Taylor was present when I asked you directly if David Rowan had been invited to become one of your speechwriters. You seemed not to have any knowledge of what I was talking about and, as I said before, I believed you. What I didn't realize at the time was that I had tipped my hand to Taylor, letting him know that there were those who knew—and remembered—*his* invitation to David to become one of your speechwriters. If I had to guess, I'd say that Taylor decided then and there that Jenkins had to be silenced. Taylor could laugh off what he had said to David's father as a joke and social chatter, but if Jenkins talked, he would be able to tell of pretty explicit promises of speechwriting glory—and historian's glory later at the White House perhaps.

"Taylor knew of Jenkins's illness and where he was from the dinner conversation at the Reuff affair, if not before. So the next night he did not go to the Parkhurst party but to Tyler Hospital, where he asphyxiated him. After which he calmly joined you at Elaine's.

"The irony, I might say, Senator, was that Jenkins was so near death that he never could have exposed Taylor. I know that because I had already tried to speak with Jenkins, who was almost incoherent from the ravages of AIDS. All I could get out of him was 'Look into Elizabeth.'"

"And what on earth did that mean?"

"I—we, those of us involved—pondered that often. Then it came to me like a revelation last Saturday. Elizabeth? Elizabeth? Of course, Elizabeth Taylor. The actress who had done so much for the cause of AIDS victims like Jenkins."

"I still don't get it."

"Senator, we are, after all, talking about Richard *Taylor*. In his extremely confused state, Jenkins had meant to say 'Taylor,' not 'Elizabeth'."

"That's the silliest thing I've ever heard."

"It may be silly. My attempt at word association may have been quite wrong. But silly or not, it started me thinking along the lines I have just laid out for you."

"Mr. Frost, my scheduling aide, Jean Selby, said she was reasonably sure you weren't a nut. I believed her then, but I'm not at all sure I believe her now. I have listened to your libels of my most trusted assistant, and your attempts to link me to them, and I find them unpersuasive. You are more fanciful than a reporter for the New York *Press*. Let alone the *National Enquirer*."

"I'm sorry. I've thought of little else but David Rowan's murder—and Jenkins's—in the last few days. Perhaps my imagination has gotten the best of me."

"I would say it has. And right now I have to get over to the NBC studios."

"Just one thing before you go. As it happens, there is a very simple way of determining whether I am justified in accusing your man Taylor. David Rowan's assailant struggled with him. In the process he got scratched, and the evidence of that scratch was under Rowan's fingernails when he died. There were traces of a stranger's blood and a stranger's skin that the Medical Examiner has analyzed and preserved. I suggest, Senator, that Richard Taylor, if he is innocent, will be more than willing to submit a blood sample and a skin sample to the police."

"That's up to him. If I were in his shoes I would laugh you and your theories out of the room."

"Let me put it another way. The police at this point I believe have 'probable cause' to get a court order to compel such tests. They can go to court tonight and do that. With no guarantee that the matter won't be publicized—indeed, if the police are so inclined, they can *arrange* such publicity. The more discreet path, Senator, would be for you to suggest, as Taylor's mentor and friend, that he submit to such tests voluntarily—and privately."

"I'll have no part of such a trick," Edmunds said.

"So be it. I have only one other thought that might change your mind. I have access to a copy of the memorandum for Justice Ainslee, dated December four, nineteen seventy-two, that you wrote in connection with the *Carrymore* case." Frost pulled his notebook from his pocket. "As I recall, in that memorandum you said something like 'Men and women *are* different. The legal rules for men are inevitably different from those for women. Under your logic, we could have women firefighters...'"

Edmunds seemed ready to grab for Frost's notebook. "Let me see that!"

"I'm sorry, Senator," Frost said, withdrawing the notebook from Edmunds's reach as a precaution, "these are only notes. I didn't bring the full memorandum with me. But it is available to me and if you do not request Richard Taylor to cooperate with the police technicians, I will see that its contents are released to the press tonight." There was no need, Frost thought, to tell the candidate that the memo itself was in safekeeping in the Princeton Library, subject to Dine Carroll's control.

Wheeler Edmunds slumped in his chair.

"Do I understand you correctly, Mr. Frost? If I persuade Richard to take these damned tests you won't release that memorandum?"

"Precisely."

"Mr. Frost, you purport to be an eminent Wall Street lawyer. That's what you told me minutes ago—"

"Let's be more precise, Senator," Reuben interrupted. "I said I was a Wall Street lawyer, a corporate lawyer. There was no mention of eminence."

"You are technically correct. That was my spin on what you said. But eminent or not, I can only say that what you've proposed to me is reprehensible—not a word I associate with the many Wall Street lawyers I've known."

"*Reprehensible* is a cheap word to throw around, Senator Edmunds. There are those, I believe, who might find your *Carrymore* memorandum reprehensible, and shall we say not entirely consistent with the liberal image you've been trying to project in your campaign."

"I don't wish to engage in semantics, Mr. Frost. The blunt fact is you've given me no choice."

"Where is Taylor?"

"He's in Washington for the day."

"Is he coming here tonight?"

"No. An early shuttle tomorrow morning. The eight o'clock, I believe."

"So if the police and I were here sometime after nine we could start the process of settling this matter—of deciding how fanciful I am?"

"Yes."

"Just two more things. There is a police officer standing by to go to Washington tonight with the idea of looking over the telephone logs of your office first thing tomorrow morning."

"For what purpose, for God's sake?"

"To trace any calls to Rowan or Jenkins."

"Is that part of the bargain?"

"It's part of the bargain. Will you arrange the necessary clearances so that the police don't have to get a subpoena?"

"This is all outrageous."

"Senator, words like *reprehensible* and *outrageous* aren't helpful just now. I've tried to lay the alternatives out for you in the way that would inconvenience you the least. Shall we meet here at nine-thirty?"

"As I said, I have no choice."

"You have a busy evening ahead. I trust it will be so busy that you won't feel the need to call Richard Taylor before he gets here tomorrow morning."

Wheeler Edmunds did not protest.

"Good night, Senator. Go back to campaigning," Frost said. He rose to leave, grasping the unused buzzer in his pocket.

CONFRONTATION: II

26

BAUTISTA, A SECOND DETECTIVE, A MEDICAL TECHNICIAN
and Frost went to the fourteenth floor of the Waldorf Towers the next morning, well before nine-thirty. Bautista and
the other detective showed their badges to the Secret Service agent standing outside the suite where Frost had met
Edmunds the day before.

He told Bautista that he was expected, but that the candidate was in conference at that moment with his aide,
Richard Taylor, and had asked not to be disturbed.

"He must have taken the seven o'clock shuttle, not the
eight," Frost said.

"They're probably in there cooking up a story," Bautista
added. "Do you think we should go in?"

Frost nodded toward the two Secret Service agents flanking the door of the suite. "I think we'd better wait. Besides,
if any damage has been done, it's probably been done
already."

"I was afraid of something like this," Bautista said.

Five minutes later, the door to the suite opened and
Edmunds looked out.

"Ah, gentlemen you're here," he said, coming out and
shaking hands perfunctorily with the group. "Richard is
ready to talk to you. Under all the circumstances, I'd prefer

217

that you talk in the room down the hall. It would be just
as well not to arrest him in my suite."

Frost looked at Bautista. The atmosphere had certainly
changed from the skepticism of the previous evening; now
the focus was on the mechanics of an arrest.

Edmunds went back into the suite, reemerging almost at
once with Taylor at his side. Both men looked terrible; it
was evident they had been crying. Taylor's face, once pink-
cheeked and youthful, was now a sallow, ravaged mask.

The Senator instructed one of the Secret Service opera-
tives to take the group to Room 3106. Then he turned to
Taylor and the two men embraced. "You're very brave,
Richard. Very brave. God bless you," Frost heard Edmunds
tell the younger man in a barely audible voice.

The procession made its way to the living room of the
suite down the hall.

"Welcome to my home away from home, gentlemen,"
Taylor said.

"Sit down, Mr. Taylor," Bautista shot back, ignoring the
man's weak attempt at humor.

Bautista sat in a chair opposite Taylor, leaving Frost to
take a third seat between them. The other detective and
the technician sat down discreetly on the other side of the
large room.

"Mr. Taylor, I guess you know why we are here,"
Bautista said.

"Yes."

"I am in charge of the investigation of the murders of
David Rowan and Horace Jenkins. You are a suspect in
the case and I want to ask you some questions. But before I
do, you should know that you are entitled to have a lawyer
present if you so desire."

"That won't be necessary," Taylor replied.

"Nonetheless, I want to read you your rights in this
regard," Bautista said. He took from his pocket the card
containing the prescribed Constitutional ritual and read it
to Taylor in a deliberate, businesslike voice. Taylor still
declined his right to counsel.

"Mr. Taylor, we also want to get from you a blood sample
and a skin sample. A medical technician is here to perform

the procedure. You can agree to it voluntarily or we can wait here while the ADA in charge of the case gets a court order. It's entirely up to you."

"A court order won't be necessary," Taylor said. "Neither will the tests. I killed David Rowan and Horace Jenkins."

"Do you wish to make a statement?" Bautista asked coolly in the face of Taylor's bald admission.

"Yes, I'm willing to do that."

"Can I talk to Mr. Frost for a minute?" Bautista asked. The two of them went out into the hall.

"Reuben, I don't know what the hell to do. He wants to confess, I'm sure of it. Standard operating procedure says I should get a camera crew in here—just like with Alan. But my side-kick's got a tape recorder, and I'm tempted to go with that."

"I agree. Can you imagine a police videotape crew getting through the network cameras downstairs? There'd be a riot. Besides, he's clearly confessed to Edmunds already, which it will be hard for Edmunds to deny. And the blood and skin samples, when they're taken, are pretty good evidence. Go with the tape recorder. But I'd ask him again about getting a lawyer."

Bautista followed Frost's advice. Once again Taylor gave permission and again denied the need for counsel. Bautista motioned to his colleague, who loaded a portable tape recorder and put it on the coffee table in front of Taylor, who watched the process impassively.

"I don't know where to begin," Taylor said. He paused, and then the words came tumbling out without hostility or defensiveness; it was as if he were relieved to be telling his story.

"Maybe I should start in Detroit in nineteen seventy-six. Wheeler Edmunds was running for District Attorney in Detroit that year. I was a senior at the University of Michigan, in Ann Arbor, and volunteered to work in his campaign. Pretty soon I had all but quit college to work for him almost full-time.

"I became part of his inner circle. Sometimes we would talk through the night about politics. It was exciting to watch him develop his views. He'd always been a Democrat, but his parents, and especially his father, had brought him up with some pretty narrow ideas, about blacks, and law-and-order, and all the social issues. His exposure to Justice Ainslee had started to change that and, when he returned to Detroit to practice law, he realized that his father's hidebound ideas didn't have much relevance in a faltering inner city like Detroit.

"Senator Edmunds won that campaign. I stayed in touch with him until I went off to Oxford, as a Rhodes Scholar, the following fall. While I was at Oxford, we corresponded about every conceivable subject, but mostly politics. We were an ocean apart, but that correspondence brought us even closer. Just at the time I finished Oxford two years later, the Governor appointed him to a vacancy in the U.S. Senate. He asked me if I would come to Washington with him, as his administrative assistant. I accepted without any question, and I've been working for him ever since. He's the only employer I've ever had, even though he's only ten years older than I am. We took on Washington and the Senate together. It was exciting and, for me, more fascinating than any marriage, or children or private-sector career could ever be.

"I don't need to tell you that the Senator was marked as a comer from the time he entered the Senate. Why not? He was the most thoughtful and exciting liberal since Adlai Stevenson, or maybe even Franklin Roosevelt himself. Hell, ten years ago, when he hadn't been in Washington very long, he would go to parties and half-drunk hostesses would come up to him and call him 'Mr. President.' Everything seemed possible, and I was ready to go the distance with him.

"Nobody was surprised when the Senator announced his candidacy last fall. They expected it. And his campaign got off to a good start, with some powerful endorsements and successful fundraising. Can somebody give me a cigarette, by the way? I've given it up, but..." His voice trailed off.

Only Bautista's colleague had cigarettes. He came over and gave one to Taylor, who then continued his story, talking in the same cathartic vein as before.

"As I say, everything was going well in the campaign. Then, about the first of the year, I noticed that the Senator was brooding a lot. This wasn't like him at all. I finally asked him straight out what was wrong. That's when he told me he was worried about some memos he'd written years before for Justice Ainslee. He'd read about Rowan becoming Ainslee's biographer and how he would have complete access to the Justice's papers. He was especially worried about the memos in three cases, which I think you know about."

"Yes, but why don't you describe them for the record?" Bautista said. Taylor did so, then resumed his tale.

"The Senator's worry just wouldn't go away. He thought Rowan's access to the Ainslee papers was a genuine piece of bad luck. He really had changed his thinking from the time when he'd been Ainslee's cocky young Turk, but he knew the voters would never believe that.

"I'd read about the J. D. Salinger case, where Salinger had stopped a would-be biographer from using his letters, and suggested that the Senator talk to a lawyer. That was a terrible mistake, and I'll always regret it. It was the beginning of the downfall. The Senator went to Fred Kincaid, a junior-grade Washington influence peddler who'd been a friend and adviser for many years. Kincaid told the Senator he didn't have a leg to stand on under the copyright law. But he drafted a threatening letter to Rowan for the Senator to sign anyway. It didn't say the Senator had copyright protection, but it didn't exactly say he wasn't protected, either. And it threw around a lot of legal jargon about the 'right to privacy.' Kincaid said Rowan was probably 'just another academic' who would be intimidated, or else so flattered at the attention from a Presidential candidate that something could be worked out.

"This was disastrous advice. To put it bluntly, Rowan told the Senator to go straight to hell. In a very bitter telephone call. So the letter failed. And, what was worse, it called Rowan's attention to the Senator's memos. I learned later from Jenkins that Rowan set him to work at once to find out just what it was the Senator was coming off the ceiling about. If that damnable letter had never been sent, chances are Rowan wouldn't have found the memos for months, or maybe even years. Certainly not until after the election.

"The Senator continued to be worried and depressed, though he refused to talk about the Ainslee papers anymore. Something had to be done. I decided to see what I could do and set up an appointment with Rowan. We met in New York. Jenkins was there, too, in that one-room office.

"Rowan was nervous when I saw him, but his nervousness soon turned to stubbornness and arrogance. He all but threw me out, accusing me of trying to 'buy him off,' though he hadn't given me a chance to say or propose anything.

"I was desperate. It occurred to me that maybe I could work something out with Jenkins. I contacted him and met with him several times. We talked 'son to son.' I was the Senator's protégé and he was Rowan's. Poor, lonely fag, he was pathetic, very worried about his health. I had no idea he had AIDS, though his condition got worse every time I saw him.

"I told Jenkins that the Senator was very interested in having Rowan become a speechwriter in the campaign—and, if he won, that Rowan would become the official biographer-historian in the White House. But of course the Senator couldn't make the offer until the matter of the memos had been resolved."

"Can I interrupt?" Bautista asked. "What were you proposing—that Jenkins destroy the memos, or that Rowan be bought off with a job?"

"We never crystallized it. I hinted at both. Toward the end, I talked with Jenkins about destroying them. He never said he would do that, but he never got up and left the room either. Then he went to the hospital and that route to Rowan was closed. I visited him at Tyler just once—before the night he died, that is—and realized he didn't have the strength to intervene with Rowan. And certainly couldn't get out of bed to deep-six the memos.

"I decided to make one last pass at Rowan. I made an appointment to meet him at his office—seven o'clock on March twenty-nine. Would it surprise you that I'll never forget the time or the date? I tried to reason with him, but he got abusively angry. He said he would see to it that the Senator's memos got circulated right away.

"You can guess the rest. It was the end of the line. An insane madness came over me. I shoved him and he shoved back. Before I knew what happened, I knocked him out and pushed his body out the window, but not before he'd shoved me and scratched me. I grabbed the three files—I knew exactly where they were. Then I happened to spot the files containing Ainslee's date books and grabbed them—I'd heard Rowan's father describe the mini scandal in those books to your wife, Mr. Frost, at that dinner the night before. In my insanity, I thought that would put people off the track if they ever checked for what was missing. There was a beaten-up attaché case in the corner. I squeezed all the files and the desk calendars in there—leaving the empty files marked 'Desk Calendars' in the middle of the floor after I'd wiped my fingerprints off them—and ran out."

Taylor paused, as if the horror of that evening were coming back.

"How did you get out of the building?" Bautista prodded.

"No problem. I went down the fire stairs. There was no one in the lobby. I guess they'd all gone outside when they found the body. I went out the door on the Forty-fifth Street side. It wasn't locked, but the fire alarm went off when I opened it. That scared the hell out of me, but I just kept walking to the corner of Sixth Avenue and nothing happened.

"We were going to Chicago that night. I got a cab to LaGuardia and cleaned up the scratches on my neck pretty good in the men's room. Then I got on the plane with my stolen papers. I was afraid airport security might see them, but of course they didn't. The attaché case was under my seat all the way to Chicago. I left it only once—when I went to the john to throw up."

"What about your cuts? Didn't anyone on the plane notice them?" Bautista asked.

"Like I said, I'd cleaned them up pretty well. And got my clothes back in order. Besides, everyone on that plane was so absorbed in replaying the day's campaign, or so tired, they didn't have time to see or notice anything personal.

"We got to Chicago about midnight," Taylor continued. "By one in the morning I'd thrown the papers I'd taken into a trash can three blocks from the Drake Hotel.

"I've never been so relieved in my life as when I threw those goddam things away. It was like a great weight off my shoulders. After that, I felt pretty safe. I had no idea you'd find hard evidence against me under Rowan's fingernails.

"That's where things stood when we met you, Mr. Frost, at that party last week. You started talking about Rowan's being a speechwriter for the Senator, and I got worried. Had Jenkins told? Then I remembered my silly ploy at that dinner, when I said something about the speechwriting business to your wife and Rowan's father. I figured I could brazen it out if you ever confronted me with that. But what about Jenkins? That was more serious. I knew he was very sick, but I was afraid he still could say dangerous things. That made me crazy again, and I went to Tyler Hospital and killed him, little realizing that he had already said enough to implicate me.

"Any questions?" Taylor asked, spent, without a trace of defiance.

"Just one," Bautista said. "How much did Senator Edmunds know about what you were doing?"

"Absolutely nothing! Nothing, I tell you! Until this morning, when we had the worst conversation of my life."

"What did he say to you?"

Taylor showed emotion for the first time since he started telling his story, holding back tears. "He told me that if I truly loved him, I should do what I had to do, to tell the truth. Maybe I'm crazy, but I've just tried to do that."

"Mr. Taylor, we're going to take you down to central booking. The rules say you have to be handcuffed."

"I guess I'm not much of a bargainer, officer," Taylor said. "If I had been, I wouldn't have made my statement unless you'd agreed to two things. One would be to wait until we got past the press and the crowd outside to handcuff me."

"That's easy. We'll go out through the basement. What's the other thing?"

"Can we keep all this quiet until after the polls close tonight?"

Horrified as Frost had been, hearing the compassionless details of his hypothesis starkly confirmed, he couldn't help but admire Taylor's loyalty to Edmunds to the very end.

"Let's consider the bargain made," Bautista said. "I can't make any promises that there won't be a leak, but we'll do our best." Frost thought that Bautista must share his own feelings of grudging admiration.

"Thanks," Richard Taylor said. "It's the least I can do for the Senator."

27

L<small>UIS</small> B<small>AUTISTA</small> <small>KEPT HIS PROMISE, AND</small> R<small>ICHARD</small> T<small>AYLOR'S</small> arrest was not disclosed until after the close of the polls on New York's Primary Day. The announcement was too late for the newspapers, but the TV commentators repeated it again and again as they announced the election results.

It turned out that Taylor's gallant gesture did not matter. Wheeler Edmunds's delegate candidates, despite all the media predictions, lost the New York primary—and decisively enough to derail his chances of becoming the Democratic nominee. The pundits, caught out wrong as they had been so many times in the 1988 campaign, attributed the loss to voter perception that Edmunds was simply too liberal a candidate.

On Primary Day, Frost had called Harrison Rowan to tell him of Taylor's arrest, and the circumstances leading up to it, receiving back warm and grateful, and tearful, thanks.

Frost did not see his old friend until a Thursday evening early in May when he and Cynthia went to dinner at Le Bernardin with Rowan and Emily Sherwood. "After all you've done, the least I can do is treat you to a four-star meal," Rowan had said. "I understand Le Bernardin is the best fish joint in America, so let's go there."

On their way to the restaurant, Cynthia remarked to her

husband that they would have a lot to talk about. Not only
the arrest of Richard Taylor (which Rowan might or might
not want to discuss), but an outbreak of scandals since
Primary Day. The first, which had been the talk of the city's
intellectual and literary circles, had been a bankruptcy filing
by the Hammersmith Press. This was no great surprise to
those who closely followed the publishing industry, and had
tracked Hammersmith's decline. But a civil complaint, filed
in short order by the Securities and Exchange Commission
against Hammersmith, was. It alleged that Hammersmith
indeed had a silent partner, as the Frosts had half-suspected.
He was, or so the complaint asserted, one Sal Manetti,
a marginal gangster to whom Stanley Knowles had sold
fifteen percent of Hammersmith's stock—presumably in
under-the-table satisfaction of a shylocking loan—without
any public disclosure that Manetti had become a major
Hammersmith stockholder.

The second scandal was also on the gangster front. Tom
Giardi and Manetti were indicted on money-laundering
charges—federal "RICO" charges under the wonderfully
titled Racketeer Influenced and Corrupt Organizations Act.
That, too, was no real surprise. What was a shock was the
afternoon New York *Press* three days later, which printed
four photographs, all taken on different dates, of Giardi
and Grace Mann, hand-in-hand at New York restaurants
other than Giardi's own. Ms. Mann's network, which had
pressed her to maintain an image as an emancipated single
woman, suddenly and cravenly found that there could be
too much emancipation. Her contract as the network's star
morning anchorwoman was not renewed.

And Cynthia, through her Foundation sources, had
learned that Peter Jewett's young protégé had recovered from
her hysteria when the police raided their Berkshires love
nest and had eloped with the professor.

All these events were rehashed, with a serving of relish,
leading Emily Sherwood to conclude that Harrison "had a
gift for assembling an interesting table" at the Reuff Dinner.
"Practically everybody that sat there is in jail, or on their
way there or fired in disgrace," she exaggerated.

Inevitably the subject of the murders came up, though not

until dessert and after a large consumption of a very good Montrachet.

"Reuben, we haven't talked about it," Harrison Rowan said, "but how the hell did you fit all the pieces together that put the finger on young Taylor?"

"You know the story," Frost replied. "I told you most of it. But maybe I can fill in a few gaps, if you really want to hear about them."

"Yes, yes," Harrison said. "It's distasteful, but my curiosity is boundless."

"Well, I thought right from the start that the person who killed David had made an appointment to see him. Grace Mann told me that he had regular habits and almost never worked late, but the night he was killed he had left a message on the answering machine that he would be late. Assuming he were going to be delayed in the office, that meant someone had arranged to see him. Who would do that? Not, I thought, a person intent on murder. Why would you risk having David tell Grace or someone else that he would be late because he had a meeting with so-and-so?

"That meant the murderer must have come with some other intention, of talking something over with David. Who could that have been? Stanley Knowles? Not likely. In publishing the mountain nearly always comes to Mahomet—Knowles would have called David to his office if there was some publishing matter to discuss. If Knowles was the murderer, his only interest was seeing David dead and collecting on his insurance. No matter how desperate, it's very doubtful that he would have made an advance appointment to kill David on his own ground.

"Peter Jewett? A possibility, but there was no evidence that his long-standing enmity for David had surfaced in any new dispute requiring a meeting or a confrontation. Their eternal dispute was conducted in print, not in person. I almost had to reconsider that one—Jewett kept popping up in odd ways—but then his little chickadee gave him an alibi.

"Ralston Fortes? Maybe. It was just possible he might have come and made a physical threat on behalf of his paramour. And thrown David out the window when the confrontation got heated.

"Tom Giardi? The least likely. From what I know of such things, Giardi and his kind do not make advance appointments to commit homicide.

"That left Alan Rowan, full of petty grievances about his father. Words leading to murder were very possible. And with a mother and step-mother being less than candid about his drug problem. But then Alan—no thanks to him, I might add—was eliminated.

"Then there were all the little clues, which proved to be wild-goose chases. We kept looking for an 'Elizabeth'—the name of Marietta Ainslee's cat and Peter Jewett's estranged wife. Red herrings both. As was the fact, significant for a while in my restless imagination, that Fortes was wearing an ascot when I saw him in Washington—an ascot covering what I thought might have been scratches.

"Then Cynthia and Francisca Ribiero, through their highly unorthodox methods—of questionable legality, I might add—eliminated Knowles and Fortes as suspects."

"Thank you for the compliment, dear," Cynthia said. "But we did manage to concentrate your thinking."

"I won't deny it," Frost said. "Your discoveries, and what I learned about the Ainslee papers, did redirect my thinking. Except that the object of that thinking, Wheeler Edmunds, was a totally improbable and impossible suspect. But then, over a second glass of wine at the Metropolitan Museum, revelation came. The wine and word association did it—Elizabeth, Elizabeth who? Elizabeth Taylor, of course. Richard Taylor, of course. Or maybe it was Richard Burton and Richard Taylor, I don't know."

"Come, come, Reuben," Harrison said. "Are you really telling us that Elizabeth Taylor was the clue to it all? That's pretty farfetched."

"Far-fetched it may be, but that's what started me down the right road. I have no doubt in my mind that we—Cynthia, Bautista, Francisca, all of us—would have zeroed in on Richard Taylor eventually. Cynthia and I had speculated all along that two people might have been involved in David's murder—an instigator and an executioner. Marietta Ainslee and Ralston Fortes, for example. Or Grace and Tom. Or Nancy Rowan and her son.

"But let me tell you this much. Without the 'Elizabeth' lead, we might not have thought about Taylor until after the New York primary. And thus missed the opportunity to bring extraordinary pressure on Edmunds and, through him, on the hapless Taylor. If we'd made our deduction later, after Edmunds's star started falling, we wouldn't have had the advantage we did and we—or the police—might still be searching for 'probable cause'."

"It's some tale, Reuben," Harrison said. "But in your omniscience, let me ask you one thing. Did Edmunds know what Taylor was doing?"

"That's complicated. Did he tell him to kill David, and then Jenkins? Of course not. Did he tell Richard to dangle the speechwriting bait before your son? I don't think so. But what he did do was tell his most trusted aide about a potentially explosive problem, perhaps even saying that Taylor would be rewarded on this earth or in heaven if he solved it. His only mistake, and a very human and I think innocent mistake, was to misjudge Richard's capacity for zealotry.

"If he knew more, if he was guilty of more, he'll be punished. Not in a court of law, but by having to sit in the vapid recesses of the United States Senate contemplating not only his political failure but his guilt."

"Or, almost as bad, contemplating his bad judgment," Harrison added.

"Yes, that's true," Reuben replied. "And let me add one other thing. I've no doubt in my mind that Edmunds, an experienced former prosecutor, coached Taylor at the end to lace his confession with references to insane behavior."

"There's only one question I have," Cynthia said. "Why did Donna Knowles eat so little at the Reuff Dinner and so much at Giardi's restaurant?"

"A mystery, Cynthia. I don't know. If I were writing a crime novel about the murders, I'm sure some pesky reviewer would call that a hole in my plot. Maybe she genuinely likes eggplant which, as you recall, Giardi's served with everything. Maybe she knew bankruptcy was coming and, like a clever squirrel, was stoking up for leaner days. Or maybe she was terrified out of her mind of Giardi, Sal Manetti's friend. But I really don't know."

"It's the only thing about this whole sordid business you don't seem to know, Reuben," Harrison said. "But enough." He motioned to a waiter as he spoke. Frost thought he wanted the check, but instead he commanded a bottle of champagne.

"My friends," he said, glass in hand. "I thought I had nothing to live for last month, after the death of my son. That scar will never heal, nor will my compassion increase for the demented Mr. Taylor. But—in addition to Mr. Taylor's arrest—there's been another upturn in my fortunes. Emily and I are going to be married in Fairfax next Saturday."

Frost's eyes filled with tears, old memories and more recent, sordid recollections swirling together through his mind. He grasped Cynthia's hand; she, too, was both smiling and crying. Then Reuben raised his glass to Harrison. And touched Emily Bryant Sherwood's with his own, whispering to her, at his side, "And may the angels sing, dear Emily."

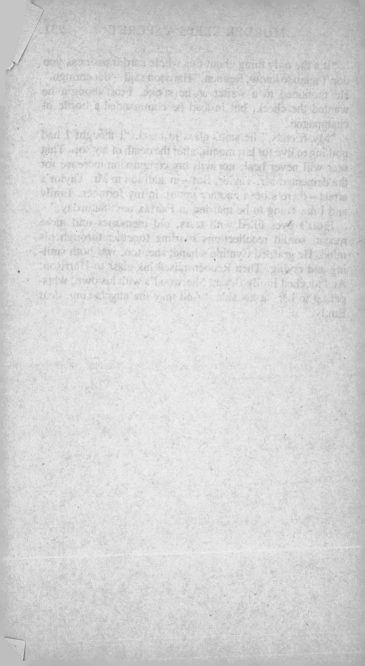

About the Author

The pseudonymous Haughton Murphy, in real life former Wall Street lawyer James Duffy, is the author of *Murder for Lunch, Murder Takes a Partner, Murders & Acquisitions, Murder Times Two*, and most recently, *Murder Saves Face*. He lives with his wife in New York City and Bridgehampton, New York.